Lindbergh's [Legacy]

'A clever and convincing look at [...] in particular, and a sharp critique of modern Ireland . . . *Lindbergh's Legacy* has a welcome edge to it, all the sharper and more welcome for being unexpected'

Pat Boran, *Irish Independent*

'A thoughtful novel exploring the threads that run through families . . . an impressive piece of work' *Books Ireland*

Gossip

'Sharp, funny and astute, Hayes is more than a match for any of her male peers on the subject of men trying to grow up'

Katrina Dixon, *Scotsman*

'Wickedly funny, Hayes' latest is unputdownable'

Cosmopolitan

'Hayes's writing is snappy and she knows how to unravel a story like a cunningly wrapped parcel' *Sunday Tribune*

Curtains

'Ms Hayes has a witty, acidic writing style, and *Curtains* takes a sharp look at theatrical cliché. But behind the melodrama there's a modern morality tale as cutting as it is funny'

Belfast Telegraph

'Katy Hayes's acerbic wit cuts right through to the funny-bone in her first novel, slicing the veneer neatly off the affectations of the theatre crowd with merciless hilarity' *Irish Times*

Katy Hayes is the author of two previous novels, *Curtains* (WH Smith Fresh Talent 1998) and *Gossip*, and a collection of short stories, *Opening Nights*. Her short story 'Forecourt' won the Golden Jubilee Award in the Francis McManus short-story competition and has been turned into a film. Her first play, *Playgirl*, was commissioned and produced by the Abbey Theatre. She formerly worked as a theatre director and has adapted and directed a stage version of *Vampirella and the Company of Wolves* by Angela Carter. She lives in Dublin with her husband and two young children.

lindbergh's legacy

katy hayes

PHOENIX

A PHOENIX PAPERBACK

First published in Great Britain in 2003
by Weidenfeld & Nicolson
This paperback edition published in 2004
by Phoenix,
an imprint of Orion Books Ltd,
Orion House, 5 Upper St Martin's Lane,
London WC2H 9EA

A CIP catalogue record for this book
is available from the British Library.

ISBN 0 75381 774 8

Printed and bound in Great Britain by
Clays Ltd, St Ives plc

For Merlin Roche – first born.

To
granny MARY
merry Christmas
from Nive, Jess + Alex
Christmas 04
x J x

1

2001

The sun shines on Ashleigh Court, showing the mixed red and yellow brick façades to advantage and glinting on the dancing fountain behind the tall iron gates. A prison exclusively for the rich.

Alison and Charlie were among the first people to move into the small and exclusive development. The semi-detached four-bedroomed house at number 12 was overpriced, but they were exhausted and dizzy from looking. It wasn't what they wanted. It lacked character. But they'd been searching for months and time was running out.

'We'll get this and it'll do us for the moment and we'll move on in a couple of years. Get something bigger. With more character. More us.'

Charlie disliked Ashleigh Court. Little finicky details around the windows and gables gave it a fairy-tale air. Lumps of bricks trying to be dainty offended his practicality. The electronically controlled gates were there to keep people out; undesirables, hawkers. But they succeeded only in making him feel trapped. What if the gates failed and I had to leave in a hurry? What if I needed to escape and was thwarted?

'It'll do us for the moment. We'll need a roof over our head when the baby arrives. And it's fully fitted out. Saves us having to bother with kitchen appliances.'

For the first few weeks, when they were alone on the estate, things were all right, but now that more people had moved in Alison was beginning to feel cramped. The new next-door neighbours, the ones to the right, from whom they were semi-detached, or perhaps, more correctly, semi-attached to, had hired a skip and immediately started pulling out the brand-new

1

bathroom and installing a pink one in its place. Annette and Gregory. They were stiff and unfriendly. Alison idly watched them from her front bay window arguing with each other. A tall thin woman, a tall broad man. Their loud voices rang out, oblivious to the proximity of others.

Do you want the bath in this corner or that?

You don't *love* me!

Damn it, woman, tell me where you want it.

You *don't* love me!

I've bought you the new bathroom, haven't I?

Pause. You don't love me.

Sigh. Shall we go out for dinner?

Sigh. OK.

Every evening their soap opera unfolded. Alison listened to them in the rear garden. Muffled through the walls. Voices floating in the front window. The noise didn't bother her so much. It filled her with horrified incredulity. To be so horribly overheard.

Number 12 is endowed with a twenty-five-foot garden, and over the fence, twenty-five feet away, is an identical house. A couple with a small boy had just moved into the house directly behind, and the child took daily delight in mooning out of his bedroom window as Alison sat at the French doors, drinking her morning tea and inspecting the beauty of the sky. Not ideal. Not exactly what she'd had in mind when she'd contemplated nesting with Charlie. She hadn't thought the nests would be so close together. Not for them. They were supposed to be rich. Privileged.

Alison, well bred and poised, had married Charlie, a rough diamond, the week after her thirty-fourth birthday. Many men had proposed to Alison over the years. She'd had six proposals in all. Something in her brought out the honourable intentions in men. She spent her twenties escaping from romances which were getting too heavy. All these men were wrong. OK for a tumble. But lifelong commitment? Not right. It looked to her as though she wasn't destined to settle down. But then Charlie arrived. A rough diamond, but *glic*. Business rich. A mechanic turned car dealer. Charles O'Brien Motors on the East Pier in Dun Laoghaire

– specialists in BMW and Volkswagen. It had started as a small garage, but the original premises were now obscured by a great silver and glass shop-front. Luxury cars perched in ornate sales-rooms. And Charlie gave you personal attention. Found the wheels that were just right for you, that fitted perfectly with your distinctive dream.

Despite Charlie's serious misgivings about the house in Ashleigh Court, he had followed Alison's lead. He felt men should obey women when it came to housing. In fact, he would submit to Alison in anything.

'At least the garden isn't too big. You aren't condemning yourself to a summer of perpetual lawn trims.'

Alison tried to sell the house to him. He made some non-hostile grunts.

'And the location is fab. If we find something better we'll sell it on no problem. Even in a slow market, it'll keep its value. Location, location, location.'

He made some more non-hostile grunts.

'And the builder has thrown in the sun room for no extra cost. In the brochure it costs an extra twelve K.'

What really galled Charlie was that he hadn't bought a house earlier. Before the boom, when all the prices went up. He had been too busy developing the business and had gone on living in some rented basement with peeling wallpaper and faulty electrics. His business was doing very well, but he was mainly rich on paper, as the expansion has cost a fortune and profits went to service the debt.

The bank manager, an old gent called Alan Cox, queried Charlie's business plan, called it 'reckless'. Charlie had sold it to him. He could be very persuasive. 'Columbus's voyage to the New World was reckless. Galileo's theory of the round earth was reckless, considering the religious climate of the time. Without recklessness, no progress.'

Charlie was determined he would be very rich. In the meantime, right now, the best they could do was this grossly overpriced Wendy house, because Alison wouldn't consider living anywhere other than Blackrock. And that rather narrowed the canvas.

Alison knew she'd made a mistake in insisting they buy this

3

house. She suspected the day after they closed the sale and handed over the bank draft. But it was only fully clear to her now when reflected in the shiny pale contours of the mooning five-year-old over their back wall.

'Tell me again why Tuesday's out?' said Charlie.

'I have a lunch meeting with the people from Saatchi and they're flying in from London specially.'

Charlie considered a moment.

'Well, can't you cancel that?'

'Of course I can, but it's my loss if I do. We're pitching them, you know. And stylists are bottom of the food chain. If I can't go, there's five young ones ready to jump into my place setting. We should've had this meeting a month ago but Lily, the production manager, had her maternity leave extended 'cos she had twins, so it put her diary back by four weeks. There are so many women in advertising now that the schedules get decimated by maternity leave. And it's all the women at the top who are doing it, as soon as their position is rock solid. The younger ones wouldn't dare; they're always weeping in the toilets over their abortions.'

'Well, what if you had to cancel it, if it was an emergency or something?'

Alison slipped a coaster under Charlie's tea mug. Really, he was quite a savage. Her attempts to instil some niceties were an on-going project. She had been thoroughly horrified by the state of the damp basement she hauled him out of.

'If I get run over by a bus, meetings with Saatchi and Saatchi are not important. In the absence of such a calamity, however, I'm going to be at that meeting.'

'And Wednesday and Thursday are out because of my meetings in Munich,' sighed Charlie. 'I simply can't not go.'

'And Friday's out because Anderson is unavailable.'

'What's his problem?'

'He was vague. I suspect it's some golf thing.'

'Jesus. He is making serious dough out of us and he's working a four-day week.'

'Of course, it could be something else. Vagueness doesn't necessarily mean golf.'

'Didn't you ask him?'

'I wasn't comfortable asking him.'

'We're paying the clinic a small fortune and you don't feel entitled to ask him a damn question?'

Charlie was beginning to get into a lather. Alison, as always, remained calm. Trance-like. The essence of serenity. Borderline glacial.

'That wasn't the reason. I didn't know your movements on the Friday, whether or not you'd be finished in Munich, so I didn't want to get him to cancel his vague appointment and agree to Friday when you might not have been available anyway.'

'Well, we'll have to wait till Monday of next week so.'

Alison remained calm, though her patience was slipping. Charlie really wasn't following this.

'Next week is completely out, because Anderson is going to Venice on Saturday.'

Charlie reeled at the dining table. He took off his jacket and loosened his tie. His tie flicked the mug and spilled some tea across the table. Alison watched a moment as the little pool of milky tea began to eat into the French polish. Then she wiped it with a tissue. This table, bought a few weeks ago, was going to be high maintenance. There was a marble-topped one she had fancied . . .

'Venice! I don't believe my ears,' stuttered Charlie.

. . . that would have been virtually indestructible. What was it that had changed her mind?

'I told you that weeks ago,' sighed Alison.

'But wasn't he in Tenerife a few months back? You remember, you had to change your monthly appointment because he was going to Tenerife, and we had to cancel closing the sale of your apartment.'

'That was about four months ago.'

'And now he's going to Venice.'

'It's his tenth wedding anniversary. His wife got the tickets for them as an anniversary present, so that's why he didn't have as much notice as for an ordinary holiday. Besides, being an obstetric consultant involves quite a lot of stress. He probably needs to take holidays to unwind.'

'Stress!' said Charlie. 'We all have stress. The cleaning lady in

5

the showroom is complaining of stress, for Christ's sake. Stress is a fact of modern life.'

'I know. Gemma says pre-schoolers are suffering from stress now, or was it their parents? Maybe it was the teachers. Yes. It was the pre-school teachers.'

'I don't understand why you're being so laid back about his capering. It's totally not on. If I was his patient I'd soon put him in line.'

Alison sat up straight, flexing her shoulders in an attempt to make herself more comfortable. It was pointless getting into a state, and Charlie always looked terrible when he got himself into a state. The reality of the situation had to be accepted and the best made of it. Railing against the circumstances was futile and a complete waste of energy. She got up from the table and heaved her huge form over to the fridge. She took out a bottle of fizzy mineral water, poured herself a glass and took a long drink. She waited a moment, held the glass aloft and stared out the window into the middle distance, a space occupied by a small wooden toolshed. Then she burped.

'That's better. You know, I am so sick of being pregnant. I have chronic indigestion, which wouldn't be so bad if I were able to take some effective drugs, but practically everything is on the contra list.'

She burped again and looked down at her belly.

'I feel so huge. I think this baby is going to come of its own accord if we don't send in the Marines pretty soon.'

Charlie got up from the table and paced the kitchen, standing up straight and doing his taking charge MD 'I am the big boss of Charles O'Brien Motors' act.

'OK, OK,' he said. 'Let's consider getting a new obstetrician and doing it next week while Anderson is in Venice. You may feel huge, but the due date isn't for another fortnight. And, and –' gleeful with his knowledge here – 'first babies never come early. I can get Sondra to find me another obstetrician in jig time.'

Alison sighed. 'Obstetricians can't be whistled up in jig time. They're booked out months in advance, like good hairdressers.'

'Money talks,' said Charlie.

'Not any more. Everyone has money now.' She sighed. 'Besides, even if we could get someone else, I'm used to Anderson. I think it'd be difficult to get to know another doctor. I trust Anderson.'

'Be logical here, Alison. Why do you trust an obstetrician who schedules a trip to Venice the week before you are due? It's hardly an act of supreme trustworthiness. We can get somebody else just as good.'

Alison shook her head. 'No. I can't be dealing with a complete stranger. Anderson knows me. He's done all the check-ups. I can't have a stranger cutting me open. I wouldn't be comfortable. Besides, we shopped around at the beginning, and Anderson was the best recommended by far. He was the only one that nobody complained about. Don't you remember? All our friends did nothing but complain about their obstetricians. They all said that theirs was a grade-A disaster. Except of course your sister, Mary, but she didn't have a consultant. She had some hippie midwife and did a DIY job with her Incredible Hulk husband – sorry, partner – standing by armed with a Native American hunting knife to cut the cord. No thanks.' Alison shuddered a little. 'Anderson is the man for the job.'

'You're a little too tunnel-visioned here. Think a bit more laterally. You're fixated. He's just a doctor.' Charlie got up and put the kettle on. Tea. He needed more tea. He was a tea addict.

'He did Donna and James's baby and, honestly, her scar is only two inches wide. You wouldn't see it at all. It's so small, you'd never believe a baby got out through there. She showed it to me last time we were over there for dinner. Don't you remember me and Donna and Gemma disappeared for a long while after the meal? That's where we were. In the bedroom, looking at Donna's Caesarean scar. Gemma showed us hers as well and, frankly, hers is a disaster. It looks like she was mauled by a wild animal.'

'Darlings, come in, come in.'

Donna Keating's larger-than-life greeting after flinging open the front door of her imposing Victorian house. It was Victorian in so far as the outside was Victorian. The inside was very modern, very not-Victorian.

Donna was Alison's best friend from school and her party partner until a couple of years previously, when Donna had produced James Keating and got speedily married. Their baby, David, was now nine months old. James ran his father's transport business. Great blue and white vans which lumbered from Ireland to the four corners of Europe to distribute this and that. His father was now retired to a life of quarrelling and gin, and James was steering the enterprise, with some dexterity.

Donna had always been a livewire, had always provided a strident counterpoint to Alison's calm. They had become friends on their first day at an expensive Killiney secondary school, shy eleven-year-olds, and remained inseparable right through. Donna the extrovert provided Alison with the social life she would never have foraged out on her own. They remained pals right through college. Donna had studied law, a very brainy girl. She now worked with a big firm specializing in employment law. Alison had gone to art college. She had a knack for drawing which she had perfected as a teenager in her own idle way, lazily spending the summers filling sketchbooks. She was indifferent academically, not from a lack of native wit but from not particularly seeing the point of working at exams. When the time came to finish school, art college seemed the natural option. Not particularly ambitious, and somewhat horrified by the extremes of some of the more avant-garde among her purple-haired college mates, Alison had drifted into the commercial art classes, where jobs were a priority and the students all had neat styles. She was hired straight from college by the advertising firm she now worked for, where she charmed and dawdled her way up the promotion ladder. Conscientious rather than hard-working, she was very reliable, and visually gifted. People liked having her on the team, because calm and tranquillity oozed forth from her and made for a very good atmosphere. She always lowered the stakes. And that was good. Tension left the room when she entered.

'Come in, come in.' Donna gestured into the hallway.

Alison gave her a kiss. Donna had dark hair and pointed features, sharp little blue eyes and a tough little chin which she carried high, an air of defiance. She was a contrast to Alison's dreamy blonde appearance and rounded face.

'How's baba?' asked Donna, placing her hands on Alison's tummy.

Charlie was always amazed at how relaxed Alison was with Donna's physicality. Alison usually couldn't bear to be touched, flinched at any uninvited invasion of her space, and Donna was a real mauler. Pawed everything. Especially when she had had a few glasses of wine. She massaged company like she was kneading dough. Charlie had mentioned it to Alison once and Alison had shrugged. 'I've known her so long, I'm used to it. She was never hugged by her parents as a kid and she feels that if she touches people enough, they'll love her.' Afterwards, observing Donna, he knew this was true. Charlie was constantly impressed by his wife. Alison was a wise woman. You had to fight past the first impression created by the blondeness and the tan and the clothes. Superficially, she was superficial. But deep down she was wise.

Donna ushered them into the drawing room, where James organized drinks. A beer for Charlie, a lime-flavoured mineral water for Alison.

'I'm so sick of this piss. As soon as I have the baby, I'm going to get jarred out of my trolley the very next day,' said Alison cheerfully.

James smiled at her.

'What terrible hardships you women have to endure for your children.'

Alison knew she was being teased, but chose to ignore it and petulantly returned, 'Yes, it's awful. How we suffer.'

'Well, the pain of childbirth is the price you have to pay for tempting Adam. Just as we're condemned to labouring in the fields.'

'We're labouring in the fields too, darling,' smiled Alison.

James poured a lager into a very tall glass, trying hard not to put too big a head on it.

'Thanks, mate,' said Charlie. He would have been as happy drinking from the can. Save on the washing-up.

'Sorry, the head's too big. I did my best but I can't get the hang of pouring lager in these skinny glasses. Management says I must use them, however, because they cost ninety quid a throw and aren't to be left gathering dust. Donna loves when you come round, Charlie, not alone for the delightfulness of your company, but for the chance she gets to break open her Polish crystal beer glasses, to accommodate your choice of malt-based beverage. If break open isn't the wrong word to use about crystal glasses.'

He passed Charlie the glass, held his own aloft.

'Cheers,' said James, as the glasses clinked together. 'Ah, that's the tinkle. We'll be pissing in crystal potties soon.'

Donna was outside, greeting Gemma and Harry, who arrived in a flurry of apologies for their lateness. The baby-sitter had been late. Lucy, the eldest, had had a tantrum. Gemma's dress had come back from the dry-cleaner's with a bizarre white streak.

'I just took the dress out of the dry-cleaning cellophane five minutes before we were due to leave the house. I don't get dressed to go out any sooner than that because, if I do, one of the children comes over to me and vomits down my front. And when I took it out, there was a white streak down the front. Like talcum powder. You know, the service industries are gone to hell. It's impossible to get a good dry-cleaner's any more. As far as I can see, everywhere is being run by kids who look too young to have sat their Leaving Certificate.'

Gemma was a chemist. She worked in the head office of a large chain. Harry was an accountant. They were a lively pair, full of talk. Alison liked their company, but thought theirs must be a very noisy marriage. No tranquillity in it. Sometimes, they both talked at once and it could be hard to converse with them as you didn't know which line to follow.

The meal was lovely, delivered to the door by a tuxedoed man from Tux Tuck – a new dinner delivery service which, despite the lowbrow name, was very *haute*. Donna was an expert on food, very well up on every kind of exotic oil and spice – she often went on gastronomic holidays, learning all the gourmet tricks. Ballymaloe, and other exotic French destinations. But she was so busy with work, she never had time to actually cook anything. She was a virtual chef. Trust her to sniff out a good delivery service.

The night was light-hearted and fun. Charlie had a knack of being popular. Alison was proud of him. It was through Harry and Gemma that Alison had met him. At least, they had recommended she buy her car from Charles O'Brien Motors. Harry had been buying his cars there for years, since the business opened in fact. They had been surprised when Alison produced Charlie as her date. They wouldn't have seen the match coming. But they liked him. Donna liked him, everybody liked him. There was something irreproachably decent about Charlie.

While James was making the coffee, Donna took Alison and Gemma upstairs to show them the new dress she'd bought in Milan for two grand.

'I just had to have it. Versace. It's the most extravagant thing I've ever done. I had to up my fee for the last job accordingly.' She stripped off happily to her bra and panties and picked up the gossamer-light lilac dress with a feather trim. She was about to throw it over her head when she noticed Alison staring at her tummy.

'What? What?' asked Donna.

'I'm so sorry,' blushed Alison.

'What are you staring at?'

'I'm sorry.'

'I know, you want to see my Caesarean scar. Fine, no problem.'

She lay down on the bed and turned on an overhead light. Alison and Gemma leaned over her. The scar was tiny, just above the knicker line. You'd never notice it.

'Gosh. That looks only two inches long,' said Alison.

'Well, I think it's longer than that,' said Donna, 'but it's a fairly neat job all right.'

'My, it's fabulous,' said Gemma. 'It's truly great. It's the best Caesarean scar I've ever seen. Who was your obstetrician?'

'Anderson.'

'Oh, yeah, I've heard he's very good. My obstetrician was a grade-A disaster. Wait till you see my scar, it's terrible.'

Gemma pulled her dress over her shoulders and then her slip and she too lay on the huge bed under the light. Her body was a good deal slacker than Donna's. Not as dedicated to the gym. Alison looked. The scar was about eight inches long, and very red and jagged.

'It was an emergency Caesarean,' said Gemma, 'but there's no excuse for this. They just hacked away. I wanted to sue, but Harry wouldn't let me. "Nobody died," he said.'

Donna and Alison bent over the atrocity.

Alison gave a sharp intake of breath.

'Nasty,' said Donna.

'Whew,' exclaimed Alison.

' "Nobody died!" As if that's a reason not to sue.'

Alison, without thinking, put out her hand and, with her forefinger, pressed the wound. The tissue was hard and a little knobbly. She shivered.

'And I wouldn't mind,' said Gemma, 'but I'd had my first two by natural delivery, no forceps, no epidural, no nothing. And then, you'd think it'd all go smoothly on number three. But you never know. I hadn't got an epidural set up, so they had to give me a general, and I was in hospital for weeks after, sick as a dog.'

'I was out of hospital after four days, and at a meeting in London a week later,' said Donna.

'When are you due?' asked Gemma.

'Two months to go,' said Alison.

'She's with Anderson,' said Donna.

'I'm going to have a section.'

'You're right, Ali,' said Gemma. 'If I had my time again, that's what I'd do. My vagina is wrecked. Harry tries to be nice about it, but I know he's faking. Not enough friction. He finishes himself off quietly in the bathroom, and I pretend not to notice.'

'Well, there's plenty of friction in my marriage,' said Donna.

'Now that we've finished our family,' said Gemma, 'believe me, girls, three is enough, I've made an appointment to have a vaginal repair. I got the number of a guy who specializes in it. My sister had it tidied up and she doesn't know herself.'

'Oh,' said Donna.

'It's the reason all the married men run off with younger women after their poor godforsaken wives have had all their children,' said Gemma. 'They think that the sex with twenty-two-year-old Suki is mind-blowingly great, but in fact it's just that her cunt hasn't been wrecked yet.'

Donna picked up the lilac dress from the floor, where it had fallen. She pulled it over her head.

'That's beautiful,' said Ali. 'It really suits you.'

It did. Scrawny little Donna looked curvy and petite and fairly gorgeous in it. It made her look like a wood nymph or a sprite.

'It's truly wonderful,' said Gemma.

'It's special, isn't it? I wouldn't have spent two grand on it if it hadn't been special. I just had to have it. Even James likes it and he has no interest in clothes.'

Gemma opened the wardrobe and started to root around. She pulled out a man's shirt, took it off the hanger and looked at the label.

'Ah, you buy James Olymp shirts too.'

'I dunno,' shrugged Donna. 'He buys his own.'

'Well,' said Gemma, 'I've tried every shirt claiming to be non-iron that's come on the market and this is the only one that works. S'funny. You spend your twenties on a quest for the multiple orgasm, or the zipless fuck or whatever. Then your thirties come along and the search is for a non-iron shirt. Still on a quest, just a different holy grail.'

'You ought to make him get his own shirts, Gem,' said Donna. 'It's not good for a man to have his shirts bought. It's not character-forming.'

When the women came back downstairs, the men were in the drawing room, all three of them smoking and drinking coffee. The au pair, whose name was Sylvie, was perched on a stool to the side, wearing a very short skirt and flirting energetically, God love her, being twenty-one. They were in the middle of discussing the property market. Alison heard Charlie make some joke about Wendy houses and the other two roared laughing. The au pair giggled loudly, a girlish tinkle. When the women came in, she excused herself hurriedly and left the room, a trail of strong perfume behind her. There was a moment of tension.

'I suppose it's time now to talk about the traffic,' said Donna with a hard edge, 'since you've just finished on the property prices.'

James turned sharply to his wife. 'I trust you had a nice lesbian romp upstairs?'

There was a tartness to this exchange which was new to Alison's ears. Possibly trouble? Related to the au pair? She was a bit unnecessarily pretty.

Silence for a moment, broken by Gemma, who took a coffee and sat down on a chair.

13

'Don't knock the traffic. It's the only time Harry and I get to see each other. One or other of us is always working late, and now we don't even sleep together any more as the kids all pile in on top of us. I generally have to leave and sleep in the spare room, because of all the tossing they do, and I'm like a *bear* if I don't get my sleep. Harry, of course, just snores through it all. So we hardly ever get to talk to each other. We have most of our important discussions on the Rock Road at eight a.m. To be honest, our marriage would be finished if it wasn't for the gridlock. Generally, I bring a flask of coffee. It's the highlight of my day.'

Charlie made himself the next cup of tea slowly and deliberately.

'And there's no way you want to wait and let nature take its course?'

'No way.'

They had had this discussion before and Alison was adamant. It had degenerated into a row. There was no way she was prepared to have this baby 'grunting and pushing and shoving like a barnyard animal'. Charlie had accused her of being 'unnatural'.

'But lots of things about the modern world are unnatural. Aeroplanes are unnatural. Why don't you swim to Hamburg for your business meetings if you want to be so damn "natural"? Or have your tonsils removed without an anaesthetic? If you wanted a "natural" woman for a wife, I was the last person you should have picked. My highlights alone should have told you that. And I told you I'd had collagen. You should have married one of Mary's hippie friends.'

He hadn't wanted someone *that* natural.

'And I don't want to have that argument again. Please. Anderson thinks that the baby is getting very big now, and even if I hadn't already decided, he said he would be nearly getting to the stage where he'd be recommending a section anyway. A Macduff it is. And I'm not discussing anything else. It's the twenty-first century. Health care is about consumer options.'

Charlie sat down at the table with his tea. The phone rang. Alison answered it. 'Hi, Cici.' Her sister Cecilia. This would be a fairly lengthy chat. Charlie went into the living room and closed the door on the kitchen. He took out his laptop and continued to work on his figures. His accountant was breathing down his neck to do the end-of-year tax returns. End of last year that was. Always busy. Always behind. The accountant couldn't proceed until Charlie gave him an account of the staff bonus payments, and this system was as mysterious as the interior of Charlie's head. The bonus system was not so much a system as a series of whims executed by Charlie. And he generally resented that the revenue commissioners had to get involved in his whims. But his accountant, Jim Dolan, hassled and cajoled Charlie onto the right side of the law.

He laboured until he got into a jumble. Figures were not his thing and paperwork bored him. It never felt like real work. He put the laptop to one side and stretched himself. He'd look at the figures again in the morning before Jim the crusader arrived. It might be easier with a fresher brain.

He went to the front door and looked out. All the forecourts were full now, as people returned from work and went into their burrows. Alison's little yellow BMW Mini Cooper brought its usual smile to his face. Beside it was his own large, sober navy-blue BMW. Then there was a little fussy flowerbed. Beside this in the next-door parking area was the blameless bathroom suite, a toilet bowl pointing forward from the prow of the skip, a shiny enamel masthead. He smiled, lit a cigarette and sat on the front step. A few kids laughed and played tag in and around the cars. He closed his eyes, and he could have been back at the little house where he grew up in Ballybrack, where his sister, Mary, now lived. Number 43 De Valera Park. His mother had hated it so much. It was so small and dark, that house. As kids, they had played tag in the cul-de-sac, just like these kids here. It was never any trouble to knock up a pal or call in on a woman renowned for having buns constantly on the bake, obsessively treating the children she hadn't had. He had liked the sense of communal living. Funnily enough, De Valera Park had never felt like a ghetto. His eye strayed to the big wrought-iron gates at the top of the estate, opening now in response to an approaching car, the electronic gatekeeper performing its invisible and ghostly function. This place felt more like a ghetto. And though number 12 Ashleigh Court was bigger than the house he grew up in, he too was bigger, and it felt smaller. He had been happy there, but his mother had soured her life away in that little house. Sat in the corner, a human chimney, puffing cigarettes as a lifetime occupation. Charlie liked the odd fag, but was always intending to give them up. He didn't consider himself a real smoker. Not like his mother. She had been a pro.

She had died of a brain haemorrhage when he was twenty. Suddenly. One day she was there, puffing like Billy. The next, gone. Charlie hadn't much mourned her at the time. His mother had been very doleful all his life, and he felt her joyless existence hadn't much going for it. He had a picture of her in his mind, her mouth set in a thin line of misery. He sometimes saw that look on Mary, and it worried him. But Mary always broke out of it. He missed his mother from time to time. Especially now. With the baby coming. It was the one thing that always surely brought a smile to her face. The sight of a baby. She would have scorned Ashleigh Court. She would have thought it represented very bad value for money, a triumph of style over substance, which of course was exactly what it was.

He stubbed out his cigarette and flicked it into the skip. As he re-entered the house, he momentarily thought how tight the hallway would be when a buggy was introduced. He mounted the stairs, two at a time, and went into the main bedroom. Chaos reigned there. He took off his suit and hung the trousers in the trouser press for tomorrow. He pulled his tracksuit from a pile at the bottom of the wardrobe and got into it. Tuesday night was one of his running nights. He put on his shiny new trainers and headed out.

He hadn't settled into a route from this area. His old flat in Sandycove was conveniently adjacent to the local GAA pitch, where he did his twenty laps. Now he set off uncertainly. Decided to try some unfamiliar back roads. The new trainers were extra springy, suitable for running on concrete.

He ran at a fast pace, his body easily adapting to the greater oxygen demand. He needed these runs. They helped him stay calm. He needed this activity. His job was now so sedentary. He sat at his desk all day, made phone calls, occasionally ambled round the showroom, only to sit down once more and drink more tea and make more phone calls. Sometimes he went to meetings where he ate big lunches and sat on bigger chairs. It was a major change from being a wiry mechanic. He jogged along the roads until he found his way to a school playing field and did his sprinting there. He loved the sprinting at the end of his jog. He loved pushing his muscles and chest until he could feel pain. Pain, then he rested and relaxed. Then he felt the absence of pain. A glorious numbness. Then he went home.

Under the shower he felt renewed again. The routine of the runs was a little disturbed because of the new location, but it was still rewarding. It still had the same calming effect on him. He towelled himself dry and got dressed in casual clothes. A jeans and T-shirt. Yob clothes, Ali called them.

He went back into the front room and, at the same time, Alison emerged from the kitchen, having finished her chat with Cecilia.

Maybe Cecilia would have managed to talk some sense into her. Cecilia had four kids, and had managed to have them all fairly naturally, as far as he was aware. She had been married very young, early twenties. Her eldest child, Sarah, had been brides-maid at their wedding, Alison's store of single friends having run out.

'Cecilia and Adrian have hired a private detective.'

'What for?'

'It's Sarah. She's become really secretive since she started col-lege. They're afraid she's getting into drugs. She's always hanging up the phone when they come in and generally being furtive.'

'Isn't hiring a private detective going a bit too far?'

'And she's lost interest in her appearance. She hasn't had her hair done in weeks and wears jogging pants all the time.'

'Can't they just talk to her?'

'Well, they've tried, but she just clams up. Cecilia says that it's all much worse than it was when we were growing up. It's all drugs and sex and the IRA. There's a big recruiting drive on in the universities. The Real IRA are now targeting the upper middle classes for membership. So are the religious cults. No one wants riff-raff any more. And as for sex, the young people are all into blow-jobs at fourteen. It's animal out there. Poor Cecilia is very distressed. And, of course, Adrian is hopeless. Head in the clouds.

Have you noticed how disconnected Adrian is? He only awakes from his trance if he can't find a clean shirt in the morning. Cecilia is at her wits' end.'

'It's all ahead of us. The problems of parenting.'

'Hopefully by the time our child grows up the pendulum will have swung back and it'll be all conservatism again. There's a lot to be said for repression. I know I gave out about it at the time, but . . .'

She handed him an ice-cool Coke from the freezer. They both pulled the rings, creating two tiny little sugar explosions.

'So,' said Alison, 'what are we to do?'

Charlie sighed. 'Well, it looks to me like it'll have to go ahead without me. Make it Thursday. There's three of us involved here. You, me and Anderson. It can't be done without you, obviously. And it looks like it can't be done without Anderson. I, however, am surplus to requirements. So Thursday it is. I'll cut the day short and come flying back from Munich and get here as early as I can.'

'There's four of us involved,' smiled Alison and walked to his side.

Charlie looked momentarily puzzled.

'Of course.' He put his arm around her broadened back and rested his cheek and ear against the side of her swollen belly. He could feel the baby move around and he smiled. A knee, or an arm, thumped him in the side of the face, quite vigorously. Eager for freedom.

'Ow,' said Charlie. 'He hit me.'

'He?' said Alison.

'I just hate calling it "it".'

'I think it's a boy,' said Alison. 'My woman's intuition.'

'I think you're right.'

2

1926

Marie Rose placed her hand on her belly in a futile attempt to quieten the bare-knuckle boxing. Her unborn child's vigorous quarrel with the world was already under way. She smiled. Around her on the train was the occasional face she knew, dotted among many strangers. She was a newcomer and people were courteous, but cautious. Her bright open face and huge toothy smile had always been a winner for her, but these craggy country faces weren't going to be too easily bought by townie charm. She looked out of the window at the countryside passing by. Late summer, a sweltering quality, even in this windswept spot. Sweltering like herself. Her sense of smell, pregnancy-enhanced, made being in a crowd very difficult. And in this heat everybody smelled. The man beside her smelled as though he had spent the day gutting fish, and a woman opposite had a box with two very pungent hens in it. Cormac had told her she must travel first class, but the train was very crowded and she had been late and lucky to get a seat at all. Another puck from the baby.

She wondered how people would react if the child decided to be born here and now. The men would hide under their caps. The women would roll up their sleeves. Not due for two months, but you never knew. Her own mother's eighth child, a girl, had come two months early and not survived. Died at four weeks. Not long enough for them all to get too fond.

But this child would survive. He, she, it was so full of life, it almost overwhelmed her. She was terrified, but gleefully giddy. People had told her so much about the pain. People loved talking about that. So many accounts of cruel, cruel pain. Of drunk doctors, of babies dying. Of women dying. Of women going off their heads with depression. Every married woman she met had a

19

horror story to tell. But Marie Rose was looking forward to it. An adventure. A struggle. She felt pretty equal to it. Her belly suddenly tightened with a light contraction. Her eyes opened wide. Was this it? No, no, some little contractions come for months before. Everyone said that. Still, it was a bit nerve-racking. Here on this tiny, elevated, half-crazy railway.

The railway line covered this mountainy terrain in a miraculous manner. It slowly strained up the mountain out of Tralee, and the view was something to behold. The precarious perch of the train and the drama of the scenery set your nerves a-jangling. A kind of beautiful terror. The viaducts were a scary triumph of man over mountain. A sheer drop on both sides.

Marie Rose didn't look to left or right, but hugged her parcel. This had been her last trip to Tralee before the baby came and she had stocked up on most of what she expected to need. Bottles, baby garments, napkins, soft blankets. Much of the stuff she could have got in Dingle, but she fancied a last dawdle round the big town. It was almost like a last visit to the mainland, so remote were they at the far end of the Dingle peninsula. At the far end of County Kerry. At the far end of Ireland.

As the train rounded the top of Glenagalt, it picked up a bit of speed and ran across the top valley into Annascaul. Here, the lady with the hens and the fishy-smelling man got out and Marie Rose could breathe easily again. A young guard she knew from the barracks in Ballyferriter got on and tipped his cap to her. She didn't immediately recognize him – out of uniform they looked so much less – but she was glad to see a familiar face. She would have happily chatted to him. The young man didn't take the seat either side of her. Shy of the sergeant's wife, he stood all the way to Dingle. A little stung, Marie Rose sighed. It was all so new for her, this new environment and these new people, and socially it was a struggle for her to find her place. Being married hadn't transformed her in the way she'd thought it would. She'd thought it would turn her into a responsible, commanding person, and it was a shock to her that she had remained the same.

The train slowly strained up to the second peak, groaning as it went, creating the impression it might never make it. Once over, another dramatic vista. Dingle Bay. A gorgeous sight on a clear summer evening. They were on the home stretch now and Marie Rose began to relax as the train assumed a new confidence.

When they arrived at Dingle Station, the young guard, O'Donnell, overcame his shyness and appeared at Marie Rose's side.

'Mrs O'Brien, can I help you with your parcels?'

Marie Rose was glad to pass them over. She was feeling spent and her arms were a bit achy. The young guard escorted her to Mullins Hotel on the Mall. She was to meet her husband there. He was in Dingle this afternoon, making a routine report to Superintendent Geraghty. She went into the gloomy lounge of the hotel and O'Donnell placed her parcels beside her on a chair. He tipped his cap to her. She wanted to invite him to join her for tea, but knew it wasn't the right thing to do. He wouldn't have liked it, and Cormac would be furious. It was funny. She had rebelled against almost all constraints forced on her while single at home in Carrig, but now married a curious docility had come over her.

Exhausted after the exertions of the day, she watched O'Donnell's clean neck and sticky-out ears retreat from the hotel as she ordered some tea. She discreetly loosened the laces on her boots to let her swollen feet breathe. Her legs had puffed up with the pregnancy and her vanity hated that. She hated looking down to find thick ankles looking back up at her from under her skirts.

The tea arrived. She sat and patiently waited for her husband. He knew the train would be in at seven o'clock, but the super was a divil and often prevailed on Cormac to stay and put a dent in a whiskey bottle. Marie Rose read the *Irish Independent* which she'd bought in Tralee. The Dublin morning papers made it to Dingle at seven in the evening, by means of the train she'd just been on. Des, the paperman who had the business of selling them, always had a large crowd gathered when the evening train came in. They congregated around him as he set up his pitch on a concrete bank around from the station and made great play of opening the twine on the parcels. The crowd good-humouredly jeered his clumsiness with picking knots. He scrupulously added the twine to a string ball in his pocket and finally, with a teasing smile, turned to his crowd of customers. News. People were mad for news. More so down here than at home in Carrig. The remoteness of the place made the hunger to be in touch more keen.

And Dingle wasn't half as remote as Ballyferriter. Only a few miles over the headland, it seemed so isolated. So windswept. A church, a barracks, a grocer's and post office, a couple of pubs and a school. And farms and fields. And when the wind blew, you knew all about it. Marie Rose had never felt wind before. Not real wind. Gentle breezes had fluttered along the streets of her home town. Not these howling, drenching tornadoes off the Atlantic that would skin you. This winter gone by had been the worst for ages. Everybody in the locality said that. But apparently they said that every year. You really did feel you were at the end of the earth. At least Marie Rose felt she was at the end of the earth.

Her mind drifted off to home, and that other life which was at once so immediate and so far away. A little over a year ago, she was a girl getting too big for her father's house. Now she was feeling lonely in this faraway place, feeling too small for her new life. She thought about her father and her poor ill mother. And she missed her dreary sisters and truculent brothers. She sighed and drank some tea. Her belly tightened again in a slightly alarming fashion. This made her smile. Her secret life inside stopped her from getting morose. Stopped her from hankering after the past and the familiar.

Her father was a grocer and she was cut from the small bricks and shops of the town of Carrig. She had taken everything for granted there and hadn't realized how important to her sense of self it was that everybody knew who she was. Her family was well to do. A cut above. Herself and her four sisters and three brothers were conscious of their standing in the town. She was the fourth child and third girl. The older two girls were fairly yoked to the house, as Mama wasn't always well. But Marie Rose had claimed her freedom. She wasn't going to become a skivvy for anyone, not least her own family, and she managed to elude almost all chastisement, bar the scorn of her older sisters. She felt deep down she had some special consequence. That her life was going to be a grand thing. That she would do something really fine with herself.

She had considered becoming a nun for a while. Liked their status in society. She had two aunts nuns in the St Louis Convent, and whenever they came to visit the house was scrubbed and the

22

front parlour tidied. All the neighbours dropped in, making enquiries in advance of the visitation. And then the nuns swooped in in flowing starched linen, and young Marie Rose sat between the two of them, marvelling at their air. Her older sisters complained bitterly about how she did nothing round the house, but she cited the Bible story of Martha and Mary in her defence. Her father always took her part. He was a stern man, strict with all his children, but there was something about Marie Rose that could disarm him. He had the air of being afraid of her. When she appeared before him, he would startle, as though seeing a ghost. The aunts said it was because she was the image of her mother as a girl. Marie Rose could see nothing of herself in the haggard grey-haired complainer her mother now was, but the wedding photo of her parents on the front-parlour mantelpiece showed a different woman. Her mother stood there, tall and shy-looking, her head crowned with thick black hair, much like her own. And underneath the image, in hand-printed calligraphy: Michael Bourke and Margaret Feeney – 18 June 1894.

All thoughts of being a nun were cleared from her head with the arrival of the recruits for the *Garda Síochána* force to the old military barracks. She was accustomed to men in uniform hanging around the streets, but she would never have gone near a British soldier. Her family wasn't political, but running around with British soldiers wouldn't have been the thing. When politics arose, her father just put on his apron and said, 'Now, I'm a grocer, pure and simple. I buy the best of goods and sell on these same quality goods at a small profit. I, literally, mind my own business. And whether it's the English running the show or the Irish, the Free Staters or the Republicans, this town needs a quality grocer who's dedicated to keeping them in quality goods.' Michael Bourke saw himself as above politics. Or, more precisely, beside politics. He'd had his fair share of hassle. The Black and Tans had ransacked the shop, thinking him too friendly with the revolutionaries, and made off with half the store's provisions, as much as they could carry. The IRA had come in and done a half-hearted job, saying he was too soft on the British, the most zealous among them putting a brick through the window. Michael Bourke recognized all of them and knew all their mothers and they let him be after that. Michael felt that as long as everybody thought he belonged to the other side, he was doing something right. And it wasn't that he was a cowardly man. He was a grocer by vocation as much as by trade. Right through the Troubles, and there had been serious skirmishes in Carrig despite the garrison, Michael Bourke opened his shop. Every day he hung out his sign bravely. And he was known for looking after the poor.

Marie Rose admired her father's quiet perseverance. She was old enough to understand what was going on, and part of her was attracted to the romance of fighting and dying for Ireland. But she had a strong practical streak and saw a little heroism in her father's careful measuring of flour and sugar into small sacks and stacking them neatly in the midst of mayhem. 'Civilization must endure,' her father would say as he polished the shop window every day, while there still was a window. 'Open for business,' he would call cheerily as he swept the path in front of the store. People couldn't make up their mind if he was mad or not, but when the Troubles settled down and Michael Bourke's shop remained open, with a new shop window, they were glad of his endurance. One old woman stood in the shop and exclaimed, 'It's just the same in here, like as though nothing had happened.' And this was true to an extent. Michael Bourke still had his slate, and arrears were carried over from the old dispensation to the new.

But something had happened. Inside the shop, the old order prevailed, but outside, on the streets, Marie Rose could smell the difference. A new police force was created. These men were our men, and this uniform was our uniform. The crowns were gone and the badge was our badge. She was twenty-four and felt a fine brave husband defending law and order in the fledgling Free State was just the thing.

Cormac O'Brien put his eye on Marie Rose Bourke soon after his arrival in the town. She stood out from the crowd. Always walked by herself. She was tall and slim and, to his eyes, regal-looking. She was cool. At twenty-seven, and with good prospects in the force, he was in the market for a wife. This was a new world. Irish men could really hold themselves up high now. Having been a volunteer in the War of Independence, and having witnessed things he'd rather not have seen, he was wholeheartedly embracing normality. Cormac believed he had a genuine feeling for fair play. And that was what was needed. Right now. The country had to get back to being civilized. So he joined the guards, believing he was at heart a guard. Not a soldier, not a fighter, but a guardian of the peace. Along with the optimism of the new force came a personal optimism. He wanted to get married. He wanted a wife and a home and some kids. Normal things. These domestic joys he would have scorned a few years earlier, but seeing chaos at close quarters gave him a sense of delight in the ordinary. Also he was sick of men. He was surrounded by them now in the *Garda*, and he'd been surrounded by them as a volunteer. He found himself hankering for the embrace of a woman. Out walking one day, he passed Marie Rose on the street and boldly winked at her. She looked to left and right, to establish she was indeed the recipient of the wink, and gave a soft slow smile, shyly dropping her head. And in that moment a deal was made. An unspoken deal for a lifetime. The future risked on a throw of the eye.

She sat on a bench on the green the next day, her lovely back turned to the barracks gate, and when a shadow fell over her, she knew it was his. He sat beside her and they talked about their backgrounds. He from a farm in West Cork, she from the largest grocer's in the town. She liked his clean hands. Her father had always had clean hands.

'Looks like I'm going to be made a sergeant,' he said. 'I'll have the running of five men then.'

'Will you still be stationed around here?' she asked.

'Well,' he said, looking archly at her. 'If I marry a local girl, I'll be sent elsewhere. They like to keep you away from your own people. You have to be impartial. Law enforcement is a serious business, and what you don't want is a bunch of madman brother-in-laws cocking things up for you.'

He laughed and his eyes twinkled. There were laughter lines around his eyes and he looked like a man no stranger to a good joke.

'And are you thinking of marrying a local girl?' she asked.

'I am,' he said.

'And who might that be? You've only just arrived a few wet weeks.'

'I have a girl in mind,' he said bravely.

'But will she have you?'

'What would you think of my chances?'

She paused for a moment and stared up into the branches of the trees above her head. A couple of crows were making a fierce row up there.

'I'd say your chances might be good,' she answered coyly. 'You're not a bad-looking man and besides . . .'

'What?'

'There's not a great pick of fellows around here.' She laughed. 'And there's nothing like a garden of daisies to make a rose look grand.'

'So you reckon I might triumph because of the lack of competition?'

'I'm teasing,' she said. 'The rose would be a fine thing, anyway, without the daisies.'

He and Marie Rose started to meet in secret near the old mill. It was disused now, had been wrecked in the Troubles, and they pursued their chaste romance witnessed only by its skeletal remains. They got a sense of each other, and after a couple of meetings Cormac decided to make his move.

It took him days to muster the courage to approach Mr Bourke for her hand. He worked himself up into a pitch and finally he called to the house on Sunday afternoon, just after his bath. Annie, the eldest, opened the door to him, and she had no idea who he was. Marie Rose had kept her trysts with him secret.

'I'd like to speak with Mr Bourke,' said Cormac, his voice wavering.

Annie showed him into the parlour and ran upstairs to fetch her father, who was reading to her mother. 'Dada, there's a guard to see you.' Marie Rose heard the voice from where she sat in the kitchen and knew the reason for the call. She buried her head in the newspaper. Cormac stood in the parlour, which was a little musty from disuse. It was full of good furniture and the surfaces were covered with embroidered linen. There was a piano in the corner. On the piano stood what looked to Cormac like a wedding picture of Marie Rose's parents, the daughter the spit of the mother. His courage nearly failed him and he wanted to run away. Something in him hated asking anybody for anything.

Michael Bourke came into the parlour and, on seeing the uniformed *garda*, supposed it was something to do with the shop. Forms or papers or something. The new administration was very tiresome in its demands for paperwork. And the rates were always inflating. It seemed the ratepayers were to foot the bill for everything. Tea and scones for the British army as it retreated. Repair jobs on everything vandalized by whoever on whatever side as the civil war raged at the pleasure of the petty vanities which fanned it. Michael Bourke was a man happy to contribute to society, but things were getting out of hand. His ability to pay rates was being undermined by his paying them. And he could never talk to anyone responsible. The administration was in such a jumble, it was always somebody else's job to talk to him. He was tired of being robbed daily, officially and efficiently. Maybe this guard could help out? It didn't occur to him that the young man was here to pilfer something else.

'My name is Cormac O'Brien, Garda, currently stationed in the barracks beyond.'

'Sir, a pleasure. Please sit down. What can I do for you?'

Cormac opened his mouth, but the words wouldn't come. He tried to find in himself the requisite humility to make the request, but it wouldn't come. He balked. He felt like a beggar. A thin thought of an elopement drifted into his head and then he pulled himself together. He had to do it. He thought of Marie Rose's beautiful dark hair and he forced himself. He looked at the wedding photograph of Marie Rose's parents. He stood up straight, stiffly, almost militarily.

'Sir, Mr Bourke, I have come to ask for your daughter's hand in marriage.'

'Which daughter?' asked Mr Bourke.

Cormac had forgotten there were a few of them, because he saw only one.

'Marie Rose.'

Michael Bourke was surprised. This was totally unexpected. He sat down.

'Have you spoken to Marie Rose?'

'Yes and no. Not in so many words, but I have gained the impression she might not be averse.'

Michael Bourke was silent. Cormac babbled on.

'I come from Glenmore near Bantry in West Cork. My father has a farm, nearly seventy acres, and my eldest brother is settling there. I've a good record with the force, and it looks like I'm going to be made a sergeant at the next promotions in two months' time. I have prospects and I'd make a good husband. I'll have no difficulty providing for a wife and a family.'

Michael wondered why Marie Rose hadn't mentioned anything about this young man to him or the rest of the family. He was stunned. This was the first time he'd been approached for any of his daughters and the absence of suitors had vaguely surprised him. The times were troubled, though, and that had explained it to him. The young men were all getting seduced by revolution. There was silence. Cormac had dried up. His courage had deserted him again.

'Sit down, sit down,' urged Michael Bourke.

Cormac sat on a chair stiffly. His position mortified him.

'You grew up on a farm? So did I,' said Michael Bourke in an attempt to make conversation and draw the young man out.

'Yes, sir. I did, sir.'

'What kind of stock?'

'A dairy herd, sir, and forty head of sheep. Some fields in grain and my mother is famous in the locality for keeping good geese.'

'And did you fight in the War of Independence?'

Cormac knew that his suit depended on everything he said at this moment. He paused and gave thought. He'd made enquiries from local members of the force and discovered that Michael Bourke had been a low-key Redmondite. Hadn't much truck with separatist warmongers. But like many of his type, indeed like Cormac's own father, he'd go along with anything so long as there wasn't too much trouble. Cormac decided that the truth was his best option – well, a nice watery version of the truth.

'I did, sir. I was a volunteer, Southern Division, Cork Company, Third Brigade, later Fifth. I felt I had to, sir. It was a question of patriotism. I joined over the conscription issue. If we were going to be conscripted to the war in Europe, I felt we should fight our own war. My own father didn't approve, but he came round to our way of looking at it eventually. The English had to go, sir, and they weren't going to jump, so they needed a little push. We were virtuous soldiers for Ireland, sir.'

'Cork. West Cork. Some fierce fighting down there.'

'Yes. Some ugly business.'

Michael Bourke joined his fingers together and looked intently at Cormac.

'Did you see much action?'

The old man was asking the questions, sure enough.

'No, sir. I was never a column member. I was rank and file. Job work.'

'Handle a gun?'

'Not really, sir.'

'Not really?'

'I cleaned a few, sir. And stored some.'

'And the treaty?'

'We backed it to the hilt. It was the best deal that could be done. And the North was always a different kettle of fish. And the oath of allegiance to the English crown? Well, the oath was neither here nor there, sir. As we saw it.'

'Cork wasn't known for backing the treaty.'

'The strong arms at the top, they were blinded with all the killing. The rest of us wanted it stopped. The footsoldiers. We were pro-treaty. Like the population at large, sir. And besides . . .' Cormac hesitated.

Michael Bourke raised his eyebrows in a gesture of encouragement.

'Besides, we had a personal loyalty to Michael Collins round our way. We felt he was the right sort of man, sir.'

Cormac had a feeling he was saying the right things. Collins had gone over with the ratepayers. Michael Bourke nodded.

'And the rest of your family?'

'My older brother is at home on the farm. My father bought out the tenancy before he was married and the holding is secure. My younger brother is also training in the guards. He's now above in Kildare. I've two sisters at home, one to be married this winter.

I've another sister gone to America. She's a private tutor to a family of girls in Boston. But she'll be back in due course. She didn't have to go, you understand. She chose to, out of curiosity. The youngest boy is still at school. They hope to make a priest of him, but I'd say the lad has other ideas.'

'I suppose you're wondering about her fortune?'

Cormac was relieved at the question. He felt he had successfully crossed the main ditch.

'To be honest, Mr Bourke, the thought hadn't come into my mind.' Cormac bristled here. He was a proud man, and haggling over a fortune was beneath him. He would ask for nothing. Except her white hand. He needed no grocer's fortune because he had wealth enough in his own ambitions. 'I'll take her with no fortune, if she'll have me. I'll take her in the clothes she stands up in. As I present myself, sir, these clothes –' and he indicated his *Garda* uniform – 'are my own fortune.'

'I'll have to talk to her. I'll have to think.'

After Cormac left, Michael Bourke sat on in the parlour and thought. He liked the look of the lad. He was clean and courteous. Had a tall figure and good broad shoulders. Handsome and would catch a girl's eye, all right. He knew he had to part with his daughters. And Marie Rose was flighty. She'd want to be getting married sometime soon before she outgrew her biddableness and got herself into some kind of mess. But something in him resisted.

Marie Rose went to work on him and soon had him cajoled into line. She also insisted on her fortune. Cormac might not stoop to pick it up, but she would. She wanted to enter the marriage with some status.

'But he said he'd take you without it,' her father teased. ' "The clothes she stands up in", was what he said, bless him.' Marie Rose's father chuckled a little here.

'All the more reason for me to have it. If he was a money-grabbing wretch, I wouldn't be bothered.'

He wrote a note of acceptance to Cormac and the match was made. Five hundred pounds he offered with her. No reason to wait around. They were married nine weeks later, just long enough for her to get a trousseau together. A week before, Cormac had been awarded his sergeant status. The ceremony was low key, on account of her mother being so ill, but when Marie Rose approached the altar rails to find Cormac waiting there for her, handsome in his uniform, proud with his sergeant's stripes, she thought she might burst, her heart was racing so fast. The stained glass of the church was alive with the glow of June morning sunshine and she had an overwhelming sense of embracing destiny. The marriage ceremony was almost physical in its power and she emerged from the church feeling like a different person. Afterwards, her father had tears in his eyes and was shy with her. Her sisters too were shy with her. But Cormac wasn't. He put his arm around her and he owned her.

After the breakfast, they took a train to Dublin to stay at the Shelbourne Hotel on St Stephen's Green. Marie Rose had never been to Dublin before and was astounded by the crowds. Cormac had been up a good many times and knew his way around. He had trained with the first *Garda* recruits at the Royal Dublin Society in Ballsbridge. The force had come a long way since. What a ramshackle bunch they'd been then, full of naked idealism, but no uniforms. He protectively shuttled Marie Rose onto a tram outside Kingsbridge Station and she marvelled at the number of people. How smart they were. How rich and varied the hats. He found her a seat and he stood by her. She thought him the finest, most handsome creature she had ever seen. She had finally escaped, from her home, from her sisters, from her life. And she was in this new life, pristine, unused, unlived. A blank future for her to map out and make wonderful.

He steered her up Grafton Street, for her to see the shops and fashions, and she'd never seen anything like it.

'I bet I look like a right country, small-town greenhorn,' she giggled.

'You look as smart as the best of them, girlie.'

She knew she looked well. Her father had spent a fortune getting her dressed up. Her coat was well cut and her new boots as neat as a kitten's paw. Her hair was pinned up on top of her head, revealing her long neck, which gave her that indefinable air of consequence.

He slipped his arm around her waist and she started. He was so comfortable with her, so casual. He had been careful in Carrig to

31

keep a proper distance, to not touch her. He had bowed as a greeting and farewell, never took her hand. Never acknowledged her corporal existence. Now he was as familiar with her as he might be with his wife.

It was taking her a while to get used to her new status. It was sinking in. He was touching her. He steered them into Bewleys for some tea and cake. He ordered from the waitress, who was saucy and cheeky. She smiled and flirted with Cormac, who smiled and flirted back. Marie Rose felt herself bristling at this liberty.

'We're on our honeymoon,' she blurted out and then felt a little foolish.

'It's well for you,' said the girl, and she winked knowingly at Cormac.

Marie Rose was outraged. Cormac laughed.

'She's a right little miss, the go of her. No class.'

Cormac laughed. 'The job is probably deathly dull. She has to keep herself amused somehow.'

'She'll never find a husband if she lowers herself like that all the time.'

'Maybe she doesn't want a husband?'

'Of course she does. All girls do.'

'No, they don't. Some girls like to be independent. Like to earn their own money and not be answerable to anyone. Just have fun. Don't want a husband hanging round their neck like a millstone.'

'What do you know about some girls?'

'Maybe I know plenty.'

It was dawning on Marie Rose that Cormac hadn't been freshly minted, like a new coin, the day he and his shiny colleagues appeared in Carrig.

'I've heard girls say they don't want to waste their lives picking up after their husbands like their mothers did. They don't want to be slaves, and marriage is all about slavery,' he said.

She was beginning to realize she knew very little about him. He was a big secret waiting to be unwrapped. He knew very little about her also, but that somehow seemed less important. There wasn't much to know about her. She had no real past. A few schooldays more than most, a few stints behind her father's counter and that was about the height of it. She stared at him,

32

her husband, almost as though it were for the first time. His face was squarish, his hair fairish, his eyes deep blue and strong, like mountain pools on a bright summer's day. He was handsome. There was no doubt about that. Marie Rose believed it, and so did Saucy Sue, who approached now, bearing their order. A pot of tea, a pot of hot water and a dish of cakes. Beautiful dainty cakes. Marie Rose couldn't help smiling and being delighted.

'Oh, thank you,' she said, smiling warmly at the girl, forgetting for a moment to be distant and superior.

That was the problem with Marie Rose, her natural warmth overtook her hauteur much of the time. The girl placed the items on the table, offering the dish of cakes to each in turn, with elaborate care.

'So how's the honeymoon so far?' she asked.

'Fine,' said Marie Rose, wanting rid of the girl.

'This is our first day,' said Cormac. 'We were married this morning.'

'It's all ahead of you so.' This was delivered with an extraordinary sympathetic leer to Marie Rose, who blushed and looked down at her cake.

A manager type walked past and barked some instruction in her ear. 'If you need anything, please ask,' she said, and scurried off to the kitchens.

Marie Rose took a bite out of her cake. It tasted like heaven.

'Looks to me like she's still a slave,' said Marie Rose. 'Husband-less and all as she is.'

Cormac smiled at his brand-new wife. She was quick. And she was beautiful. The two things you wanted in a woman. Easy on the eye and easy on the ear.

The girl buzzed about, attending to other tables, hardly stopping to exchange pleasantries.

'It's great to be away,' said Cormac.

'Yes,' smiled Marie Rose. 'I feel like I've escaped.'

'Carrig is grand, but it's small. Every corner I turned I ran into one of your family, or one of the guards. It's great up here, nobody knows us. We can do what we like. Nobody's looking at you saying, "There's Michael Bourke's daughter," and nobody is looking at me, saying, "I believe young O'Brien has a bright future with the *Garda Síochána*." I feel feckin' free and I feel feckin' marvellous.'

Marie Rose didn't like that language. He may feel free, but she'd soon rein in his tongue.

When Cormac settled the bill, he left the girl a tip. They continued on up Grafton Street. Marie Rose was still bristling a little after the waitress encounter.

'Did you like her?'

'Who?'

'Saucy Sue, the waitress.'

'Oh, well, she was fine.'

'Did you like the look of her?'

Cormac considered for a moment. 'She had a nice face, but she had a broad arse and thick calves.'

Marie Rose bristled a little more.

'Well, you took a good look at her so. I hadn't realized you were taking so many notes, that you'd have as many opinions as she had limbs.'

'You asked the question. No need to get annoyed because I answered it.'

'I asked the question because I wanted to find out what was going on in your head.'

She was nagging him now and picking an argument. Cormac hoped they weren't going to be the kind of married couple who bicker all the time. Marie Rose was getting nervous as they headed closer to the hotel and soon were to be alone together. Cormac stopped walking and held her at arm's length.

'She had a nice face but she's not a patch on you. You're a true beauty in every way. And that's the honest truth.'

Marie Rose smiled, reassured. Cormac chuckled. He was getting the hang of her. Figuring out how to make her work. They proceeded to the hotel and Marie Rose stood shyly aside while Cormac requested their room. He gave orders well, in a courteous but firm way. He had a natural authority. Some people were like that. They just had a way about them that made them leaders. Some air of wisdom. Marie Rose felt a warmth inside. She had chosen well, she was sure of it. He was a fine man, standing there in his suit, looking handsome. Looking like he belonged there, ordering people about. She felt so small and lost as she stood to one side, fingering her bag, the grandeur of her surroundings dwarfing her spirit a little. Her feet were sore from the walk, the stiff new shoes unkind to feet unused to such constriction. Cormac was enjoying himself hugely. He sensed her shyness and was happy to show off his urbanity. He put his arm around her and steered her to the lift. He kept his hand on her waist as they ascended, and this alone stopped her yelping in discomfort at the lift's petty battle with gravity. She had never used one before and hated it. She would avoid it for the rest of her stay, preferring to climb the stairs 'since God has seen fit to give me knee joints'.

He led her to their room and opened the door. It was huge, and in the middle of the room was the biggest bed she had ever seen. Their two cases were placed on the bed, opened. Marie Rose was glad to see them. She had felt worried when she parted from her cases at Kingsbridge Station, felt she might never see them again. Now their reappearance comforted her. She fingered the new garments inside, then cast her eye about the place. Over to one side of the room were a table and two chairs. She took off her hat and placed it carefully on the table. The window looked out over St Stephen's Green.

'It's nice to have a park like that in the middle of the city. A little bit of countryside. It reminds me of the green at home. Only it is fancier.'

'It's the one damn thing the English are good at. Planting flowerbeds. You've got to hand it to them for the pansies and the gladioli.'

Cormac took off his shiny polished shoes and through a hole in one sock poked a big pink toe.

'Give me that, Cormac O'Brien. You are a disgrace.'

He took off his socks and handed them to her. She went to her case and produced a little box of threads and needles. She was a fine neat darner. It was the one feminine art she had mastered. The socks were blue and she had only a grey wool, but it would look all right. He sat sockless, kneading the carpet with his toes. His feet were pink and babyish-looking. Small feet.

'My feet are sore,' she said. 'These shoes are pretty, but I'm afraid my vanity made me buy a size too small.'

'Take them off,' he said.

She blushed.

'Take off your shoes if they're uncomfortable.'

She looked around, nervously.

'Nobody will come in. This is our hotel room. Anybody who comes will have to knock and we can deny them entry.'

She buried her head over the darning of his sock. He got down on his hands and knees and started to unlace her boots. Slowly. She darned furiously. When he had removed one, he held it up and admired it.

'They are pretty. Good leather. Nice colour.' The boots had a reddish tint. He removed the other. He stroked her feet. She was terrified. She stared at him. He was a stranger. She had spoken to him maybe ten times in all prior to today. And now they were married and he was stroking her feet. It had all seemed like such a good idea. When he proposed, she knew she must have him. She was sure of that if she was sure of nothing else. But now all certainty deserted her, as his hands stroked her feet and her heart began to race and suddenly, for the first time in years, she missed her mother. Her old well mother. Before she became the tiresome invalid.

'Here's your sock,' she said, knotting the last bit of thread and biting off the stray ends with her teeth. She had always been in trouble for doing that at the convent. But she liked doing it nonetheless. Liked using her teeth for something practical. Who was it decreed that biting thread is a bad idea? Who decided that? Little details brought out a belligerent streak in her.

He went over to the bed and sat on it. He patted the bed beside him for her to join him. He bent forward and kissed her and she shyly returned the kiss. His lips were so soft and gentle. He started to unhook the back of her dress and touch her in an intimate way. He laid her back and gently but authoritatively slipped the top of her dress from her shoulders. She was frozen in shock.

'What are you doing?' she finally gasped.

'Well, we're married now, so we can make love. We're not properly married until we do it.'

'What do you mean make love?'

'Well, you know, make babies and so on.'

'What are you talking about?'

Cormac raised his head and supported it on his arm. It only dawned on him now that she hadn't a clue. 'Well, hasn't somebody told you about being married? Your mother, or your sisters?'

'Mama's ill. And my sisters are single, and never talk to me except to scold.'

'Your aunts?'

'I don't see most of them, except the nuns.'

'Has nobody told you?'

Marie Rose thought for a moment. There had been whispered conversations among her schoolfriends about the terrible things men did to women when they were married, but Marie Rose had always had too much pride to admit she didn't know and never went off behind the shed for the secret conversations. She was aloof even then. Besides, she wasn't particularly interested, as her practical mind had no curiosity about things she hadn't experienced.

'So you'd better tell me,' she said. 'I know there's something here I need to know.'

Cormac sat up in dismay. He didn't quite feel equal to this. He thought she'd know what was expected. He didn't feel able to confront her bodily integrity without having her as an accomplice. He was suddenly shy with her. And the room was bright with evening sunshine and her gaze so clear.

'Let's go down for dinner.'

They sat at a quiet corner table and Marie Rose was delighted with the grandeur. Cormac ordered a bottle of red wine and poured some for them both.

'I'm not allowed wine,' she said.

'What do you mean?'

'Well, Dada hates drink. It's the one thing he gets very worked up about. He'd let any poor person off their bill in the shop, but people who were poor because of drink, he billed them mercilessly. So he never has drink in the house, even when the parish priest calls and my mother always felt the priest should be given a whiskey.'

Cormac tasted the wine.

'It's good, have some.'

'I'm not allowed.'

'Your father isn't in charge now. You're a married woman, and you can do as you please. You don't have to obey your father. Have some wine if you want.'

She lifted it gingerly to her lips. It tasted strong and she liked it. She gulped it down, like a lemonade.

'You're supposed to drink it slowly, sip it.'

She rapidly became quite giddy. The meal was good, course after course, and Marie Rose felt just grand. The shock of her changed circumstances receded and she began to enjoy the sense of being quite grown up. For the first time in her life, she was no longer her father's daughter. She was her husband's wife. And in time, she would become her own woman, she was certain of that. But for the moment, it suited her to be owned.

'Where would you like to be posted, now they've made a sergeant of you?' asked Marie Rose.

'Well, I won't be sent near my own home town, or yours. Where would you like to go, Mrs O'Brien?'

Marie Rose thought for a moment and looked around at the glamorous surroundings.

'Here. Dublin. Policing St Stephen's Green would be fine. Keep those ducks in line.'

Cormac laughed.

'I'm afraid not. The Dublin Metropolitan Police do the capital. None of us *gardaí* will be sent up here.'

'Cork then. I'd like to go to a city and be in the thick of things. Or at least a good town. So long as we aren't sent to the back of beyond. I can't stick too many cows and fields.'

After the meal, they went upstairs, avoiding the lift at Marie Rose's insistence. They walked along the corridor to their room, giggling and holding hands. Cormac opened the door, and then picked Marie Rose up and carried her through, kicking the door closed behind them. He deposited her on the bed. His courage wouldn't fail him now. He had had some wine and a whiskey after, and he felt up to the job. Marie Rose was light-headed and giggling, and a kind of wantonness had crept into her demeanour. He removed some hairpins and the monument of her hair collapsed around her shoulders, like a decimated frontline defence. She was beautiful in the lamplight, her perfect skin glowing and her eyes sparkling with a hint of desire. He was on fire and held her tightly to him.

'We'll have to do it now, we'll have to do it now,' he said, feelings and desires swamping him.

'Tell me what it is.'

'I'll show you,' he whispered.

He sprang up, turned off the lamp and, the darkness hiding his shyness and her terror, they consummated the marriage. Afterwards, he collapsed asleep and she lay there, eyes wide open, unsure. It had been so confusing in the darkness, and his hands had been everywhere at once and she had felt aroused all over and finally he had done something, she wasn't precisely sure what, something hard at first but then she had started to tingle and waves washed over her and a noise came out of her and then he grunted, frighteningly, like someone in real pain. And that was it. And she wasn't sure precisely what had happened, but she knew there was something about it she had liked.

3

Charlie tapped gently on the door and pushed it open. The baby had been born at two thirty in the afternoon and he had got there as fast as possible, stopping only to collect a huge bunch of red roses at the airport florist. Alison lay on the bed, her blonde hair sweaty and clinging to her head, and beside her a tiny creature with a massive head of black hair slept peacefully. Charlie, strangely awkward, held out the flowers for his wife to see, before popping them onto a side table, beside two other enormous bunches. Charlie glanced at the cards. One was from Alison's office. That was fast. The other was from Guinness, one of her major clients. That was scary fast.

'Oh, red roses. I just love red roses. There's only one thing more beautiful than a red rose.'

'What's that?'

'Your new-born son. He's the image of you,' said Alison in a low husky voice.

Charlie kissed Alison and stared at the baby.

'It's real. He's come. I'm speechless.' The tears started to roll down his face. He took Alison's hand and squeezed it. 'How are you, my love? How did it go?'

'Fine, not a bother.'

'Are you in pain?'

'No. I think I'm doped up to my eyeballs, so I feel nothing –' she smiled – 'except a warm maternal glow. It's like the glow you have after three strong whiskies.'

Charlie bent over the infant. Yes, he did look like himself. Long-limbed and dark-haired and a little cross-looking.

'Babies always look like their fathers on the day they're born. It's to reassure the dads, because, of course, men can never be certain.'

'He's so tiny.'

'He's not tiny. He's ten pounds ten ounces. In paediatric terms, he's a giant.'

'Michael. I want to call him Michael, after my father. That's it. Michael O'Brien. Like my father.'

Alison smiled. She had wanted Charlie to name the baby. To give him his first gift. She had read through loads of books of babies' names and become bewildered at the array. One name seemed just as good as the next. She fancied a name on a Sunday and went off it by the following Wednesday. So she abdicated the decision. She had told Charlie to surprise her with a name on the day the baby came. She was surprised. Charlie rarely mentioned his father, who had left Charlie's mother high and dry when Charlie and Mary were very small. Gone to England. Never heard of again. Charlie's mother was too proud to chase him for maintenance and had reared the two children in a state of near destitution. It was strange to Alison that Charlie should want to call the baby after his absconded father.

'You sure?'

'Certain.'

'Hmmn. Why?'

'I don't know. I feel I want to. I don't know why.'

Alison thought a moment. At the beginning of their romance Charlie had given an account of his family and told her about his father's absence. That had been it. Nothing until now. Really, Charlie was very untransacted. He worked such long hours and with such passionate absorption, he never gave anything personal much thought. Alison would have to push him on that. Increase his emotional literacy. Make him think. Have a good emotional spring-clean from time to time.

'I want to give Michael O'Brien another chance.'

Alison shrugged. She had left choosing the name up to Charlie and he had chosen. That was that. The baby was Michael. Fine. It was a good name. Solid. Immediately, she decided she liked it.

Baby Michael started to shriek and Alison called the nurse. Charlie was astounded at the powerful anger of the child.

'What's wrong with it?' asked Alison.

'We'll give him a bottle,' said the nurse. 'He might be needing a feed.' The nurse set to heating a bottle.

'Have you eaten?' Alison asked.

'No.'

'Order some room service. You look dead beat.'

Charlie sat in the chair by the bedside and was overwhelmed. He had been terrified something would go wrong. He hated being absent, felt stupidly that somehow if he was there he could help, which of course he couldn't, as he knew nothing about obstetric surgery or babies or anything. But being far away seemed like bad karma. Inviting disaster. He was relieved to see Alison looking so comfortable and the baby so perfect. Alison was in better shape than he was. He picked up the infant, so tiny and light. He held him close and started to cry again.

'It's just the relief. I hadn't realized how worried I was.'

'You're a big goose,' said Alison, smiling. 'There was nothing to worry about.' Alison was always so calm and serene. It was impossible to rouse her to anxiety. Her somnolence seemed even more appropriate than normal here, in these hospital surroundings, the air heavy with tiger-lily pollen and the tangy scent of lochia.

'The flowers arrived fast.'

'Yup,' said Alison. 'Because you weren't here when we came up from theatre, I was lonely, so I called the office. And within twenty minutes, those lilies arrived. I tell you, Jenny, the new PA, is a wizard. Then I sent a text message to everyone, so I'd expect the hordes to descend soon.'

A clickety-click of high heels in the corridor.

'Here are the hordes.'

A gentle tap on the door and Donna burst in, staggering under a huge bunch of yellow daisies. She pawed Charlie and embraced Alison and goo-gooed at the baby. 'Oh, he's beautiful. Alison, I'm afraid there isn't a scrap of you in him. He's the image of his dad.'

Charlie smiled. 'Without the flaws and defects.'

'With the flaws, especially the flaws,' muttered Alison, 'because they're my favourite bits.'

'They do that, you know. New-borns are very crafty. They look like the father on their first day, to give the father a bit of reassurance,' and Donna gave him her cheeky grin. Charlie smiled back. Donna was only pretty when she smiled.

'He's big,' said Donna.

'Yeah, ten pounds ten ounces.'

'Wow. That's big, all right.' Donna winced and gave a sharp intake of breath. 'But, sher, aren't you the fine big girl!' and she hugged Alison a little vigorously.

'Ow, ow, careful.'

'Sorry, stitches.'

Donna went off down the hallway to the room where the vases were kept. She knew her way around the clinic as this was where she'd had David less than a year before.

More clickety-click in the corridor and another tap on the door. Alison's mother, Miriam, appeared, waving a little French designer sailor outfit for the new-born. Miriam was a tall, thin, beautifully dressed woman who looked a lot younger than the sixty-three years Alison ascribed to her. She had the olive skin Alison had inherited, which tanned well, and her hair and jewellery shone in the sunlight which fell across her from the window. She was a tense beauty, without any of Alison's sensuousness. More exclamations, more exaltations. 'I stopped in Becky's shop for this. I had two outfits on stand-by, depending whether it was a boy or a girl. The girl's one was lovely, a little shepherdess outfit. But I thought this would do. It's so much nicer buying presents for girls, don't you think, but boys, well, boys are fine, aren't they?'

'It's lovely, Mummy,' said Alison. 'Thank you.'

'You see, I know nothing about boys, because I had only girls.'

'Well, at this stage they're both the same, except the boys wear blue Baby-gros, Mrs Jackson,' said Donna.

'Miriam, please, Donna.'

'I'm sorry, Miriam.' Donna couldn't break the schoolgirl habit. She had been so fond and grateful for Mrs Jackson's kindness to her. Donna was in the house so much, it was like she was a third daughter. Miriam had been fond of her, the skinny, freckled ugly little thing, and thought she needed more love than she was getting.

'Show me, show me my grandson,' declaimed Miriam.

Charlie angled around with the infant, who was sucking well on his bottle.

43

'Oh, look at him,' squealed Miriam. 'What weight?'

'Ten ten,' said Alison.

'A good size. Ali was big. She was nine ten. We always had big babies in our family. It killed my mother, of course. She died in childbirth. Maternal mortality was still high then. Nineteen thirty-eight.' Miriam sniffed. 'Sorry, I shouldn't be getting maudlin. It's just I'm sorry. At times like this it's hard to forget everything. Let me see him. Oh, he's a little pet.'

Charlie displayed the infant with pride.

Miriam recovered herself. 'He's the image of you, Charlie. You know, they always do that in the first week. It's to reassure the dads.'

'I hadn't realized I was in need of so much reassurance,' quipped Charlie.

'Well, I didn't mean that, Charlie.'

'I'm only joking,' said Charlie.

'Oh, no, I've offended Charlie,' said Miriam. 'Alison, what'll I do? I've offended Charlie.'

'No, you haven't, Mummy. Don't be silly. Charlie never gets offended.'

'He is, he is.'

'I'm not, Miriam. I assure you.'

'Charlie, I'm so sorry. I didn't mean –'

'Mummy, shut up and stop being such a drama queen.' Alison always treated her mother like a child.

Then Cecilia appeared with an even more enormous bunch of tiger lilies. 'My first nephew, I'm so delighted.'

Cecilia's Adrian appeared behind, with a bottle of champagne and a roll of paper cups.

'May I?' he asked of Alison.

'Mmmmn, bubbly,' muttered Alison.

'Oh, I'm so glad you've had a boy, sis. Girls are such a worry.'

Adrian opened the champagne and distributed it to the assembled. The room was getting very crowded now. There were huge bunches of flowers everywhere and the place was beginning to resemble a botanical garden. It wasn't designed for entertaining on a grand scale, for the champagne parties which erupted as a matter of course among Alison's entourage.

'Have we a name?' asked Miriam.

'Michael,' said Alison. 'Michael O'Brien.'

'That's a lovely name,' said Cecilia.

'Mmmn. Lovely.'

'Why Michael?' asked Miriam.

'Charlie's dad's name,' said Alison.

'Your dad, that's lovely,' said Miriam. 'He's passed away, hasn't he? God rest him. It's a lovely way to remember your father.'

Charlie said nothing.

'More champagne for the hard-working mother!' said Alison.

'Thanks, dear,' said Miriam, raising her glass to be filled.

'Mummy, I meant myself.'

'Oh, sorry, dear.'

Adrian filled up the glasses for his mother-in-law and sister-in-law.

Charlie was relieved when everybody had left and he could concentrate exclusively on Alison and the baby. Alison's mother and sister constantly teetered on the brink of well-bred hysteria and they were very tiring. He stared at the baby, transfixed. His little fists were tightly curled and his mouth was curved in a half smile.

'He's smiling,' said Charlie. 'He's glad to be here.'

'Well, I'm glad to have him here,' yawned Alison. 'I'm so relieved that he's out safe and sound. I hadn't realized, but I was very worried about it.'

Alison was such a serene personality, she hadn't seemed particularly anxious.

'What did you tell your mother about my father?'

'Oh-oh. I knew you were going to ask me that. I'm sorry, it's just that Mummy wouldn't understand why your father wasn't at our wedding, so I decided, rather than get her into a big fuss about nothing, I'd issue him with an RIP certificate, along with your mother. Absent and unaccounted for fathers would give her the willies. She'd start coming over all Cassandra about bad blood. Whereas dead parents bring out the concern for orphans instinct, which is very pronounced in her. That's why she was always so kind to Donna. Donna was practically an orphan.'

45

'Hmmn.' Charlie didn't mind. He was just curious. And for all he knew, it was probably true. His father might well have died at some time in the thirty-odd years since he'd last seen him.

'Well, he's not around and, you know, she's hardly likely to meet him at the golf club. A little white lie makes things simpler for Mummy. I'm sorry, I thought you wouldn't mind. We've always had to protect Mummy from the harsh realities of life. And around the time of the wedding she was in such a state. And Daddy was being so difficult, insisting that Hazel come and everything.'

Alison's mother had made a very big deal about their wedding. She was in her element. Her previous outing as mother of the bride and director of ceremonies was at Cecilia's wedding, over fifteen years previously, and it had faded almost beyond recall. The stakes were much higher now. Miriam had been invited to so many of her friends' weddings since then, or rather their children's weddings, and the pomp had escalated over the years. Flowers, gowns, receptions had all come on a lot, as each occasion topped the previous. Alison was happy to hand over the responsibility to her mother, seeing it as a relief not to have to bother about booking sopranos and looking at flower arrangements. Miriam was delighted and took over the role with great glee. It had all reached epic proportions before Charlie really grasped what was going on, and it was too late to put a stop to it. Miriam had been a little put out at his lack of relations, but put a brave face on it. Charlie had to beg and cajole his sister, Mary, and Brendan to adhere to the black tie stipulation on the invitation as they railed against fashion fascism. Charlie had been nervous they wouldn't come, or that Brendan would wear his gardening clothes and wellies just to make their point. But when he arrived at the church, the first person he saw when he entered was Brendan, looking very handsome in the regulation black tie, and beside him Mary quite regal in a silky green gown, her long dark hair piled high on her head. Charlie was glad of them among the sea of strange elaborate hats, all of which turned to inspect him.

When alone with Alison, in the intimacy of their life together, he could forget their class difference. But at that moment, before she arrived in the church, isolated among her people, he knew that they remarked him as a sort of astonishingly superior insect who had climbed the ladder out of the pond and learned to walk amidst the pleasure gardens. He became suddenly self-conscious and dragged his best man, Declan, outside for a cigarette.

Charlie stood at the front of the church, watching the guests arrive, and smoked, bringing his nervousness under control. Declan kept slapping him on the back, as much to reassure himself as reassure Charlie. Declan himself had been married very young and had four children. His wife, Shelley, and the scrubbed kids were seated in the church, in fine form for the 'day out'. He ran a bathroom installation company. He and Charlie had been the two from their class at school who had done very well.

'You can always change your mind and make a run for it,' joked Declan.

Charlie laughed.

'I wouldn't be doing my duty as best man if I didn't offer you a last-minute opportunity to avoid the ball and chain. You could leg it over that wall there. I'll create a diversion by doing a striptease.'

Among the cars that pulled into the car park was a preponderance of Charles O'Brien Motors stickers. This was natural up to a point – his colleagues and employees, all invited, mostly had cars belonging to the shop – but there were many more. Strangers. He pulled on his cigarette in puzzlement. Then it dawned on him. Many of the guests, friends of Mrs Jackson, had made up the inexplicable stream of new clients he'd had over the past six months, after he got engaged to Ali. There was a general boom in business across the board at that time, but Charles O'Brien Motors experienced a super-boom. A business bubble. And this explained it. Couples entering the church greeted him and smiled and he smiled back. They looked eerily familiar. Customers. The church was full of customers. Miriam had recommended him to all her friends, from the golf club, the sailing club, the bridge club. They had all come down with fistfuls of cash to buy cars and procure a sneak preview of the groom. 'My son-in-law-to-be is a self-made man, you know, and an orphan.' Up to forty cars of his were parked in the church lot, representing near a million pounds of business. These guests had paid hand-somely for their wedding invites, and paid it voluntarily without noticing. Charlie's business had been the beneficiary. Mrs Jackson arrived and kissed Charlie on both cheeks. She'd had a couple of whiskies to stiffen her nerves and was giddy and skittish. More than usual. She'd left her ex-husband to accompany the bride.

'They'll be at least another fifteen minutes,' she sang at Charlie, and headed into the throng to mingle. Persuade the remainder of her friends that they wanted a new car and send them down to the East Pier. For an apparent airhead, she was quite an operator. Charlie stared at her bobbing pink hat and he marvelled. He prided himself on being quite the salesman, but it had never occurred to him that marrying somebody with rich connections would generate business for him. And all in this natural, un-strained, pink-hat-bobbing fashion. He wondered if Declan noticed. Probably not. He wouldn't have such a sensitized eye for the black and gold Charles O'Brien logo.

'We'd better go back in,' said Declan. 'We look like a couple of corner boys out here. All we need is a bag of chips.'

They went back inside. Charlie passed Miriam talking to an older couple whom he remembered selling a car to a few weeks past. They smiled and greeted him cheerily. Charlie sat down in the front pew, both amused and appalled.

But it all went out of his head when he rose to the tune of 'Here Comes the Bride' and, looking down the church, he saw Alison make a steady progress in his direction. She walked tall and voluptuous in a white and silver dress which hugged her figure and accentuated her loveliness. The formality of the dress, the music and the lights from the stained-glass windows made her look like she was from another world. Miriam dabbed her eyes. She'd thought she'd never get Alison up the aisle, given how picky she seemed to be. Thirty-four. She was getting on. Miriam did like Charlie. After some initial hesitation, she'd been won over by his obvious decency. But she felt deep down that a truly nice boy wouldn't have spoiled the line of the wedding gown by having her several weeks pregnant as she went up the aisle. Ali denied it, but Miriam wasn't a fool and the dress no longer had that perfect fit.

Alison's father walked beside her with obvious pride. Colm Jackson was now beginning to look elderly. He had finally agreed to leave Hazel behind, and this had lowered the temperature generally. He was duly allotted father of the bride duties.

Miriam had overspent her budget by a long shot. She was reasonably well off in that she had an expensive lifestyle, but she hadn't great reserves of cash. She had forced her husband to sell much of his property, including the large city centre pub, the foundation of their wealth, in order to make a settlement with her when they finally separated after years of a non-marriage. Hazel, the young thing, now no longer so, had been on the scene for thirty years. Miriam had engaged a clever lawyer to argue her separation agreement. She insisted that she had worked in the pub and built up the clientele. This had a certain truth. She had advised the interior decorators over the years and swanned around when they started getting the lunch trade moving. In fact Colm Jackson hadn't done much work there either. He mainly came in at the end of the evening and supervised the managers' till receipts. The pub had been sold just before the boom and the resultant money not terribly wisely invested. Miriam rued the fact that she spent so much on a lawyer but cheesepared on the accountant. The same pub would be worth millions now. Alison's father cursed his ex-wife for this above everything else. When Miriam announced she'd overspent her budget, a figure to which he had contributed half, he said he hadn't anything spare and couldn't help. This was possibly true.

Charlie had ended up picking up the tab for most of it.

'Poor Mummy, she got carried away.'

Charlie didn't mind paying. The business bubble had left him with a bit of spare cash.

The nurse took the baby and Alison drifted off into a deep sleep. The exhaustion of the experience was just hitting her. Charlie made his way down to the coffee dock. There was a peculiar atmosphere in the clinic. Part hospital, part five-star hotel. He got himself a coffee and a pastry and dialled Mary's number.

'We had a boy.'

'Congratulations, Charlie. That's great.' Real warmth in Mary's voice. 'It's just great you've had a kid.'

'Ten pounds ten,' volunteered Charlie.

'Super. It's nice when they're big. They're more confidence-inspiring. Especially the first. How's Alison?'

'Seems fine.'

'Did she have the Caesarean in the end?'

'Yeah.'

Mary had been horrified by Alison's 'birth plan'. She had thought that Alison needed her head examined. They weren't really a take, Alison and Mary. Very different types. Charlie hoped that the wariness between them didn't blossom into full-blown hostility. Mary was very important to him.

'Tut-tut. Foolish girl. Unnecessary surgery. But what's done is done. Make sure she keeps wriggling her toes. Watch her circulation. There's a high danger of thrombosed clots post op. The morbidity rate is quite high.'

Charlie didn't want a medical lecture. Especially from a failed nurse.

'And make sure her wound is kept clean and dry.'

'Michael. We've called the baby Michael.'

There was silence at the other end of the line.

'Oh. Why?'

'Well, I just thought I wanted to.'

'Oh. Well. That's a nice curse to put on the new-born.'

'Mary, stop.'

'Sorry, that's a terrible thing to say. I'm so sorry. It's a lovely name. And you're brave to choose it.'

Mary had always been the one who had more difficulty talking about their father. She remembered him much more clearly than Charlie, and mourned his loss all her young life. She had been five to Charlie's three when 'Dada' left. Charlie recalled a childhood filled with her obsessive laments about his absence. It was these lamentations which silenced their mother on the subject. Charlie's attempts to extract information about his father were rebuffed with suggestions that it would just get Mary going again. Photos had to be removed from mantelpieces. Charlie's mother had erased all traces of him to avoid the childish hysterics. It was like he'd never existed. Mary wasn't happy until she teamed up with Brendan and had children of her own, now three, five and seven. She loved her children, but even more, loved watching Brendan love them. One of her favourite pastimes was to sit on the back step of the house and watch Brendan digging the vegetable garden with the children 'helping'. She spent her life witnessing daily demonstrations of paternal love. Each spade and shovel handed to Daddy by the kids, another small patch in the repair of her filial wound.

'I'll come in tomorrow. Can I bring the kids? Only if Alison is up to it. They're dying to meet their only cousin. Well, they will be as soon as I tell them. Susan's mad about babies. She's at that age.'

'Sure. Ali's fine. She seems very fit.'

Mary hung up. Charlie felt relief. She took the name OK. When he made the final decision on the plane back from Munich that afternoon, he knew Alison would like it and take it in her stride. It was Mary he felt might have had difficulty with it. But she'd taken it OK. A bit gracelessly, but OK.

Charlie was shaken from his reverie by somebody halting at his side.

'Congratulations, Mr O'Brien.'

It took Charlie a second or two to recognize Dr Anderson, who stood by his side, a tray of coffee aloft. Dr Anderson sat down. He was Australian and very informal. He wore his hair long and in a ponytail, and was immediate and friendly. That was why Alison liked him. His accent was still very pronounced, despite having lived here with his Irish wife for almost ten years.

'Oh, Dr Anderson. Thank you.'

'Please call me Jonathan. A fine big boy. Have you named him?'

'Michael. For me da.'

'Solid traditional family names. My favourite. Nowadays people are calling children Pepper or Cobweb or Tamasin Chutney. I bet your father's pleased.'

'Yup. Delighted.' Charlie didn't want to go into it.

Dr Anderson's phone rang. A merry series of beeps.

'Fine. Ten a.m. tomorrow. Is everybody on? Great. Yes, the weather sounds fine.'

51

Dr Anderson smiled at Charlie. 'I'm in a regatta tomorrow. Some friends of mine have bought a boat and I've been roped into the team. It's great fun.'

So this was the mysterious engagement on Friday. It sounded very cancellable to Charlie. Anderson conformed to the Australian stereotype. All outdoors and water sports.

'How's Alison?'

'She looks OK. I was just up with her. Tell me, Dr Anderson, is it dangerous to have a Caesarean, like she did?'

'Not really, for a woman in such good health.'

'People have been saying to me –' what was it they were saying? – 'eh, something about clots.'

'People, people. People are always full of uninformed views. Sure, there's a marginal risk. But, on the other hand, I wouldn't fancy a ten pound ten battering ram doing a job on my pelvic floor. Incontinence, intercourse problems. It's swings and roundabouts.'

He bit into his pastry and drank his coffee.

Charlie wanted this line of conversation to cease. He was in over his head. He'd have to stop worrying about things he knew nothing about. Anderson's phone rang again.

'Sorry. Sorry. I've told everybody to ring me after five 'cos I'm just out of surgery.'

Charlie was glad of the interruption. He drank his coffee and ate his bun. He felt changed. He knew that fatherhood would affect him. How could it not? But he thought it would affect him in more tangible ways. He thought he would become more cautious crossing the road, more protective of Alison perhaps. But now he felt the change at his core. Everything looked different. The cup of coffee, the bun. It was all new. He smiled. Inside and out, he smiled. He was grinning like a fool. Dr Anderson's tanned face smiled back at him. He was listening intently to information being relayed to him on the phone.

'Yes. How much is that? And how much is the BMW? OK. I'll have to think about it. I can't test-drive next week, I'm away. I'll try the week after. I don't have my schedule in front of me.'

Charlie's ears pricked up.

Anderson put his phone away and sighed. 'I'm trying to get a new car, but I play golf every Saturday, and my weekdays are usually chock-a-block with work. I can't skip the golf, because without the exercise I get a stiff shoulder during the week. Surgery tension.'

Charlie took a card from his top pocket and handed it over.

'A BMW you're after, eh?'

CHARLES O'BRIEN MOTORS
East Pier, Dun Laoghaire.
Specialists in
BMW and Volkswagen.

'Why don't you come and see me? I've got some fine babies at the moment,' said Charlie.

Charlie wrote his personal mobile number on the end of the card.

'Call me any time. I'll happily let you test-drive after hours.'

Charlie specialized in the personal touch.

Ashleigh Court was even more unbearable than normal when he let himself in that evening. Without Alison inside, it felt completely pointless. Charlie looked at the empty and bare kitchen, all shiny appliances and digital displays. It looked equipped to traverse galaxies rather than boil a potato or fry an egg. He wandered out into the sun room. Alison had got some pleasing wickerwork furniture with Japanese writing on the cushions. He wondered idly what it said. It could be saying 'You're an arsehole' for all he knew. He sat in the chair that Ali normally sat in. She loved this room because it had plenty of light, and she could look up at the sky through the Velux window. He felt the ghost of her embrace in the chair. His eye drifted to the crossbeam which ran from one side of the sun-room roof to the other, little curlicued carvings at each end. The roof was way too narrow to require a crossbeam for support. It epitomized what he disliked about this house. It seemed to have an embedded dishonesty.

Charlie went upstairs, changed into his tracksuit and picked up his kit bag. On Thursday evenings he met Declan in the gym, where they did a workout together. They used to go for drinks instead, but Declan had to stop. Some liver problem he'd developed. So now they cemented their friendship pumping iron. They booked adjacent weights machines and pumped away for half an hour. Then they played squash. Finally a swim. This routine was the same every week.

When Charlie arrived, a little later than normal, Declan was already hard at work. Charlie didn't disturb him to tell him about the baby's arrival. Just got on his own machine and worked away. Charlie loved the strain of this. He loved the feeling of strength. He worked away until he felt pain. Muscle ache. He had a nice routine going now, working on each group of muscles. Working them until they protested.

In squash, they indulged in some marvellously colourful competitiveness. They teased each other beforehand and worked themselves up into a pitch of ambition. A huge investment was made in each stroke. They swore at each other and fought over the calls. It was a sight to behold. Anybody watching would never have taken them for the great friends they were. Declan had won the previous two weeks, and Charlie was getting annoyed about it now. He was beginning to suspect that Declan was sneaking to the gym and getting training behind Charlie's back.

Then they showered and swam. This was the most relaxing bit for Charlie. He ploughed through the water with ease, long strokes bringing him up and down the pool with comforting monotony. A cold shower and then down to the bar for a juice. Declan had showered and changed faster than him and was waiting for him below, the juices ordered and sitting on a barstool.

'We had a boy.'

Declan slapped himself on the head.

'Oh, of course, it was to be today. I'm so stupid to have forgotten. It's just I had a very big job on.'

'Lovely little kid. And Alison's fine.'

'Jesus, pal, welcome to fatherhood. They drive you mad, the little brats, but you'd die for them.'

Declan insisted that Charlie drink a whiskey and he bought two cigars for them. Charlie smoked his happily.

Now that their Thursday evening was spent in the gym, rather than the boozer, Charlie wondered what they'd talked about in those long beery hours. Shelley used to arrive for a last drink just before closing time. She was so thin, Shelley, her arms and legs looked brittle. She was a bit of a comedienne and knew everybody in the pub. Declan would have been lost without her.

Now, in the twenty minutes they spent over their juice and whiskey, they seemed to have less and less to say to each other. Charlie's ability to communicate was deteriorating. He was drifting further and further away, from Declan his best pal and from himself. It was like he was being sucked backwards out of life. And it made him feel very uncomfortable, this constant sense of slippage. He had a strange and vague feeling that he was clinging to Alison like some sort of life raft.

4

Marie Rose howled. The pain was beyond anything she had ever imagined. It was like being struck by lightning. Repeatedly.

'There, there, Mrs O'Brien, you'll be fine.'

'I think I'm dying.'

'No, love, you're going to be fine. It always gets really bad just before the baby appears.'

'Stop the pain, please.'

'Open your eyes, love, don't close them. It'll trap the pain inside you.'

Marie Rose felt like her body didn't belong to her. Instead her head had been attached to a pain machine which was involuntarily going into spasms over which she had no control. And the pain, the pain.

And where was Cormac? He had been here a moment ago but had now disappeared. Where was he? Why wasn't he here? At that moment Marie Rose hated him. Hated him for not experiencing the pain, for leaving her to it. She was almost out of her mind. Cormac had fled downstairs in panic when the going got rough.

Bean Uí Cartaigh was the local woman who 'did' the births. She was self-appointed but very experienced as the nearest doctor was eight miles away. She had attended the majority of the births in the locality for the past twenty years. Her own family was grown and mostly emigrated, but she busily delivered grandchildren for the two remaining, her son on the farm where she lived and her daughter married on a farm beyond in Dunquin.

Cormac had initially declined the offer, but Marie Rose had insisted, as she rightly suspected there'd be little chance of getting a doctor unless she moved to Dingle for the end of her confinement, and she wasn't inclined to do that. Also she liked the bluff and brusque Bean Uí Cartaigh and was impressed by her knowledge and submitted to her. Cormac hated getting too involved with the locals. He hated the idea of this woman playing such a central role in the intimacy of their family life. He had wanted to send for his mother, who performed the same function in her own locality in West Cork, but Marie Rose wouldn't hear of that. It would mean she'd have to fuss and bother and entertain a mother-in-law she scarcely knew when she was quite exhausted and bedraggled at the end of the pregnancy. So Bean Uí Cartaigh was running the show.

She came downstairs to replenish her basin of water and put on some more kettles. Cormac was pacing the kitchen in front of the range.

'Is she all right, Mrs Carthy? She sounds terrible.'

Cormac insisted on using the English form of Bean Uí Cartaigh, as that was how she introduced herself to him. Marie Rose had fallen into the Irish form, as that was how she was referred to by everyone else.

'No, she's fine. They all sound terrible. I never once knew a woman to birth a first baby without a fuss. It does get easier on the second.'

'Are you sure she's all right?'

'Look, Sergeant O'Brien, so far there's nothing out of the ordinary to be getting yourself alarmed at. She's a grand healthy girl and everything is going ahead as normal. If she's moaning a bit louder than some, it's probably because she's a town girl and not used to hardship.'

Cormac was not ignorant of biological reality. Growing up on a farm, he'd assisted at the delivery of myriad lambs and calves, but the calmness and serenity of those procedures had made him all the more shocked at the violent intensity of what was going on upstairs.

'But the howls. She's howling fit to break your heart.' Cormac was very worried. His face was white and his lips bloodless.

'Don't be getting yourself into a fuss. Here, go for a walk out the road and say a prayer for a healthy boy.'

She put some rough black rosary beads in his hands and got his cap and coat from the hook for him.

'Go on, out, out. You're only under my feet here. I've to get things ready as the time is coming. I'd say we'll have a result in another few hours.'

Cormac stood uncertainly, the howls from upstairs increasing in intensity.

'Out,' she ordered.

He turned to go.

'You might catch some lawbreakers lurking about the streets.'

Cormac ignored the cheek and fled. He walked down the garden path and stepped out into the village, where he stood smoking a cigarette, listening to music coming from one of the pubs. There was a warm glow of lamplight from the premises opposite, and for a moment Cormac keenly felt the lack of fellowship he experienced here in this remote place. He couldn't mix with the locals. It was his job to enforce the law and too much familiarity wouldn't be good. Also, this was a staunchly Republican area, and he was known as a Free State man. The Free State police were in this area under sufferance, and he knew it. In theory, the new police force should have had automatic authority. Irishmen policing Irishmen. But now it was boiling down to what particular kind of Irishman you were.

People in the vicinity spoke Irish among themselves, though most could and did use English when it suited them. His mother was a native speaker, but his father wasn't. His mother spoke Irish to his aunts and uncles, but they didn't bother with it in the home. Its usefulness hadn't been predicted. Cormac had worked hard at learning Irish from the gramophones while training. He could manage with aplomb the *cúpla focal* which were necessary, and all the paperwork in Irish was easy to him. His prowess in classroom Irish was partly responsible for his promotion and totally responsible for his posting to this *Gaeltacht* area. But he hadn't the humility to speak the language and fail, and his proficiency never progressed off the page. He was no match for the local thick Kerry brogue. He might as well have been policing a district where the people spoke Greek.

Cormac wasn't comfortable mixing with the guards in the barracks. His status as sergeant made them awkward with him. People in the area, the local priest and publicans, who would have been typical company for him elsewhere, looked on him with suspicion. The parish priest had been running his own little law and order dispensary from the confessional, with the authority of the man above, and wasn't keen on being displaced by a fella in a Free State badge. The bitterness of the civil war was still palpable, especially in an area like this. So he was alone. And happy to be mostly, but at this very moment he would have given anything to have the company of one of his brothers to share a whiskey with.

He walked south out of the village and the little buzz of activity soon faded behind him. The night was still and clear, and an almost full moon lit the path in front of him. He could feel the rosary beads in his hand and he was going to put them away in his pocket, but decided against it and clutched them still. He wasn't much given to prayer, his nature too practical, though his mother had instilled in him a fondness for the rites of religion. Also, he saw the sacredness of the beads for others and thought it would be bad luck to bring that down on his head, tonight of all nights, so he handled the beads with care. It was a mild night and he walked until he'd gone for a few miles. He couldn't bear to go back to the intensity of the barracks and couldn't bear to listen to his wife's cries. Better to be away. Better to arrive back and the event would be over and he would have a baby, something he was desperately looking forward to. All this business of having a son, he didn't care. He'd happily have either a boy or a girl. A boy'd be nice, but a little girl running around looking like Marie Rose would be something as well. At the headland, he sat for a moment on a drystone wall and looked out to sea. In the moonlight he could see a small boat working its way along the coast. Probably poteen makers, he thought. Good luck to them. He wasn't about to go harassing them now. Let the poteen makers of the Dingle peninsula have their day, or night, with their friendly moon. He sat there for a long time and watched the progress of the little boat. It met another boat and something was passed from one to the other, the boatmen sure they were unobserved. By the light of the moon Cormac could see it was a keg. He smiled at the activity. Though he meticulously upheld the letter of the law, as was his duty, he privately didn't agree with a lot of the temperance attitudes that were fashionable. Not since the case of the

mountain man which had come to court only a month previously.

Cormac and O'Donnell, the youngest guard in the barracks, had
found an illegal still in a farmhouse up the hills. It was in a room
off the kitchen which had formerly been used as a dairy, and so
was well equipped with sinks and the like. They were acting on a
tip-off received by O'Donnell, who was a great mixer and
footballer and got a lot of information from the loose tongues of
the young. When Cormac entered the house, the equipment was
in full swing, the furnace roaring away and the cylinder bubbling,
poteen issuing forth into a bucket like the river of Hades, while
the wife was in the kitchen stirring the family supper on the fire.
Really they were an unfortunate bunch. Children everywhere.
And the poor missus so bedraggled-looking. The accused was
a fine figure of a man, and exceedingly courteous to Cormac
and O'Donnell, conceding that they were only doing their job.
Cormac developed a liking for the tall Kerryman.

Nevertheless, Cormac prosecuted the case, as was his duty. He
did his best to ameliorate the details. District Justice Walshe, who
heard the case in Dingle court, handed down a sentence of three
months' hard labour. The wife, with the infant on her lap, started
to sob in the court. The justice asked had he anything to say in his
defence. The mountain man piped up in his gruff gentle voice.

'Your honour, I have a wife and thirteen children to support.
I've only one acre of bad land and I was "stilling" only to put food
in their mouths.'

There was a silence after the defendant's little speech, broken
only by the semi-controlled sobs of his wife. The judge looked at
the man.

'I have extreme sympathy for these unfortunate congests in
their terrible struggle, but as this man could get no work, it would
be no loss to his family to take him from them for a time. People
must understand that this evil practice must stop before there is
any prosperity in the country.'

The man was led away, and Cormac had a bad feeling about the
business. Justice can taste sour sometimes. Was it so wrong? What
was the difference between this man's enterprise and Arthur
Guinness's brew or John Powers's whiskey? Apart from scale.

And location. And by appointment to the king of England. Was this true justice that was getting dispensed? Why were we locking up a poor man in order to protect the business of a rich man? Everything was supposed to get better once we were running things for ourselves, but this father of thirteen was going off for independent Ireland hard labour, and his wife was sobbing bitter independent Ireland tears.

Superintendent Geraghty clapped Cormac on the back. He was in a terrific boil about seizing illegal distillation equipment and Cormac had to feign some enthusiasm for the whole caper. But Geraghty was a bit of a softy, and Cormac thought he'd get to work on him and get some strings pulled. Put the liquor criminal back onto his mountainside with his unfortunate wife sooner rather than later. There was nothing to be gained by having him breaking stones in jail. This whole puritanical business was just an attempt to be holier than the English, on account of the Black and Tans having a reputation for running round full of drink. Cormac thought it a bit foolish. They were their own force and should make their own laws, taking into account natural justice, not some imagined social enemy left behind after the British colonial tide had gone out. But Eoin O'Duffy, the big *Garda Síochána* boss beyond in Dublin, was a great man for being a holy temperance Catholic. He had a fondness for marching the force up and down in front of Marian shrines, like so many dollies in shiny buttons. It gave Cormac the right pip. This and other things. The Utopia of a free Ireland had to be accommodated to the deficiencies of the individuals. Pity we couldn't get in all those perfect heroes out of the storybooks. Cú Chulainn and the likes. Ferdia and Oisín. Pity we were stuck with mere mortals. Cormac sighed. Maybe the next generation will be better, he thought, his mind returning to the noisy struggles going on upstairs at home. Maybe if they grow up in a free Ireland, they'll be better people than we are.

A man progressed along the road, whistling to himself and carrying a big stick. Cormac recognized the distinctive shape of him. It was Frank Duignan, originally from Dublin, who was down here learning Irish and renting a small place out the road. He took lessons from the locals and was popular with everybody, splashing his money around. He was affectionately known locally as Froggy. Froggy was a tall man, with a very round belly and skinny legs. He was about ten years older than Cormac, and fond of food and drink. Apparently he claimed some sort of a living writing books, but it was rumoured he made his real money as a landlord up in Dublin. Cormac had always found him friendly. He hailed him.

'Sergeant! Is that you? And what are you doing in the ditch? Holy God, you gave me quite a scare.'

'Would you join me for a cigarette?' asked Cormac, his need for company overcoming his pride.

'Happy to, happy to.'

Cormac lit their cigarettes.

'So, what are you doing here? In the ditch, on your own. Some sort of covert operation? Law-breaking rabbits watch out!'

'Marie Rose is having the baby. I'm afraid I couldn't stand it and I've scuttled off to cool my nerves.'

'Well, good God, man, you need a drink.'

Frank steered him back towards the village and into a pub. Cormac went along with it. This was the first time he'd entered one of the pubs for any reason other than to enforce the licensing laws. Frank was well known in there and was hailed on entering. There was quiet when people realized who was with him. Then the hum started up again.

'Two large whiskies, Sean,' he requested of the barman. 'This man needs sustenance!'

Sean nodded. They all knew what was going on above in the barracks. Someone had seen Bean Uí Cartaigh hastening up the road, all her things under her shawl, and reported it in the pub. For once, they felt kindly towards Cormac. Though he wasn't exactly friendly to any of them, a prickly character by all testimonies, a man expecting his first baby was a man under pressure. Sean put the whiskey in front of Cormac.

'That one's for luck.'

He charged Frank Duignan for the other. The little act of solidarity meant a lot to Cormac. Right at that moment, he needed it. Needed some indiscriminate act of kindness from the other side. Humanity had a way of breaking out, despite people. And babies brought out the humanity in all. Cormac had read in the paper that on Christmas Day in the trenches of the war in Europe, the Germans and the Allies took the day off and played football to celebrate the baby Christ's birth. Then returned to the slaughter the next day. He drained the whiskey and asked for another.

'I'll pay for this one, Sean. Against the rules of the *Garda Síochána* to be seen to accept free drink. Except the one for luck for the baby.'

Frank Duignan turned out to be very conducive company. They sat quietly in the corner and Frank steadily worked his way through a fair few whiskies, Cormac having difficulty keeping up with him. Cormac soon realized that politically Frank was close to him. Praised the *Garda*, praised the new administration. Cursed the foul-mindedness of those who opposed the treaty. Did all this in hushed tones, only for Cormac's ears. Otherwise he kept to more general subjects: literature, music, poetry. Subjects that didn't get people so hot and bothered.

'There's great things going on above in Dublin in the Abbey Theatre.'

'It's hardly a day trip from here.'

'A young nation needs its own drama and storytelling. It's a mark of mental health. Have you seen the plays of Johnny Synge?'

'No,' said Cormac.

'He's the man, now. I met him a few times when I was a lad. My father knew him. Fine fellow. Not at all like a Prod. In fact lots of them Prods aren't like Prods. Take Lady Gregory now. She's a fine woman. Sad about her son.'

'What happened to him?'

'Died in the war. A pilot. Disappeared over France. Dangerous business, flying around Europe.'

'Dangerous business, war,' said Cormac.

'Did you fight?' asked Froggy.

'A bit, not much,' answered Cormac.

'Very modest of you. Everyone I meet in Dublin claims to have occupied the GPO single-handed, and personally done away with at least five English soldiers.'

'Maybe being in the GPO was glorious, seeing as they all got butchered afterwards. But where I come from, there was many deeds that weren't claimed by anyone.'

'Like what?'

'Like nothing.'

The young maid came out from the back and whispered something into the barman's ear.

Sean the landlord came over to Cormac. 'Our girl says that your maid is after coming over to get the crib. Your wife left it over here because she was spooked looking at it.'

This was news to Cormac. There had been a crib, a gift from Carrig that had arrived by cart a few weeks ago, and it had stood in their bedroom for a while. Then it had disappeared. Cormac had never enquired where. Cormac stared at Sean, a bit bewildered. The whiskey and the emotions of the day had left him befuddled.

'Well, if they want the crib it only means one thing,' said Sean.

Cormac stared at him confused. And then the penny dropped.

'The baby.'

He grabbed his cap from the table and left the pub.

He was a little unsteady on his feet as he made his way in darkness through the village to the barracks. He let himself into the living quarters and everything was very still. Worryingly so. Panic surged in him and he ran up the stairs to the bedroom and threw open the door.

Marie Rose lay there, calm, serene and beautiful. Her face was glowing and her hair had been combed and tidied and she was wearing a white lace nightgown which buttoned up to her throat.

'You want to look well when you show the baby to your husband,' said Bean Uí Cartaigh, tidying her up after the baby had been settled and swaddled.

'He's a boy,' said Marie Rose, her exhaustion showing in her voice.

Cormac crept over to her side and peered down at the little puckered face of the infant.

'I'll leave ye a minute,' said Bean Uí Cartaigh as she departed with her knitting needles. She always knitted a jersey for the new-born after it was delivered. She'd done it every time and was now superstitious about it. She went downstairs and left the proud new parents in privacy.

'I always knew he was a boy,' said Marie Rose.

Cormac picked the infant up and the baby's eyes opened and looked at him with a serious and accusatory stare.

'I'm your father,' said Cormac. 'Pleased to meet you.'

'Michael. I want to call him Michael after my father,' said Marie Rose.

They hadn't discussed names, and Cormac was a bit taken aback at Marie Rose's declaration. The baby was the first in Cormac's generation in his own family. He was the second eldest, but he was the first married and he'd wanted, if the baby was a boy, to name him John for his own father. But he said nothing. He didn't want to upset Marie Rose. She wasn't usually so adamant about things. And Michael was a good strong name. A hero's name.

Marie Rose loved being a mother. A pile of beautiful baby clothes had arrived in a parcel from Carrig and little Michael was the swankiest baby for miles around. Marie Rose was careful of people's feelings, though, and she often covered him with Bean Uí Cartaigh's *bánín* knitted cardigan and other gifts she'd received from the local women. She was proud of her baby son and brought him everywhere with her, showing him off to everyone she met.

Somehow, now she had a baby, she was becoming more and more accepted. Before, as a newlywed, she didn't have much in common with the local unmarried girls, but hadn't fully become one of the local married women. She worked up her Irish language so as to fit in all the better. Cormac became unhappy with her ingratiations.

'We should stand a bit aloof, Marie Rose. Be civil but strange. We don't belong here. We'll be moved in due course to some other place, where we'll have to police another lot of different people. I am the sergeant here, and you are the sergeant's wife, and you'd want to remember that,' he said gently. 'You haven't married a farmer and moved into a locality where you're going to put down roots and join a family plot in the local graveyard. Marry your sons off to the local girls.'

'That's all right for you to say, Cormac. I need company.'

Cormac was busy all day at work, where he had the company of his *Garda* colleagues. Then he came home to her and the baby at night. Read the papers for a bit of diversion. He could as easily be living on the moon. It was different for a woman. Marie Rose felt she couldn't be alone all the time. She'd go out of her mind here looking at fields and sea and sky. No entertainment except for weather formations.

'You weren't a great mixer in Carrig.'

'That was different. I was waiting for my life to begin. Also, I had my family back there, and they were company enough.'

Marie Rose put a plate of dinner on the table in front of her husband and settled down opposite him, mashing a little bowl of potato and carrot to give to Michael. He was weaned now and took to the new fare with great gusto.

'Well, let's hope that I don't have to go arresting any of your gossipy friends' husbands.'

'You can arrest whom you want. I don't care,' retorted Marie Rose with spirit.

'That one, Mrs Carraher. Her husband came within a hair's breadth of being one of the executed. Geraghty told me there was a warrant for him and he hid out for two years. Only recently slunk back down the mountain.'

'I don't give a fiddler's what her husband did or didn't do. The woman is civil and friendly, and I return that.'

'Tim Carraher was a real die-hard.'

'Maybe she doesn't agree with her husband's politics.'

'Women always agree with their husband's politics.'

She shot him a sharp look.

'I don't agree with yours.'

'That's because you have no politics, like your father. Women either agree with their father or their husband.'

'My father is a fine man.'

'A man without politics is like a tree without a trunk. A bush. No stature.'

'My father gave the poor a helping hand.'

'He lined his own pockets and kept on the right side of everyone.'

'He might have had no politics, but he had humanity. Jesus Christ had humanity.'

'Oh, so your father is Jesus Christ now.'

'Well, closer to it than some. Handing bread to the poor is a finer thing to do than lurking in a ditch with a long knife waiting to do in the next unfortunate to come strolling along on the wrong side of "politics".'

There was silence for a while. Cormac was always slightly taken aback by his wife's spirited argumentativeness. It surprised him. Marie Rose was sorry she let the row develop. They got into bickering arguments easily, but they got out of them easily also. Marie Rose changed the subject.

'I was listening to a talk on 2RN about the Atlantic flights.' She was fascinated by the attempts being made to fly the Atlantic. It was such an amazing thought, that people could actually fly to America from Europe. She avidly read the newspaper reports on the subject. 'The Frenchmen are feared drowned. Captain Nungesser and Captain Coli. They haven't been seen since they left the French coast ten days ago. People have given up on them. It's sad, though. To be lost in such a big ocean as the Atlantic.'

Marie Rose had been sent a wireless set by her father. She had hankered after one since they'd had one installed in the barracks. Cormac and she had arguments about it because she wasn't supposed to be listening to the barracks set. Marie Rose couldn't understand why she couldn't have a little listen to it, rather than have it gather dust all day. None of the young guards minded her about the place. Cormac was supposed to be the sergeant and make the rules, so why couldn't she be let listen to it? The argument was settled by the arrival of the present from Carrig.

'Imagine that. Imagine flying all the way from Europe to America. They must be madmen or geniuses.'

'There'll always be men who'll take a risk for glory, Marie Rose.'

'There's a load of airmen just waiting to take off from America to try the flight. They're only waiting on the weather to be right. There's a queue of them all chasing the prize. It's a bit indecent, with the Frenchmen still missing. A bit heartless.' Marie Rose had memorized their names and incanted them now, like a litany of the brave. 'Commander Byrd and his crew. Captain Chamberlain and Captain Bertrand. Captain Charles Lindbergh – he's going to do it on his own.'

Marie Rose had spent the day talking about it with her friends Ellen and Kate and they both thought these fellows were mad. Ellen was the priest's housekeeper, and Marie Rose had spent an hour of the afternoon over there with the baby drinking tea. The two other women were gloomy about all the airmen's prospects. Thought they'd all wind up in the Atlantic, never be heard of again and break their mothers' hearts. They said that the Americans didn't have enough real trials in life. Life was so cosy over there that they weren't losing sons to the sea or emigration, so they had to invent risk-taking activities in order to dispose of them.

'That's daft. These airmen are all very brave,' Marie Rose had said.

'Sometimes it's hard to tell bravery from thick-headedness,' replied Ellen.

Marie Rose didn't mention to Cormac her visit to Ellen in the priest's house. Cormac had had a row with the parish priest and was angry with her if she went there. A few months ago they had gone over to Father O'Keefe to enquire after arrangements to have the baby baptized. Father O'Keefe didn't like Cormac. In the early days, the priest had a habit of calling in to Cormac and leaning on him in minor matters of policing and generally getting on Cormac's nerves.

There had been a dispute about a right of way to a pond over O'Grady's field. The field used to be in grass for years and years, but O'Grady's son had taken over the farm and had put the field in vegetables, and that was where the trouble started, as the cow usually had a little vegetable snack for herself on the way to the pond. O'Grady felt the cow owner should be able to keep the cow from 'stealing the cabbage out of my children's mouths', or else could go around the field, a route which would extend him by no more than an extra few hundred yards. Father O'Keefe came into the barracks to plead on behalf of the pious cow owner and

Cormac had listened patiently to his spiel, but followed his own course of actions.

On another occasion, malicious fire damage had been caused to the post office in a strange and isolated incident. This caused the priest to come and repeat whispers and slanders, all the products of his housekeeper's fevered imagination as far as Cormac could see, about the section of the community who weren't fully devout in their attendance at Mass. Cormac got sick of the sight of the priest and discouraged him. He wasn't a great man for priests at the best of times.

When they approached him about the matter of the baby's christening, Father O'Keefe sat down at his big book to see about dates. 'Michael, huh. That's a nice name for the child. A nice West Cork hero's name.' He smiled oleaginously.

'It's my father's name, Father,' said Marie Rose softly.

Cormac got up and stormed out of the priest's house. He'd flown into a rage over the incident. 'I'm not letting that Republican crawler maul his grubby hands over my son.' Marie Rose tried to calm him down. Priests were priests, a mixed bunch. And this one wasn't a charmer by any manner of means. But you had to look beyond the individual priest to the function they performed. 'We kicked the English out and I think we should send the damn priests packing after them.' Marie Rose hated when Cormac spoke this way. She felt it would bring them bad luck. She normally gave in to Cormac, but she decided to fight her ground on this one.

'Look, does it matter? Surely the important thing is that the job is done. If O'Keefe has insulted you, so what? Rise above it.'

The next day O'Keefe called round to apologize. He knew he'd upset the young sergeant and wanted to make amends. Marie Rose welcomed him and plied him with tea and scones. Cormac, annoyed to find the priest in occupation of the best chair when he returned from a patrol, accepted the apology with dubious grace. The situation had gone into stand-off. Meanwhile, the baby languished, unbaptized, in a state of sin.

Cormac ate his meal with relish. It was a lovely bit of fish pie, cooked up real nice with onions and milk. Marie Rose had become very adept in the kitchen. She had claimed to know nothing about culinary matters when they married, but soon got the hang of everything, and her brand-new range in the barracks was the envy of all her friends, most of whom were still cooking on the hearth.

'Cormac, do you think Captain Nungesser and Captain Coli are foolish or brave?'

'Brave, but dead,' said Cormac, chewing the food.

'And would you be proud if Michael did something like that? Brave, but risky at the same time.'

Cormac thought for a moment. 'The trick is to be brave, but alive. If any of these Americans land in Paris we'll think that they're great men altogether, but if they ditch into the ocean and are never heard of again, we'll think they're fools. You can't separate the deed from the result.'

'Imagine flying in an aeroplane. That must be a marvellous thing to do. I'd love to try it, even though I know I'd be afraid,' said Marie Rose.

'You might get a chance,' said Cormac. 'Aeroplanes are only getting going now. People say that their design will be refined and become much more common, that every country will have its own fleet. They'll be used to deliver mail to godforsaken remote places like this place, rather than that rickety train that comes out to Dingle.'

Cormac had never really settled in here. He hadn't started to belong. Marie Rose felt a little sorry for him. He was very alone. At least she had managed to create a little community of friends for herself. The only person he ever had a friendly evening with was the superintendent over in Dingle, and the odd time with Froggy Duignan, whom Marie Rose disliked and felt Cormac only encouraged because he was as much a misfit as himself. Marie Rose couldn't see the point of Froggy Duignan. What did he do all day? Idleness was bad for a man.

'I've the christening organized,' said Cormac. 'It'll be on next Saturday over in Dingle.'

Marie Rose went silent. Cormac was dishing out orders here and his tone annoyed her.

'He's a nice priest over there, Father Moore, a friend of the super. This is a lovely fish pie.'

The balance of power between them wasn't fully established, and Marie Rose knew that in some matters she got her own way, in others he did. But she felt very strongly about this. Why trek all the way over the mountain to Dingle to baptize Michael? It defied reason. She was not only annoyed by Cormac's behaviour on this topic, she was baffled by it.

'Cormac, I just don't understand you. I want Michael baptized here, at home, in our own parish.'

'This isn't our parish. We don't belong here. There might be some sense in taking him home to Glenmore, or back to Carrig to be near your people or mine, but we owe that priest nothing and that church nothing.'

Cormac looked at Marie Rose. Under no circumstances was he going to go back into the priest's house with his tail between his legs, inviting him to baptize Michael. So he just smiled at her. In a slightly sympathetic way, as though she didn't understand. This maddened Marie Rose. But she couldn't go against him. She could hardly take the child over on her own. Since Cormac was so set against it, she would have to give in.

'Just give me a reason. Apart from the fact that Father O'Keefe annoyed you with the Michael Collins remark. He apologized for that, and you have to accept a man's apology. It's only fair.'

'I accept his apology, all right. I'm just not going to let him baptize the child.'

'But I want a reason.'

'All right, girlie, I'll give you a reason.' He got up from the table and put his napkin down. He went over to the range and lit a cigarette from a coal and stood up tall.

'This is a story, more than a reason. But it should explain things in an allegorical way.'

His eye twinkled. Marie Rose smiled. He had a way of winning her over.

'This is a story about my great-great-great-great-grandfather, Tim O'Brien. Further back than you can imagine, he was living away on our farm back home. He was a hard-working farmer and husband and my great-great-great-great-grandmother was a good and dutiful wife, who kept a very clean house and very clean geese, and they begat us all, as the Bible would say. They were among the finest people in the townland of Glenmore, and many said the actual finest. But Tim O'Brien was a proud man.

'And the floods came. God was angry and wanted to punish the people for sins of sloth and disobedience, and worshipping every other thing but God. So it rained for forty days and forty nights, and the seas rose. Every day, Tim O'Brien would walk up to Vaughan's Pass, in the hills above Glenmore, and look down on the rising flood and the devastation of Bantry Bay. He was six and a half foot tall, so the view he got was splendid. Whiddy Island was covered without trace, the town of Bantry sank, and the palaces and pleasure gardens of Garinish Island and Glengarriff were no more. And every day, Tim O'Brien, my ancestor, wondered would the waters rise as high as Glenmore, and take them and their farmlands too, and he returned every day to his wife with an increasingly more worried face.'

Marie Rose put a cup of tea into Cormac's hand, and he smiled a thanks to her.

'One day, he went up to Vaughan's Pass and looked out, and saw a large boat sailing around the area that used to be Bantry town, and Tim walked down to the water's edge and hailed the man on board. It was Noah.

' "Are you Tim O'Brien?" asked Noah.

' "I am," said my great-great-great-great-grandfather.

' "I have come to save you from the floods," said Noah. "You and your wife. God sent me to save you."

'Tim O'Brien looked at the cosy boat as it bobbed high on the seas and from where he was standing he could smell a good stew cooking on board. He looked around at the rising floods and the enlarged Bantry Bay. He looked up at the grey sky, heavy with the prospect of a renewed deluge.

' "Thank you kindly," he said, "but I'll decline, for the O'Briens have their own boats."

'Noah sailed off, puzzled, scratching his head. And that's the story.'

'That's a funny story,' said Marie Rose.

'It's an old family story. My father tells it often, and he does a great job embellishing it. I'm afraid I didn't do it justice.'

'And what's it got to do with O'Keefe?' asked Marie Rose.

'It explains the proud streak in us, that's all.'

5

Charlie tilted back on his chair and put his feet up on the desk. The cheque for the Volkswagen Passat from Anderson lay neatly folded in his breast pocket. A simple sale. Charlie had given him a discount, but the deal was still very worthwhile from his point of view. The premises were empty, save for himself and Phil the cleaning lady. It was now nine o'clock and he had come down specially to open the place up for Anderson. People liked the personal touch. They liked having salesrooms opened exclusively for them. They liked the convenience of being exactly catered to. Anderson had driven off a happy man. Happy with his deal. Charlie sat at his desk, also a happy man, also happy with his deal. He got up and walked out onto the balcony and looked down at the salesroom. Lots of sleek lines and shiny glass. A palace of diagonals. His office was like a crow's nest, overlooking the shop floor and the two-storey glass shop-front that looked out over Dun Laoghaire harbour. Busy with boats.

The front façade of the shop consisted of two chunky verticals straddled by a giant Charles O'Brien Motors logo. This sloped away onto great angular haunches, giving the impression of a Sphinx crouching and looking out to sea. The premises looked very well from offshore. Looked commanding and inviting. Boat owners had lots of dough to spend on luxury cars. Charlie found the activity in the bay hypnotic. He found himself occasionally standing there on the balcony staring. Transfixed by some tiny figure on a water-ski, or a person sunning themselves in mid-afternoon on a boat. It had become very prosperous round here. Not like when he was growing up. There had always been a few yachts, but now it looked like every local teenager had a water-sports vehicle.

The silence surrounding Phil's scratchings was filled with the tinny sound of latent electricity and lots of glass. A snatch of poetry came to him from school. 'My name is Ozymandias, king of kings:/Look on my works, ye Mighty, and despair.' He flexed his shoulder blades to try and settle an itch. It didn't work, so he took off his jacket to try and scratch it. That didn't work either, so he stood against a wall and rubbed his back against it. That gave him some relief. I am proud of my shop, he thought to himself, and then wondered why. Why was he proud? He didn't know.

From several rafters hung fronds of greenery. Charlie wasn't sure about them. Thought they looked like triffids. The architect had insisted on them, insisted that the original drawings wouldn't have been as attractive without the greenery, but Charlie wasn't sure. The architect felt the 'photosynthetic opportunity' provided by all that glass was too good to miss. It all seemed a bit pointless to Charlie. Great green rubbery thongs. This wasn't a bloody greenhouse. And Phil was always muttering about how dusty they got. They had been so expensive to purchase and install, Charlie couldn't bring himself to simply remove them. And everybody said they looked good in the brochure.

The new building had been finished about a year ago, but it still felt massive and unfamiliar to Charlie. He liked when he worked late alone. He liked wandering about in the quiet glare of the place, looking at the sleek lines of cars. This was beauty. Perfect new cars in a perfect new showroom. Phil would be finished soon, and then he'd have the space totally to himself. He found himself eager for her departure.

It was all so clean now. Originally, when he was training as a mechanic, and later when he started Charles O'Brien Motors as a maintenance facility, it had been dirty. Scruffy and oily and messy. Then cars were about getting stuck in. Cars were about filth. But now cars are about inciting esteem. Cars are about security and prosperity and position. Cars are no longer a method of getting from A to B, where a man would buy a car and keep it for ten years. Now, they're a reflection of the soul.

'I'm off, Mr O'Brien. I gave the kitchen area a special scrub like Sondra asked.'

'Bye, Phil. Thanks.'

Phil put on her coat and scarf. Charlie was afraid of her. He always dodged her when she was about, and gave her untoward bonuses at Christmas and holiday time. Sondra, the office manager, dealt with her. Phil was 'saved'. She had explained to Charlie once about how her life had changed since she found Jesus. 'He comes with me everywhere. He sits on my mop handle and brings me an extra bit of strength when I need it.' Charlie had been horrified at this speech. He wasn't much into religion. And as time had gone by he got scared of Phil. She did seem different from other people. There was indeed something 'saved' about her. He would have been more comfortable with her not around, but she was a very good cleaner, or so Sondra reported. Sondra had a nose for shoddy cleaning jobs. No slackers would get by Sondra. 'These days it's easier to get a good managing director than a good cleaner.'

'Goodbye, Mr O'Brien.'

'Goodbye, Phil.'

She let herself out the side door. Phil insisted on calling Charlie 'Mr O'Brien'. He had pressed her to use Charlie, but she refused. She liked the formality, she said. He had asked her would she rather be called Mrs Durkan, but she refused that. Phil would do fine. It reminded Charlie of his mother. She had always used the formal address to the women for whom she'd cleaned house. Mrs Nolan and Mrs Smith. And they'd always called her Deborah. A special cleaning-lady social code. Charlie was glad Phil was gone, with her mops and detergents and witches' brew of cleaning stuff. He would much rather get contract cleaners who came in anonymously in yellow suits, did the job anonymously and left anonymously, the only sign of their presence a sterile invoice in tomorrow's post.

Phil's head popped round the door.

'I've a present for the baby. I meant to bring it down today, but I hadn't got wrapping paper. I'll bring it on Friday.'

'You're too good, Phil.'

'Goodbye, Mr O'Brien. Don't work too hard. That lady of yours needs a bit of help now.'

She shuffled off. Charlie waited a while to see that she was really gone. Then he lit up a cigarette. Now that baby Michael had arrived, he had decided he'd better stop smoking. He had absolutely stopped smoking at home. Can't be giving the nipper a bad example. Got to be a better person so that he'll be proud to have me for a da. He relished the fag, knowing their days were numbered. He could feel his focus shifting from the business to his home. He had lived his whole life for this place. It had been his only real interest until now. But Alison had made a powerful intervention in his life, had drawn him away. He had met her here. Sold her a car.

Two years ago. He'd had a phone call from a lady who introduced herself as a friend of Gemma and Harry Sinnott and asked if she could come in later that evening. He'd happily obliged. Harry Sinnott was a regular customer. Had updated the last two times from him and regularly had his service done. Occasionally a customer would come his way saying he was recommended by Harry Sinnott. Word of mouth. Charlie appreciated it and always acknowledged it to Harry. Often did minor repairs for him for free as a kickback. A nice symbiosis. Alison had arrived half an hour later than the appointed time, and Charlie was close to giving up on her. 'I am so sorry,' she had breathlessly cried when she arrived. 'My meeting ran on and I did try to phone you but my stupid phone's battery was dead. Am I too late?' She smiled her dazzling smile at him. No, she wasn't too late. He had all the time in the world.

It was a warm August evening, and he walked her round the compound, showing her various models and discussing how much she wanted to spend. Did she want a new car or a used car? How much space did she need? It was before the new building was completed and the yard resembled a building site. Charlie's office was in a Portakabin. 'I want something dinky,' said Alison. 'I've just been allocated a parking space in the office lot, but last in, smallest space. So, eh, compact is what I want. Compact, but irredeemably stylish.'

Charlie showed her a BMW Mini Cooper. It was yellow and had a sun roof.

'This has my name on it!' she exclaimed. 'Yellow is my colour.'

'It's a nice little car,' said Charlie. 'Perfect for round town and very easy to park.'

He fetched the keys and she took it for a test-drive. He sat in beside her. The best time to make the sale was on the road.

'Where'll I go?' she asked. 'I've never done a test-drive before. My old car was one of my sister's cast-offs.'

Charlie glanced at the great silver Honda Accord she had arrived in. A fairly fancy cast-off.

'Wherever you like. Take the coast road. Go to Dalkey. It's a nice run.'

She made herself comfortable and put on her seat belt. It was at that precise moment that Charlie started to find her attractive. At the moment when she stretched the seat belt across her front and secured it in its clasp. He noticed how lovely her body was. Full firm breasts and a flat tummy. Her T-shirt was scoop-necked and short-sleeved and a purple silky skirt stopped above the knee. Her skin was tanned and covered with little blonde hairs. Her long blonde hair was tied back in a careless scrunchie. Now that he was so close to her, he found her stunning. This was unusual for him. Charlie had never been a great man for the birds. He hardly noticed them. He'd had a few girlfriends over the years, in an almost dutiful fashion. None of them had worked out very well. In his early twenties, he'd got half-heartedly engaged to a young one who thought she was knocked up. But it was a false alarm and Charlie soon scrammed. His finding Alison attractive took him by surprise. He hadn't been with a woman for ages, certainly over a year. It was as though he'd forgotten about sex. Maybe it's the heat, he thought. It was a very balmy evening.

Alison took off, the kick in the car taking her a little by surprise.

'It *is* a baby BMW. It can go from 0 to 62 miles per hour in 10.9 seconds.'

She crunched the gears as she changed from second to third. Charlie shuddered.

'Pull in.'

She did so, apologizing.

'Here,' he said. 'You need the seat further forward. The gears crunched because your clutch action is imprecise. You're too far away. The size of the car is deceptive. It's got a lot more legroom than you think.'

He slid her further forward.

'Thanks. That feels much better.' She took off again. She drove to Dalkey and then turned on to the Vico Road, its view splendid in the evening light.

'I love it here,' she said. 'I grew up around here and I think this is the most beautiful sight in the world.'

It was true. Charlie didn't much look around him and he took this area very much for granted. He too had grown up not too far from here. She pulled in to the kerb at the Vico.

'Open the sun roof!' she said excitedly. He did so. And she stood up and looked out.

'Just look at that blue sky. It's gorgeous and it's going to be gorgeous tomorrow. I'm a bit of a sun worshipper.'

Charlie thought she was liking the car. She sat back down and once more pulled the seat belt across her breast. Charlie had to look away.

'This is a good little car.'

Charlie couldn't read her. Was she going to buy? At this stage he couldn't say. More sell.

'The range was just launched this summer. It's got very striking styling, all-important nowadays. The chrome touches are innovative, but have that classic-car mood. Yet it's a very comfortable car to drive. I particularly like its handling because it's like a go-cart. You really feel in control. It's the way cars used to feel, in touch with the road. It's an outstanding performer on winding roads.'

Alison smiled. 'Well, let's test it on the Vico Road, because that's nothing if not winding.'

She took off again, more smoothly now, accustomed to the new machine. She went on along the Vico and down the twisty descent into Killiney. She banked sharply into a lane and under the railway bridge, arriving on the grassy verge at Killiney seafront.

'Yes, it hugs the road, sure does.'

'It's roomier than you think. Fold the fifty-fifty rear seats down and there's plenty of room for kit bag or shopping.'

'I like the car. The price is within my budget. I'm going to take it.'

'Fine, that's great.' Bingo! It was always worth the late opening.

He invariably made a sale. People who asked you to stay on late were serious about purchase. Weren't wasting your time.

'Do you mind if I get out and have a quick paddle? It's just I love this beach so much, and I hardly ever find time to come down here any more.'

Charlie shrugged. He didn't mind at all. She kicked off her sandals and picked her way across the stones to the sandy area of the beach. Charlie got out of the car and sat on the bank. He removed his tie. He didn't like the shirt and tie routine, but felt he had to go along with it. Car sales were all about confidence, and his preferred casual clothes put off the type of clientele he was after. He lit a cigarette and watched Alison. A light breeze fluttered her skirt. She really was quite something to look at. Slim waist, but curvy elsewhere. Her calf muscles were strong and her hips broad. She waved at him and splashed lightly in the water. He waved back. All of a sudden he was overcome with desire for her. It felt strange. She wouldn't look at the likes of him though. She was what Declan called toff totty. He was a scruff, and he knew it. He looked down at his hands, which were still a little grimy from working on an engine that afternoon. She wouldn't look his way.

He walked down to the water's edge.

'Happy feet,' she said, jumping up and down, doing neat little ballet steps. 'My poor feet needed to be cooled down.' She gestured to Bray Head. 'We used to come and swim down here almost every day when we were kids and I used to draw Bray Head. Obsessively. I have piles of old sketchbooks of the head in every different light.'

'We used to come down here at night,' said Charlie. 'And have cider parties.'

'Oh,' said Alison. 'You from round here?'

'I grew up over in Ballybrack.'

'I grew up on Military Road.'

Charlie nodded. Big houses in their own grounds. Toff totty was right.

'Come on in the water,' said Alison.

Charlie was startled. Was she flirting with him? It was hard to figure out. She just had this very informal way with her.

'OK.' He took off his shoes and socks, rolled up his trousers and followed her into the water. His suit was incongruous, and he felt a little foolish. He felt wrongly attired. But he always felt wrongly attired. He felt wrongly attired in life. Whereas Alison looked so natural and relaxed. Her nipples had hardened in the breeze and now peaked through the light T-shirt. Charlie didn't know where to look.

'There now. You'll have happy feet too.'

Charlie felt very uncomfortable.

'Relax,' she said. 'You seem very uptight. It's not good for you. Let it all hang out.'

'It's hard to relax in a suit.'

'Take it off.'

Jesus. Charlie wasn't up to this. But he took off his trousers and belt, then his jacket and stashed them with his shoes.

'That's better,' she said. 'You look almost human.' Charlie's hairy legs were strong and muscular. Alison gently teased him with splashes of water.

'It's funny, you take things so much for granted when you're a kid. It was only after I grew up that I realized this was one of the most beautiful places on earth. You can keep your Mediterranean or your Alpine peaks. This is the Utopian landscape.' She gestured to the expanse of Killiney Bay and the Wicklow hills in the background.

Charlie looked around and tried to enter into the spirit of what she was saying. He suspected she created the beauty of the landscape herself. It was beautiful to her because it surrounded her. But that beauty was becoming infectious. And he was looking round and beginning to think he too was in paradise.

'I suppose we'd better go back,' she said. 'Do the paperwork for the car.'

Charlie nodded docilely, though he was in fact now quite happy gently paddling in the water. He put back on his trousers and shoes with as much formality as he could, feeling uncomfortably observed. He looked around and she was gone, back up to the car. He slung his jacket over his shoulder, followed her and sat in beside. She pulled the seat belt across her and he could restrain himself no longer. His hand dangled in the air for a moment and then landed on her breast, gently clutching the extroverted

81

nipple. She gasped. Firstly she seemed shocked. He thought for a moment he'd made a terrible mistake, misread the situation. She looked stunned. But he felt an overwhelming compulsion. He had often thought he had a low sex drive, but now he was on the business. He leaned over and kissed her, then slipped his hand up her T-shirt, opened her bra and touched her flesh. And then she was on him. Like an animal. She tore open his trousers and caressed him, kissing him hard on the mouth, eating him. She managed to pull a condom from her bag, put it on him. Then she straddled him and took him and he gasped. Her head and shoulders sticking out the sunroof. They shuddered and juddered and he held on as long as he could, trying to wait for her, but he exploded, and then so did she. A brief brutish convulsion. He couldn't believe it.

She got off him and sat back in her seat and breathed heavily. She calmly put on her seat belt. Started the car, put it into reverse, turned it and headed back out under the railway and through the lane. Dusk was now all around them and the trees overhanging the Vico made it very dark. She drove quickly back to the shop. Charlie was speechless. He went into his office. The strip-light lit the tawdry interior of the Portakabin mercilessly. He was sweating and almost panicked.

'Do you want a whiskey?' he asked her.

She nodded and he poured them both a small whiskey. She took out her chequebook.

'Who do I make the cheque out to?'

'Listen, steady on, you can't just buy a car off me, after –' he paused, searching for words – 'after what we just did.'

'Why not? I still want the car. Need it in fact, 'cos I can't park that great hulk over there in my brand-new parking space.' She smiled bravely.

'It's just.' Charlie didn't know what to say. 'It feels wrong. Maybe I should give you a discount or something. I always give discounts to friends.' That had come out wrong. Discount! He had a bargain-basement mind. He wanted to give her the car.

'How much discount? How much is a fuck worth? No, thanks. I'd rather pay the full price. If you gave me a discount, I'd feel like a whore.'

She carefully wrote out the cheque. Seventeen thousand nine hundred and ninety-five pounds. Payee: Charles O'Brien Motors. She pulled the cheque from the book and put it on the desk.

'That makes me feel like a whore,' said Charlie. And he ripped the cheque up.

'I want the car,' said Alison.

'I'm not selling it to you.'

'I wanted the fucking car more than I wanted the fucking fuck,' she said, a little teary now, sounding for the first time spoiled. Panic was setting in. This was getting out of hand.

'Take the car. I want to give you the car,' he said. 'Here, give me your details for the logbook. These are the car's details.' He handed her a piece of paper. 'Phone your insurance company tomorrow and get them to insure it. You can come and collect it tomorrow. It's yours. The car is yours. Here's the key.' He put the key in her hand.

'I can't take it without paying for it.' She put the key back on the desk.

'They always say, "Never mix business with pleasure," ' said Charlie, 'and we've just done that. And I've never done anything like that before. I'm sorry. I hope I didn't offend you.'

This was going all wrong. The atmosphere was souring.

'You didn't offend me. But I obviously have offended you.' And with that, Alison left.

The next day Charlie called her at her office, and the day after, and the day after that. He persisted and eventually she took his call. He asked her out to dinner the next weekend. She agreed.

She arrived to meet him at the shop, wearing a long black strapless dress and a huge red silk orchid in her hair, which was twisted up on top of her head. If he'd found her beautiful on the previous occasion, she took his breath away now, dressed like a model. She put a bank draft for seventeen thousand nine hundred and ninety-five pounds on his desk. 'I got a bank draft because I know if I gave you a cheque you wouldn't cash it.'

The draft sat uneasily in the middle of the desk.

'And another thing . . .' said Alison.

'What?'

'It *is* roomier than it looks.'

She turned to leave the office. Charlie smiled. He let the draft sit on his desk. He wasn't going to argue with her. He got his coat and locked up the office, placing a mechanical manual over the draft to hide it from view. A bank draft is like cash. Can't be left exposed to view. He wasn't that casual. He took her to the restaurant she had chosen.

'I'm sorry about the other day,' he said. 'I wanted us to go on a proper date.'

'I'm not really sorry about it,' said Alison. 'I liked it.'

'We were like savages.'

'That's what I liked about it. The savage element.'

'I've never done anything like that before. I just wanted you to know that, in case you think . . .' he said earnestly. Her good opinion was of the utmost importance to him.

They had a lovely time over the meal. They clicked somehow. Charlie felt transformed. He was in love with her and he knew it. He felt compelled, felt he was being guided in his actions by some external force, beyond his own control. She liked him and it made him feel great that she did. She took him home to her apartment, a small single-gal pad in a complex at the back of Blackrock. It was very crisp and stylish, all beautiful furniture and *objets*.

'What exactly does a stylist do?' asked Charlie.

'Well, on a campaign I've got responsibility for the overall look. The art director comes up with the concept, and the copywriter writes the lines if there are any, but I put the gloss on it all. I'm part of the creative team. For example –' and she showed a picture from a magazine on the coffee table advertising a homewares department – 'I did that. The jewellery, the flowers, all the detail. It's a nebulous task, but believe me, it shows if your stylist ain't any good.'

Charlie looked around at the apartment. It was as stylish as her. The essence of style and civilization. And Charlie was surprised by feeling loved there. He felt loved with his rough hands and accent, and slightly awkward physique. She took him to her big fresh bed and loved him there, quietly and calmly. Now with his clothes off, Alison could see what a lovely body he had. A stylish body. A masterpiece of nature. A beauty. He took his time with her, got to know her, and when he entered her, he put his weight on her, and gently pinned her underneath him, and he knew he'd have to have her. Not just once, not just now, but all the time and for ever.

'Will you marry me?' he whispered into her ear.

'Are you serious?' she asked.

'I have never been more serious in my life.' He stroked her, hard.

'How do you know?' she gasped.

'I just know. I feel I'm being guided. You are for me. I know. If you need time to think, that's OK.'

'Yes, I'll marry you, Charlie, yes yes yes.'

He withdrew, took off the condom and entered her again, feeling totally connected to her. They moved in total harmony and he gave himself to her with a roar, spraying her with his seed. His secular heart felt something sacred, like a violent prayer.

'I want to give you a child,' he said.

'I wondered how I'd know you when I found you. But I do know you. I know I know you,' she said.

There was consternation in the Jackson household when Alison announced her engagement.

'How long have you known him?'

'A few months,' lied Alison. It was in fact two weeks.

'And who is he again?'

'Well, he owns Charles O'Brien Motors. Down at the East Pier. He's a friend of Harry Sinnott.'

'And who are his parents?'

'Mummy, that's a stupid question nowadays. People's parents don't matter any more. It's all a meritocracy now.'

'And the best man is a plumber!'

'He owns a plumbing business, Mummy.'

Miriam was uneasy about the whole thing. She had a bad feeling about it. Why couldn't Alison have found a husband among people of their own sort? Cecilia did. She married a brother of a schoolfriend. Adrian was a fine man, even if the schoolfriend sister had gone to America and married a hippie. A boy who grew up in a council estate in Ballybrack? Miriam was sure the omens were bad.

'But, Mummy, you and Dad didn't exactly have a great marriage, despite him being "your sort".'

'I know. And my aunt tried to talk me out of marrying him and I should have listened to her. She didn't like his lip.'

'His lip?'

'Yes, his upper lip. She thought it thin. And cruel-looking. She tried to talk me out of marrying him on my wedding day. I should have listened to Aunt Julia. But no, I knew it all.'

'But Dad's not cruel.'

'No. Your father's flaw is weakness, not cruelty. Aunt Julia's assessment was correct in that the lip was peculiarly thin, but wrong to diagnose cruelty. Your father was about as cruel as a lamb. Perhaps had he a little more cruelty, he would have got rid of the trollop. She trapped him, you know. She left her husband for him and after she'd done that, he hadn't the heart to drop her. Trollop. She's lower class too. Must be some streak you've inherited from the Jacksons. They were very well to do. Landed, going back centuries. In the habit of affairs with the servants. There was some story about your father's grandmother and the gardener. Some scandal going back to the Victorian era. I remember some story vaguely. It's breaking out in this generation now.'

'Mummy, you haven't even met Charlie. You can't be having views on someone you haven't met. He's very nice. And special.'

Alison arranged a date. Dinner in her apartment. She invited Harry and Gemma as icebreakers. Her mother knew Gemma very well and approved of Harry. The evening went off reasonably well. Miriam was won round. Charlie was charming. Low key and gentlemanly, if his accent was a little rough and his nails a bit grimy. And he didn't use the fish knife for the prawn starter. But there was something nice about him. The face was open and the eyes clear. And Miriam saw devotion in the way Charlie's eyes followed Alison round the room, admiring her in every attitude and light. And Gemma and Harry were very friendly with him. And the world was different now. She'd have to get with it.

After the main course, she lifted her glass. 'To the happily engaged couple.' Alison sighed with relief. It would all be so much simpler if Mummy was on side. Alison loved her mother. She didn't approve of her, but she loved her. And Mummy was part of the picture. Charlie would have to take that on board. Once every week, without fail, Alison had dinner and spent the evening with her mother. And once a week Miriam spent the evening over at Cecilia and Adrian's. The two girls thought that their mother would be unbearably lonely without them. Dad had Hazel, but Mummy was alone. And though Alison felt no rancour towards her father for leaving, she had no pity for him. She thought him fine. But she pitied her mother. And she appreciated the fact that her mother had kept the marriage charade going for years to shield Cecilia and Alison. Her mother and father left the house together to go on holidays, and unknown to the two girls Miriam had gone for an annual holiday alone. While Colm had gone off with Hazel. They coordinated to return together, one a Mediterranean bronze, the other a Jamaican tan. One year they'd returned from holidays, Daddy with a tan, Mummy without. 'I used too high a factor suncream and didn't get much colour.' In reality, it had uncharacteristically rained in Corfu, while the sun baked down on Dad in Lanzarote. It didn't strike Alison as peculiar until her mother later told her of these charades, and little details started to fall into place.

Charlie hadn't particularly taken to Miriam. He found her fussy and tedious, but he made the effort because he knew it was required. And quite simply, he would do anything for Alison. If she asked him to stand on one leg for a year, he would have done it, and liked it.

Charlie walked around the salesroom. It smelled of Phil's polish. He relished the clean sound of his shoes on the floor. The squeak of expensive shoe leather on marble. He was fulfilled. He had everything he wanted. A booming business of which he was the sole boss, surrounded by the machines he loved: cars. A fabulous wife whose presence in his life gave him a sense of delirium. She was as beautiful as any supermodel. Sometimes he closed his eyes and pictured her draped across a car: the perfect ad. And now, a thirteen-day-old son, a gorgeous tiny little helpless mite. He had everything he'd ever known he wanted. But he didn't feel quite right. He felt there was some great weight on top of him, pressing him down. It was Wednesday. Not his running night. He might have a run. An extra run. He was doing that a lot frequently. Having an extra run. Alison was beginning to get annoyed about it. Now that she had the baby, she liked to have more of him in the evenings. He sat down on the bottom step of the flight which led up to his crow's nest and stared transfixed at the shiny paintwork on a red BMW 7-series, seeing a distorted reflection of himself and the shop behind him. He sat there in a trance for a good while until he was woken up by the phone. He could tell by the tone that it was his line. He picked it up on Sondra's desk.

'Yes?'

'Darling?'

'Yes.'

'Would you get me some cotton buds in the chemist on the way home?'

'Sure.'

'How did it go?'

'It?'

'Anderson. Did he buy?'

'Oh, yeah. It was so long ago I'd forgotten.'

'Hurry home.'

He felt the tug. Alison could always pull him up out of himself. He wanted desperately to get home. To see her and him. To see the two of them. He alarmed the shop and left, then went into the chemist down the road to fetch the requested cotton buds, an urgency in the task. Then, fast along the coast and into busy suburban streets. Then the back roads behind Blackrock, Charlie getting unreasonably agitated by slow drivers in front of him. A tiny old woman in an Opel Corsa drove so slowly round the bend, Charlie almost went into the back of her. He chastised himself for his impatience and held well back, though regretted it when a young woman in a Suzuki Swift brazenly cut in front of him from a side road. Suzuki Swift. A Japanese stripper. Who doesn't waste your time. The Suzuki turned off and he was behind a light green Mitsubishi Colt. It pulled in to the kerb without signalling and stopped inexplicably. Charlie gave him a reprimanding beep. Then he signalled, pulled out and passed it. The driver was an eighteen-year-old youth, in his mammy's car probably. Cars, like dogs, assume the characteristics of their owners. He was once again behind the Opel Corsa and the geriatric corner-turning. He kept well back. It seemed like an age before he got to the gates of Ashleigh Court. He waited as the gates opened slowly and lugubriously. They failed momentarily at two feet, and just as Charlie was considering getting out of the car to give the gate a good kick, it started up again. 'Teasing fucker,' he muttered to himself as he passed through. He pulled into their parking fore-court and braked sharply, allowing himself the petty violence of that single jerk. Then he jumped out and made his way in to them, an urgency in the journey as though he was returning after a long, long voyage.

Alison stood under the hot jets of the shower and relished the sensation on her skin. She hadn't showered in days. It was difficult to find the time, and when she had the time she was usually too exhausted. But now she had baby Michael asleep in his pram, she grasped the opportunity, plugging the baby monitor in her bedroom so she could listen to his slight and pleasant snores. She didn't feel herself yet. But that didn't surprise her. The baby was only thirteen days old. Michael. Michael. She was having difficulty switching to Michael from 'the baby', which was what he had been called for nine months. She stripped off and went into the en-suite, leaving the door open so she'd hear the infant if he woke. She washed her hair and rubbed shower gel all over, making a nice soapy lather. Then had a final cold blast to give her a bit of a zing, and got out.

The new house still felt strange. Nothing was where she expected it to be. She would stretch out her hand to pluck the shampoo from a shelf and find herself grasping air. The shelf was elsewhere. The temperature of the shower was difficult to set. The top shelf in the hot press was too high to reach without a stepladder. She must make a list of things they needed. Nothing remained in her head for long any more. She wrapped herself in soft towels, lay on the bed and flicked through a baby manual. She dried herself off, got out her hairdryer and sat at her dressing table, her face framed in the oval mirror. She hadn't had her highlights done for a while, and little strands of grey were beginning to show through the blonde. Fine lines were forming round her eyes and mouth, like little dried-up rivers. Age advanceth. Not twenty-one any more. She dried her hair and tied it back, putting on face cream. Her face was uncomfortable after a shower without the cream. She pulled out some red pyjamas and was about to get into them, but stopped, and stood naked in front of the mirror. She was fat. Always inclined to be a bit fleshy, the pregnancy had put up a fair bit of weight, and she now felt too exhausted to exercise. She placed her hand on her tummy, which drooped and felt like a great loose sack. She stood in profile and thought she looked like she had a kangaroo's pouch. She did her best to hold in her tummy muscles, but it had little effect. Her tummy muscles felt like they were no longer there. She put on the pyjamas, and felt she looked much better.

Charlie had gone down to the salesrooms after dinner, which Alison resented, even if it was to open the shop for Dr Anderson. They'd eaten a very nice lamb casserole, delivered by Cecilia, who was keeping the freezer stocked up with home-made meals. Alison, alone and overwhelmed during the day with the baby, wanted Charlie to stay home in the evenings for the moment. She'd get back to her normal independent self in time. But tonight she begrudged him. She pictured him down in Charles O'Brien Motors in splendid isolation, sitting in his giant jam-jar looking out over the bay. He'd been gone ages. Surely it didn't take that long to sell a car? Anderson was the efficient type. He exuded informal efficiency. He'd either buy in five minutes or be gone. Alison felt herself getting unreasonably grumpy. Tears welled. Hormones, she cautioned herself. Do not expect to be rational for several weeks. And she was exhausted with the night-feeding. Originally they'd agreed that they'd share the night feeds, but Charlie slept like a stone and never heard the baby wake up. Michael, Michael. She checked the baby monitor to make sure the infant was still breathing. She was terrified he'd just stop. She went to bed with the newspaper and drifted off into a light doze.

She woke a half an hour later, feeling very refreshed, and then panicked. She lurched to the baby monitor and listened. Yes, still breathing. He was so small, his grasp on life so recent, she found herself in a state of wonder at the fact that he kept breathing. She went down the stairs and into the kitchen, where he slept peacefully, snug in his pram.

She started to buzz around the house, gathering up clothes and generally tidying. She put on the radio and played classical music. And then went into the sitting room and put on the television for the news. She gathered armfuls of clothes and stuffed them into the washing machine. The washing machine was new and very perplexing. It had arrived accompanied by a lengthy manual, which Alison felt she didn't have time to read. She set it to some sort of programme, guessing at the meaning of the symbols. She loaded up the dishwasher and turned it on. It was getting very late now. What could be delaying Charlie? She didn't want to seem a pest, but she wanted him home. She phoned the showroom.

'Yes?'

His voice was uncertain and dislocated.

'Darling?' she asked, sure it was him, but feeling he didn't sound like himself.

'Yes.'

He still sounded distant. Almost drugged. She started to feel irritated.

'Would you get me some cotton buds in the chemist on the way home?'

'Sure.'

He had warmed up now. The voice was becoming alert.

'How did it go?'

'It?'

'Anderson. Did he buy?'

'Oh, yeah. It was so long ago I'd forgotten.'

'Hurry home.'

Alison went through to the sun room at the back. There was a feature pillar and wooden crossbeam which supported the vaulted ceiling. Alison felt the sun room was crying out for some greenery. It looked so bare. She wanted to train some sort of vine up the pillar and along the crossbeam. And she wanted some big rubber plants. She fished out a plant catalogue from a drawer and looked up the vines. There was a rapid-growing indoor one that she thought would do nicely.

The phone rang. It was Cecilia. Cecilia had taken a new-found big-sisterly interest in Alison since she became pregnant, and this was only enhanced by the arrival. The sisters had always got on well, but the difference in their lifestyles had meant they didn't see so much of each other. Cecilia spent her life ferrying her children here and there and working hard to make sure they and her husband had and continued to have the perfect life. It was a full-time job, all that perfection. Gardens had to be kept up, roses had to be dead-headed, interior decor had to be applied where necessary. The petrol tank needed to be topped up. This was a neurotic twitch. Cecilia felt the tank was getting low when it dropped near the half-full mark.

'He sleeps all the time, Cici. Is that normal?'

'Be grateful, sis. Some of them are sleepers and some not. You're lucky if you got a sleeper. Sarah, now, she never closed her eyes from the day she was born, but Philip slept as soundly as can be for the first four months. Michael must be like Philip. Then you're lucky. I didn't know myself, the peace of Philip, of course I was expecting a second Sarah . . .'

Alison's mind wandered off while Cecilia talked. She found she could keep one ear on conversations with Cecilia and devote the other half of her brain to another matter, which, in this case, happened to be the perusal of plant catalogues.

'I've got to go, Ali. I can hear Adrian's car on the gravel. I'll call you back once I've got him settled.'

Alison pictured Cecilia 'settling' Adrian.

'Thanks for the casserole, Ci. It's very good of you.'

'Oh, that old recipe. It's nothing. Takes three seconds to prepare. Literally, zap, and it's done. Gotta fly. Bye.'

Charlie let himself in the front door. The house hummed with activity. The washing machine was going at full tilt, and the dishwasher. In the sitting room, the TV was on and in the kitchen the radio played. The phone rang and Alison's mobile chirped its sweet spring birdsong at the same time.

'Darling, I'm back.'

He made his way to the kitchen and through the arch into the dining room, where Michael was asleep in his pram. The phones kept ringing. He went through the kitchen to the sun room, where Alison sat looking through a magazine, the picture of unworriedness.

'Aren't you going to answer them?'

'No, let the machines take them. It's only Mummy bothering me about this herbal compound she dropped round. She's on this fad about herbal remedies, and of course if Mummy takes an interest in something, we all have to get involved. I don't want to be cruel and tell her I'm not interested, but at the same time I'm not drinking herbal crap that looks and smells like horseshit. I poured the stuff down the toilet.'

The phones gave up on trying to reach Alison, and Charlie turned off the TV and the radio. All that was left was the hum of the laundry machines. Alison was in her dressing gown, a long silky gown which trailed the floor, and a set of red Chinese pyjamas.

'The problem with being on maternity leave is you're defence-less. If Mummy bothers me in the office about something, I can always get off the phone by saying I've to go to a meeting. But here, she knows she can get me. And she's coming round to help far too much. And Cecilia's round all the time. I'm exhausted entertaining them. They come round to "help", but all they do is create washing-up.'

Charlie went and stood over the pram. Baby Michael was fast asleep, his little fists clenched and at the ready, like a boxer. Charlie took a beer from the fridge. Alison smiled. It was a sign that he wasn't going to go for a run and she was glad of that. She found his running disturbing. There was a desperate quality to it. She went and sat on Charlie's lap and he put his arm around her. It had all happened so fast. They met, married, moved and had Michael so rapidly it was as though they hardly knew each other. The initial euphoria of their meeting carried them along for a while, then the wedding had become such a major event thanks to Miriam's interventions, and all the fuss had driven Alison to distraction. Then there was the panic of the baby coming, and them needing to buy a house as Alison's apartment was so small. That occasioned a whirlwind of activity. Every moment they weren't at work was spent organizing money and life insurance and mortgages and stuff. Then the baby's time was near and they had to gear up for that. It was all shopping for prams and cots and Winnie-the-Pooh lanterns. They had lurched from crisis to crisis. The attraction continued very strong, but Alison, now that all the panic was over, looked coolly at Charlie and felt she was looking at a stranger. He was reserved. He held back. And she wasn't going to let him do that. She was going to get him, climb inside his encrusted state and find him, and pull him out with a little crochet hook. As she had sucked Michael out of him, so she would extract him from himself.

6

Cormac sat in the corner of Tig Sheáin with Froggy, the gloomy interior of the pub warm and smoky and cave-like. He had started in the past few weeks to join Froggy here for a couple of pints of stout. The clientele had got used to him, were no longer sitting up straight and silent when he walked in the door. Cormac knew that when closing time came, particularly at the weekend, there was a charade of exits and table wiping, and after he left people reappeared and continued with the night's talk and sometimes song. He didn't mind. So long as the charade was adequately energetic, he accepted it. He knew Froggy was among the performers in this antic. Sean would stand up straight, take off his big green apron, grunt, 'I suppose it's time so,' and start rattling bottles in a purposeful manner. Caps were pulled down over ears and collars raised, and men, mostly farmers from the houses around, muttered, '*Slán*,' and headed for the door. Froggy walked Cormac home, virtually escorted him to the barracks, said good night, and then returned to the shuttered pub to report the sergeant's safe arrival. Froggy was then readmitted. It was a game. Cormac acquiesced in it. He thought the licensing laws were a lot of nonsense anyway, and he felt he needed the occasional night with Froggy. They had tried to sit in Cormac's kitchen, but Marie Rose resented them there, and banged around the place pointedly, cleaning under their feet, until they fled and sought shelter in the pub.

Froggy was full of talk about Dublin. He always spent six months of the winter up there and even during the summer he went up from time to time to deal with 'business'. He read every newspaper daily, and occasionally foreign ones. Because he didn't do any discernible work, that head of his just sat around all day absorbing information. In the opinion of Cormac, he was excellent company. Froggy had set himself the task of learning

Irish, and was becoming increasingly proficient. Cormac was puzzled about Froggy's lone status. He seemed interested in women all right, certain comments of his made that clear, but he never produced anyone. He occasionally waxed lyrically envious of Cormac's marriage to Marie Rose. 'Aren't you lucky to have such a fine woman keeping the house warm for you, Sergeant?' Cormac was surprised at the warmth in Froggy towards Marie Rose, as she treated him with haughty contempt most of the time. Froggy probably thought it was good breeding, but that wasn't Marie Rose's style at all. She was warm as newly baked bread with someone she liked. Cormac once ventured an enquiry to Froggy about the matter and was answered glibly, 'I'll keep my eye out. There's some fine young ones coming up in the next batch.'

Cormac couldn't picture Froggy with a local girl, all they ever talked about round here was fishing and children, and that wouldn't do Froggy's great big egg-head, but he was surprised that nobody was ever produced from Dublin. One of these girls who'd been to university. That's what Froggy needed. A great brainy girl to come and cook dinner for him in a very educated way.

'I'm thinking of buying the cottage,' said Froggy. 'I rent it every year and feel like it's my own. The fella owns it would happily sell it. It belonged to his mother-in-law, and his children aren't interested in it. He's cosy in a big house in Dingle, and if I didn't take the place every year it'd be a ruin by now. And every year I say to myself I'm not going to take it, I'm going to go to the south of France, but something inexplicable draws me back here.'

'It's a nice little spot, all right.'

Froggy's place, Duntobbar Cottage, was about two miles out the road, in an elbow created by a fold in the hill. It was nicely sheltered from the worst of the winds, and from the front door you could look out over the sea.

'And would you have the money to buy it?'

'I would. I'd have to do a bit of rearranging, but I could manage it, and in the long run it'd be cheaper than renting.'

Cormac felt a sting of envy. Now, with baby Michael in the

house and Marie Rose so domestically settled, he felt the lack of a place of his own. The married quarters in the barracks were fine, but it didn't ever feel wholly theirs. It was an aspect of his job that hadn't bothered him before. In fact, in the early days of their marriage, they hadn't foreseen that it would ever bother them. But now it made him feel insecure and never wholly private. On his occasional visit from Dingle, the superintendent always hung his hat in an irritatingly familiar manner on the hall-stand crook, when Marie Rose invited him in for tea.

It was a mild evening. The year had just started to warm up and the evenings were beginning to have a good stretch in them. Froggy had returned a number of weeks ago and Cormac was surprised at the lift he felt on seeing him. Over the long months of the winter, the occasional pleasantries exchanged between them had blossomed in memory to a warm friendship.

The pub was busy tonight. Yesterday had seen the monthly fair in Dingle and most people had had a minor swelling in their coffers. Coins a-plenty had returned from over the hill and trickled down like a mountain stream, some of them pooling in Sean the landlord's drawer. It was always a cheerful time of the month. There was a group of strangers in one corner of the bar, a road-building crew from further north. The roads round here were badly in need of work and there had been talk for a long time that they were going to be improved by the government. Long delays had ensued, and the locals made smart remarks in Cormac's hearing that the Free State government wasn't up to the job, and there was nothing like the Republicans for getting the finger out, unlike the Free Staters, who were only good at getting their fingers in the till.

And now the road crew had arrived, and Cormac smiled at them in a nice bit of Free State smug satisfaction. In fairness, the locals were so glad to see the road menders, they were getting treated royally in the bar. Very drunk now, they had been singing for a while. They all went quiet and one of their number, a tanned, wiry, black-haired man, rapped a knuckle on the table in front of him four times and a gentle, almost trained-sounding tenor voice sang out:

'On the twenty-eighth day of November,
The Tans left the town of Macroom,
They were armed in two Crossley tenders,
Which led them right into their doom.'

Cormac sat up straight, the change in his mood apparent to
Froggy.
'What's wrong?'
'Nothing.'
The singer continued:

'But the boys of Kilmichael were way-ay-ting,
And met them with powder and shot.
And the Irish Republican Army
Made bits of the whole shaggin' lot.'

The song sounded so strange, sung in this manner. It was a
rebel ballad, and usually sung by groups of men barely clinging to
the tune, like drowning men dropping like flies from an upturned
lifeboat. Rarely did the tune survive its rendition. But this man
sang it in a fine pure voice. Bizarre. The pub went quiet. A few
eyes on Cormac. It would be well known that he was from near
Kilmichael. That the actions being celebrated in song at this
moment were actions he would know something of. They
wouldn't be sure, though. People from home, from West Cork,
were discreet. Nobody knew anything. That was the drill. And
even if you did know something, you were never sure. And
sometimes you didn't know what you knew.
The lone voice rang out and people listened respectfully. But
when he got to the chorus again, one by one, a few other voices
joined in the ballad. They restored the song to its usual savage
tunelessness.

'Then here's to the boys of Kilmichael,
Who feared not the might of the foe,
The day they marched into battle
They laid all the Black and Tans low.'

All the other voices happily drowned the original voice, and gave the song more body. Froggy too lent his voice to the chorus. Cormac stared sullenly into his pint.

> 'The sun in the west it was sinking,
> 'Twas the eve of a cold winter's day.'

Everybody was quiet while the lone voice held the song again. So Cormac and Froggy too sat quietly.

> 'The lorries were ours before twilight,
> And high over Dunmanway Town,
> Our banners in triumph were waving
> To show that the Tans were gone down.
> We gathered our rifles and bayonets,
> And soon left the glen so obscure,
> And never drew rein till we halted
> At the faraway camp of Glenure.'

Then the whole room joined in for the chorus. Including Froggy. He nudged Cormac to join in, but Cormac wouldn't. He was aware that his abstention was noticeable, but he didn't care. He was a police sergeant. He didn't have to join in.

> 'So here's to the boys of Kilmichael . . .'

There were raucous cheers and clapping. The thin, dark-haired singer looked over at Cormac and nodded. He did look familiar, but Cormac couldn't place him. Then the penny dropped. He had grown his hair, but the tenor voice belonged to a young man Cormac knew from near home. Cormac nodded back and smiled. The other man was from Drimoleague in West Cork. Strange to see someone from there wandering round here with a road crew. Keep smiling at everybody. Particularly at the Republicans. He turned away, not wanting to encourage the other man. He hated that song, 'The Boys of Kilmichael'.

It was a ballad commemorating a battle during the War of Independence between Tom Barry's flying column and a bunch of Black and Tans. The Tans were ambushed on their return from a patrol and none were left standing. Even the fellow who managed to escape was hunted down a few fields away and a bullet was put in his neck. Cormac had occasionally acted as a scout in this area, but on that day he had been replaced as a bad cough had rendered him useless as a lookout. His friend Owen O'Halloran had filled his place. Everyone had been shocked by what happened. Owen never spoke to Cormac after that, left the volunteers and went to England, to Liverpool. His mother said he got a job there and shut the door in Cormac's face. Accounts of the battle filtered down from the active unit. The Tans tried to escape; they made a false surrender and shot two of ours; they wouldn't surrender and fought to the death; half of them surrendered and, while we were arresting them, the other half went crazy with battle-madness and started shooting us; they got confused and shot themselves. All manner of explanations had been produced to put a shine on the butchery, but the end result was that every Englishman wound up with fatal bullet wounds, save one, who was paralysed.

Cormac had walked the ambush site a few days later. A crisp cold December morning. Christmas was in the off and a frost in the early light made the scene beautiful. The blood remained on the road, a wicked staining in a quiet countryside. It had been the turning point for him in his attitude to the war. It was when he decided it had to be stopped. It wasn't so much that he felt sorry for the Tans. It was the column men he felt sorry for. It was too much. To mow them all down. The fighting had to stop. They were learning only how to be savages. Afterwards, in his mother's warm kitchen, he felt a huge depression. Surrounded by the trappings of civilized family life, he felt a tremendous sorrow. Nobody in the house mentioned Kilmichael. His mother fussed over the hearth, cooking meals and cleaning the house. She kept giving him little jobs to do. Fetch the water. Get me some turf. Get some potatoes from the store. Cormac knew she was having difficulty talking to him, but made herself keep communicating with him because, if she stopped, she might not start again. Get the water from the well. Fix the wheel on the cart. Sink a pole for the line. Mend the well wall. Feed the chickens. Cormac's father had agreed to differ with his sons in their tacit support for the IRA. The subject was off limits in the house. And the evenings round the fire were often very quiet, because things couldn't be talked about. But nothing was clear at that time. It's easy to be wise after the event, as the wise man says. But one thing had then become clear to Cormac. It had to be stopped.

'So, were you about Kilmichael?' asked Froggy. Froggy loved a bit of gossip.

'No,' said Cormac. 'I was very much a bit player. But I visited the site a few days later.'

'I hear the song was written by a local schoolteacher.'

'A local fool. The fools all became schoolteachers in those days. Glorifying butchery is what it was.'

'I see,' said Froggy.

'It was pure savage. They mowed down the poor miserable English fuckers. I never felt sorry for an Englishman in my life until then.'

'I see what you're saying. There's a wide gap between a fine song and a dirty deed, as my friend Mr Synge might have said.'

'He might have been a clever man.'

'That man has a good tenor voice,' said Froggy. 'It was like he was singing a prayer. Quite beautiful. Before the populace joined in and dragged the performance down.'

'I didn't like it,' said Cormac. 'It sounded like sacrilege. That song should be sung by savages, because savagery is what it is.'

Froggy looked at Cormac. 'You have strong feelings about this, my friend.'

'It's why I wanted to be a policeman. I wanted to be civilized.'

'Like the playwrights and poets wanted. Civilization.'

'A police force armed with nothing more than moral authority. You can't get more civilized than that.'

'I'd be nervous if I was a policeman round here. I'd say I'd like a little gun tucked into my pocket. They'd turn Turk round here real fast with little provocation.'

'It'd just make you a target, Froggy.'

'They hid de Valera round here, during the civil war. Ran him out to the islands for safekeeping.'

'The reason the RIC became the enemy is mainly because they

were ambushed for their guns. And people got hurt. And then there was reprisals. And that was that. Before you know where you are, you're in the middle of a bloodbath. The government knows that, because they were on the streets, like the rest of us. I'm only sorry Michael Collins didn't live to see it.'

'Did you know Collins?'

Cormac shook his head. 'Not well, but he was from round my way. He was a real leader, because he knew when to call a halt.'

A tear in Cormac's eye startled Froggy. He hadn't expected it. Cormac was usually a cool customer.

'He saved Ireland. He led us out of slavery, like Moses. Both kinds of slavery. To the English and to the bloodbath. And they slaughtered him for it. It was all right while he was fighting the English, but not while he was fighting the bloodlust. Padraig Pearse ranting about blood sacrifice and Dev going on about wading through blood. Could they not have copped themselves on?'

Froggy busied himself getting two more pints of stout. Cormac got a grip on himself. Talking to Froggy was very demanding, because he trusted him. Talking to other fellows was grand, you never said anything to them, but Froggy had a way of making him sing. Froggy returned with the pints.

'When I was a young *Garda* recruit, just after my training in Dublin, I was sent to Wexford for a while, for a bit of breaking in. The civil war was in full swing and things were pretty hot and heavy down there. There was a prisoner in the *Garda* barracks, an irregular. He'd been surrounded in some remote farmhouse where he was minding a big stack of rifles. He surrendered. Why he was being kept in the *Garda* barracks I don't rightly remember, but he was in a cell. There was a local sergeant, a big lug of a fellow, and he was doing the interrogations, and let me tell you, it was bloody rough. I was young and junior, but it was sickening what was going on. You'd have to be sorry for the IRA man. I heard somewhere it was personal between the sergeant and the IRA man. Some local business. Something to do with a row over a boundary. In Ireland, it's always personal. And the more political it is, the more personal it is. They're all fighting and dying for Ireland, but really it's a row over a ditch.

102

'Well, a young one came down from Dublin, a Sinn Feiner. The women were the worst, I needn't tell you. This one had a loud voice, like a foghorn, and demanded to see the prisoner. Read out some charter about rights or something, and some thick guard let her in. Of course, she got a right land when she saw the state of the prisoner. It was much worse than she had suspected. It was wrong what was being done. You understand me.'

Froggy nodded. 'Bad business.'

'So the Sinn Feiner saw the prisoner and left to return to Dublin. I was about the barracks, but I wasn't in uniform. I'd been to a funeral, so I was in my Sunday clothes. It took a while for it to dawn on the guard in charge, but the prisoner was missing his jumper. A filthy grey jumper he'd been wearing. The harpy had run off with the jumper as evidence, covered as it was in dried blood. The Dublin train wasn't due to leave the station until five o'clock and it was most likely she would be on that. I ran over to the station and went into the waiting room. And sure enough, there she was, a brown parcel at her side. I sat down opposite and opened the newspaper. She was very agitated, hopping up and down and running out to the platform to see if the train was coming. On one of her absences, I whipped the brown paper parcel and slipped out past her. I had crossed the footbridge before I heard her shriek of discovery. I crossed the square, moved swiftly to the bridge on the main street, placed a few heavy rocks in the bag and tossed it into the River Slaney. And that was the end of that.'

'You moved fast,' said Froggy, impressed.

'I felt sorry for yer man. I wanted to do the right thing. In this one instance, the sergeant was in the wrong and the IRA man needed help. You always have to look at the larger picture. But it was hard, Froggy. Hard to know what was the right thing to do. Moral certitude deserts you in a time of civil war. The little picture is so often at odds with the big picture.'

'It sounds to me like you did the wrong thing for the right reasons. Or the right thing for the wrong reasons. Or something like that.' Thank God for the stout, thought Froggy.

'I ratted on the sergeant later. We had a high-level visit from

Dublin and I ratted on him. He couldn't be doing things like that and getting away with them. Giving us a bad name.'

Cormac steadied himself. It wasn't like him to get moralistic in this way. He prided himself on his pragmatism. But it had been hard, the war, and finding the right thing to think wasn't easy at that time. And you couldn't allow yourself to get too emotional about things. Now, with peace and a new beginning, sometimes the feelings you couldn't afford to have then came and ambushed you now. Or maybe it was being married and having Michael. Things affected him in a different way. He felt differently now. More deeply.

'What would you have done, Froggy?'

'Me?' Froggy took a sup of his pint and considered the question. 'I wouldn't have done nothing, because I wouldn't have been there.'

'But if you were there?'

'Well, I am a man of thought, not action. So I would probably have sat down and thought about it. And by the time I reached a conclusion, it would have been too late. Wisdom takes time.'

Cormac smiled at Froggy. Froggy wanted to change the subject. He felt Cormac was getting mired in the past. Looking backwards. His mind turned to the present.

'What do you think of this Lindbergh caper?' asked Froggy. 'Do you reckon he has a chance? *The Spirit of St Louis*. That's a nice name for an aircraft.'

It had been reported that morning that Captain Charles Lindbergh had taken off ahead of his two rivals and was airborne at that moment, setting his cap at the North Atlantic crossing.

'I s'pose he does. We might see him. He's aiming to cross the southern tip of Ireland.'

'We should keep an eye out for him tomorrow,' said Froggy. 'It'd be amazing if we saw him.'

''T'would.'

'Whatever happened to that plan the Free State air force had of crossing the Atlantic? There was talk of it about a year ago.'

'It was shut down for financial reasons. The country is on its last legs financially, repairing all the war damage. No money for glory projects.'

Froggy supped his stout and got into a patriotic splutter.

'Why don't we Irish capitalize on our geographical location as the gateway to the Atlantic? It'd be great for morale in the Free State. Once upon a time Ireland had pioneers to court the perils of the Atlantic in a cockle-shell boat, following the very track that these airmen are following today. Nowadays we leave it to Dutchmen, Frenchmen and Yanks.'

'I agree with you, Froggy,' said Cormac. 'All our heroism got used up in the stupid civil war. It split the Irish people and the heroism sort of leaked out the middle. You couldn't have a Free State aeroplane hero, without a Republican hanging on to the wing trying to capsize it.'

Froggy sighed. It was hard to get Cormac off the split. Hard to try and pull him into the present, and steer him to the future.

Marie Rose stood over a hot tub, steaming the baby's clothes and Cormac's shirts. This was her third and final batch. The two previous loads flapped happily on the line out the back, basking and bleaching in the May sunshine. Tasks such as this had been anathema to her at home. She would duck out of sight to avoid them every time, but now she didn't mind it at all. She loved the cleanness and whiteness of everything. Her hair was tied up and her face red from the boiling water. When she caught sight of herself in the little mirror she kept over the stove, she thought she looked like a washerwoman. A boily-faced washerwoman with a lock of hair falling damp down her neck. This is my beautiful future, she thought, and smiled, not bad-humouredly. She had been listening to a reading of *Pride and Prejudice* on the BBC and the cheekiness of Miss Austen's observations made her smile and put her in a good mood.

A tap on the door and the latch lifted. Kate came in with the eggs. Kate ran a little business with her eggs, and Marie Rose was glad of them. The highlight of today was to be cake-baking! And fresh eggs were what she needed.

'I'll take four eggs, Kate.'

Kate put the eggs in the blue-striped dish on the dresser.

'I won't disturb you, Marie Rose, I can see you're busy.'

'Oh, please do disturb me,' said Marie Rose, and she filled the kettle from the bucket and put it on the range. 'If you don't mind the steam.' She took the cloth off her head and let her hair down. 'I'm dying to be disturbed. Have you any news?'

'No news today. I got a letter from Maisie in America two days ago. She is fine and wants us all to come over, but that's just a mad dream she has. She sent money and a headscarf.'

Kate's sister and two brothers were in America. It seemed that everyone round here had family in America. It was strange and exotic to Marie Rose. America sounded like a grand place to go. Full of excitement and opportunity. She enjoyed Kate's company, but she couldn't understand Kate's contentment. Kate, one of the most delicate and refined creatures you'd ever meet, was married to a great thickhead of a man called Donal, who could hardly speak. Marie Rose was mystified by the marriage. They never appeared in public together, and Marie Rose knew Donal Carney only because she saw him from time to time in the village. Kate rarely mentioned him, but two children, aged fourteen and sixteen, testified to marital intimacy. Kate was still a young woman, early thirties, so the marriage had been young. On her part at least – Donal had the look of a man of fifty. Kate said she had been set up with Donal by Davey the Hare, a matchmaker who came from over by Ventry. Marie Rose had tried to get more information out of her without much success, until one day, visiting Ellen in the priest's house, Kate had produced a bottle of sherry she'd been sent by way of thanks from a girlfriend she'd helped out. 'I don't want Donal getting his hands on it, it'd be like a daisy in a bull's mouth.'

They all joined in the sherry. It was strange to Marie Rose's palate, but the other two seemed accustomed. The sherry oiled Kate's tongue and she described seeing Donal for the first time. Davey the Hare had come looking for a wife for Donal Carney, and Kate's sister Maisie was on offer. Maisie was two years older. Donal Carney's mother had followed his father into the hereafter during the summer just gone, and after a few months of proper mourning, he felt the house needed a woman, so word was put out and Davey the Hare set himself to the task. Carney was an only child – well, only surviving child. Two others had died in infancy. So the farm was his, making him a good prospect. Kate's father was keen on the match. Davey the Hare and Donal Carney called over and drank whiskey with Kate's father and got into a good mood. After a time, Maisie was sent for and she sat with them at the fire. Kate peeped through the door and watched. It was the most exciting thing that had happened in their house, ever. Donal Carney was a fine man, she thought, through the crack in the door. He glowed nicely in the firelight. And Maisie was the luckiest girl alive, having a chance at getting married and living in her own place.

There was a fierce row after, as Maisie wouldn't have him. 'There wasn't a word out of him, it'd be like getting married to a stone. I'd sooner marry a block of wood.' Pressure was put on Maisie to take him, but she refused, and when Muiris, the eldest boy, sent passage money from America, she begged to be allowed to go. And she went, her father fuming about the loss of a good farm. Kate had piped up that she liked the look of him, and her parents initially dismissed it as a childish fantasy. She was only fifteen and too young. But Davey the Hare got wind of her wishes, and he was a man who couldn't countenance failure. There were many faint-hearted men and women on the Dingle peninsula who found themselves propelled into marriages by the tenacity and whiskey of Davey the Hare. He put the prospect to Donal Carney, who was also agreeable, and a second night of drinking whiskey by the fire was organized. Kate was duly sent for and no longer had to watch the scene through a crack in the door. She liked the look of him once more, as he sat and once again glowed in the firelight. It was true that there wasn't much talk out of him, but a quiet man would be restful. It was arranged that they'd wait for her sixteenth birthday. And a week after that, they were married.

'And the glow soon wore off him,' squealed Kate in laughter, her mirth fuelled by the sherry.

What mystified Marie Rose, after hearing this story, was the fact that she was convinced that Kate was happy. Not in love with her husband, but happy nonetheless. Actually liked her life. Marie Rose couldn't understand it. And Ellen, she too was happy, basically as a glorified servant to the priest. A dead-end job. She'd be got rid of when O'Keefe died or when she outgrew her usefulness, and she'd have no children to care for her. But Ellen also exuded contentedness. And she, Marie Rose, truly loved her husband, despite his difficult streak and occasional moodiness. Lived happily here in great comfort, but always felt a slight itch of discontent. She wanted to do something. What it was she didn't know, but she wanted more.

Baby Michael stirred in his pram and Marie Rose sat him up. He raised his arms and fiddled with imaginary wireless knobs in the air. He'd had a good nap after lunch and now looked happy and refreshed. And clean. Marie Rose loved how clean he was, his bright face shining up from among his feathery pillow and fluffy white sheets.

'How's the *gossún*?' asked Kate.

'Thriving,' said Marie Rose as she scalded the pot and emptied the water in the sink. She measured the tea carefully, poured in the water and set the pot to draw on the range. The range was too hot and the water started to hop, so she moved it to the very edge, where it was hardly warm at all. If there was something she couldn't stand, it was stewed tea. She set out cups and saucers on the scrubbed kitchen table, and Kate began to relax.

'Maisie says she might be getting married. She's met some man over there, a Protestant, an Episcopalian or something, and she's thinking about it. He's a porter at her hospital. McCrea is his name. Family is originally from Scotland, but he was born there. I don't know if she will though. She's getting a bit old now.'

'What age is she?'

'Thirty-six. If she's going to do it, she'd want to get on. I think she's a bit unsure because he's a Protestant.'

'Surely that wouldn't matter over there. They're all different religions in America. It's only here that people give tuppence for that kind of thing.'

'She'd be afraid she wouldn't go to heaven, and we'd never meet up when we die.'

'That's nonsense talk. Tell her to marry her Scot. If that's her heart's desire, it's a sin not to follow it. She'd be sent to hell for that quicker.'

'I'll say that to her. Hey, I'd better write it down. You've put it so well, it'll go out of my head when I get home, and I won't remember the actual phrase.'

'You'll remember it,' said Marie Rose.

'No. You've put it so well. Here, write it down.' She took a small notebook from her egg basket, her egg accounts, and pulled a page from the rear.

Marie Rose took the pencil and paper and wrote, 'Marry your Scottish Episcopalian doorman. It's a sin not to follow your heart's desire.'

Kate took the paper and added, 'My friend says that. It's a bigger sin than marrying a Protestant. And she's very well informed. She was in school until she was seventeen and she's the sergeant's wife.'

Marie Rose laughed at the attribution of her wisdom. She poured the tea and took down a tin of ginger biscuits and fetched some milk from the pantry, which was still thankfully cool, despite the heat generated by the stove.

Young Michael opened his mouth and let out a loud bellow, sounding a note of weary boredom. It startled the two women, the adultness of it. Marie Rose laughed and gave him an old snuff tin with a stone in it, and the child rattled it delightedly.

'He's starting to complain already. They start early. My two are grumbling about the work they have to do for their father. The farm's beginning to get busy, with the potatoes just ready, and we've taken the younger one out of school early. Young people now are always complaining. Not like in our day. We thought we were lucky to have the chance to work on our parents' land. Nowadays they just take it all for granted. "I don't want the farm, I want to go to America like Auntie Maisie and Uncle Muiris." That's what they both say.'

Marie Rose heard the familiar distinctive sound of Cormac's bicycle coming up the drive. She was startled. She wasn't expecting him until tea time. He'd been in for his lunch and gone off about his business. Kate hopped up. 'I must be off.' Marie Rose never said it, but Kate had nous enough to know that Cormac wouldn't be pleased to see her around the place. Kate sniffed a streak of general misanthropy. She put her shawl over her head, collected her egg basket and made for the door. Marie Rose put the teacups to one side and the biscuit tin back on the top of the dresser. Then something in the acoustic alarmed her. Normally Cormac put the bicycle safely in the shed, but it crashed to the ground, and heavy boots thud thud thudded to the door. Marie Rose's heart seized. It sounded like an emergency of some sort. Cormac pushed open the door and burst into the kitchen.

'Would you believe it? It's Lindbergh.'

'Hello, Sergeant, I'm only delivering the eggs,' muttered Kate, not having listened to him.

'I'm sure of it. I've to wire Dublin.'

Cormac ran into the radio room in the barracks, ignoring the presence of Kate. He had just finished his swim below at Whitestrand and was getting dressed when he saw it. A slate-grey plane dancing in the air as light as a feather. It came in over Three Sisters headland, then across over Smerwick harbour and was headed straight for him. He hopped up on his bicycle and pedalled like mad for the village, the aeroplane directly above him as he flew along on his bike, his heart racing. He rang his bell to draw people onto the street. He had been idly keeping an eye out but hadn't expected to see anything. And now that he'd seen it, it was like he'd been touched by some sort of miracle. He wanted to wire Dublin. He wanted badly to be the first.

'Did he say Lindbergh?' asked Kate.

'Lindbergh!' said Marie Rose, almost a spell, an incantation.

Marie Rose picked up the baby and the two women ran out the front into the village street. People were running out of their houses. The words 'It's Lindbergh,' 'Lindbergh atá ann,' being intoned by various voices. People were making the sign of the cross. Young boys were waving handkerchiefs as flags. Above the din of the people, and unmistakable, a thin hum of a plane. Marie Rose couldn't see anything. She looked up but couldn't see anything. 'Where is he? Where is he?' The people on the street surged south, all running as one to catch a glimpse of the man and the machine. Then they stopped and turned, and the surge was in the northerly direction. Marie Rose couldn't see the reason for the change of direction, so she stood still, trying to assess the situation. Just then, a young lad, running along, his eyes glued to the skies and not looking where he was going, ran smash into Kate, sending her basket of eggs flying. There wasn't more than a half-dozen left, and they all fell to the ground in a scramble.

'Oh dear,' said Marie Rose.

'I'll just think of it as luncheon offered to Mr Lindbergh after his long voyage,' laughed Kate.

Marie Rose was torn between wanting to help her friend and following the surging crowd north to get a glimpse.

'Run on,' said Kate. 'There isn't much can be done for these eggs.'

Marie Rose looked at the crowd for a moment, then formed her own plan. Clutching the baby on her hip, she ran up the drive of the barracks and around the back. Her shirts and baby garments were decked out like bunting on the line and on bushes. She ran up the steep hill beyond the garden, a place she often came to sit because of the view, which was beautiful. She turned on the brow, and then she could see him. The strange metal thing. A car with wings. A metal bird. He was circling above, uncertain. Probably doesn't know where he is, the poor man. It was somehow incongruous, this manifestation of engineering genius and physical bravery against the familiar backdrop of islands, headland and sky. Michael looked up and gurgled with glee. This was some fine toy, up in the sky. He stretched out his hands to reach for it. Marie Rose cuddled the infant on her hip. Bless you, Lindbergh, you're a brave man, she thought. I'd love to do something like that, something glorious. But I never will. For me it's washing and cooking and minding babies and sweeping kitchen floors. But maybe this lad will. She held Michael up high over her head and offered him. This great aeroplane god had come here all the way from America, had appeared in the skies, in her skies, and she wanted a blessing for her baby son.

That night the pub was humming with excitement. People were beside themselves. They couldn't believe it. America had always seemed so far away. Most households in the area had family over there. In fact many had more family in America than they had in Kerry. Cormac was the toast of the pub, having seen the airman first. He had to relate the story over and over again.

'And did you hear him first or see him?'

'I saw him. I thought it was a bird.'

'Queer-lookin' bird.'

'Very queer-looking bird.'

'And then what?'

'Well, then it dawned on me, as I was half expecting it.'

Cormac enjoyed the attention he was getting. Suddenly, everybody was Lindbergh crazy. Cormac was sure most people in the village had hardly known who Lindbergh was a few days previously; now the airman was a celebrity. In fact, Cormac himself was becoming a celebrity.

'I believe they saw him crossing Dingle Bay, and they saw him beyond in Skibbereen,' said Cormac, who had been kept informed by the superintendent.

'But we saw him first, Cormac, what do you say?' said Sean the landlord.

'My wife has some sort of fancy for him, I think. She talks of little else, and now she's seen him I'll never hear the end of it,' said Cormac quietly to Froggy.

'Oh, the ladies like the look of him all right. He turns heads. He's still single, you see.'

'Well, Marie Rose isn't.'

Cormac had meant that as a joke, but it came out in an annoyed tone.

'And it is a truth universally acknowledged that ladies are tormented by the sight of a single man, feeling strongly the need of procuring him a wife.' Froggy too had been listening to Jane Austen on the BBC.

'I'm surprised you've escaped their scrutiny, friend.'

'Oh, how do you know I have?' Froggy's eyes twinkled.

This was new. Froggy was never coy about women. Something in the offing?

'I wonder how many croissants you can buy for twenty-five thousand dollars?'

'What's that in pounds?'

'In truth, I don't know. It's the amount of the prize Daniel Orteig is giving. Some French American.'

'And I thought Lindy was doing it for the glory.'

'Glory, my arse,' said Froggy. 'He's doing it for the money. Nobody does anything for glory alone. The money has to be split, though. His backers. The St Louis crowd need to be paid off.'

'Quite a risk they took.'

'Pity it wasn't some Irish American who put up the prize,' said Froggy. 'Let's call it the Murphy Prize. Then he might have landed here.'

Froggy was very well up on the Lindbergh quest. He had followed all the preparations. He'd nothing to do all day except read newspapers. No wonder he knew everything. He had cuttings from the papers over the previous few days of all the coverage of the flight preparations which he brought down to the pub for everyone to look at.

'He's quarter Irish, you know,' said Froggy.

'Lindbergh. That's a fine Irish name,' said Cormac.

'That'd be the Swedish side. He has an Irish granny. He's one of ours,' said Froggy, puffed up with a little distant patriotic pride.

Cormac was paid five pounds by the government for reporting the first sighting of the plane. Dublin had confidently wired Paris that Lindbergh was on his way, and Paris readied itself for a wild reception. Flying at one hundred miles an hour, he'd be in Paris six hours after crossing Kerry. Dublin was proud to announce Ireland as the gateway to Europe. A few months later, Marie Rose took the five pounds and went into the big toyshop in Tralee and bought Michael a beautiful model of *The Spirit of St Louis*, made from carefully polished wood. The most beautiful toy she'd ever seen. It cost almost two pounds and was the type of toy that would be found only in big rich houses. Marie Rose didn't care how much it cost. Cormac suspended it from the ceiling in the nursery to keep it out of harm's way until Michael was big enough to play with it carefully. When Marie Rose checked the baby at night, entering the room with a flickering lamp, the gust caused by the door opening set the plane in motion on its slender string, and it cast a shadow on the wall above her son's head, a brave winged angel hovering over him as he slept.

7

'*It's Joe Duffy. Talk to Joe,*' advised the jingle. '*Eighteen-fifty, seven-one-five, seven-one-five.*'

The glories of daytime radio were new to Alison. The radio was a constant companion as she and baby Michael navigated the shell shock of her maternity leave. The pace of life at home was so much slower. It hadn't occurred to Alison in advance how odd it would feel not to be rushing round doing things. She had worked for the same company for fourteen years, knew the running of the place intimately, and to be cut off from it was a bit of a shock. She delighted in the baby, but it was a whole new experience for her. And Charlie's life remained the same as it had before. Well, almost. He went to work every day like normal. He came home from work much in the manner he had before. His routine hadn't changed one bit. OK, they went out to eat less. Saw less cinema. But otherwise, it was business as usual for him.

But for Alison, it was like she had been born, not the baby. And it wasn't very comfortable feeling like a new-born when you were nearly thirty-five. It was strange for her to get up in the morning and not dress for work. She tried dressing smartly for a while, but baby Michael regurgitated quite a lot of his bottle and all her favourite clothes were getting wrecked. Also, it seemed a little silly for her to sit around the house in a smart suit. So she had resigned herself to jeans and loose, machine-washable cotton shirts. Her stylist's sensibility had often been offended by the clothes that Cecilia and the other mothers wore, but now it was all beginning to make sense. She had thought that being on maternity leave would be a delight, like being on constant holiday, but it was all stretching endlessly around her. Holidays only worked because they happened so seldom. Valuable like diamonds, because of their rarity.

After the first few weeks of quiet, Michael cried a lot and woke frequently in the night. A colicky baby, they said. It didn't bother Alison. She took a nap in the afternoon to make up sleep if she felt tired. And if he was cranky during the day, she took him for a walk. The motion of the pram soothed him and rocked him off to sleep, and Alison walked and thought. She was taking the baby in her stride, no bother at all. It was herself and her inactivity she was having trouble with. Often she walked for hours, bringing her Walkman and listening to the radio. She had become hooked on the news. Voracious. And the phone-in shows. Where they talked about the news.

Walking around the back roads of Blackrock with the pram, she had given things a lot of thought, and formed a plan. Now that she had time to think about things, all the panic being over and nothing to do all day, she had come to a few conclusions. She reckoned that Charlie was troubled. At first she was resentful of his distance. He had this way of sitting there and staring into the middle distance, almost trance-like. She had to call him back from wherever he was. 'Penny for your thoughts,' she would say. 'Oh, nothing. My mind was a blank,' he would answer. He was a good guy, there was no doubt in her mind about that, and her annoyance with him subsided into concern. And this prompted her to form her plan.

Alison had been very surprised by Charlie's decision to call the baby Michael. It had come out of the blue, and it occurred to her that it might help Charlie with the jumbled jigsaw of his life if he got some sense of where his father had gone. It might give him closure. Or it might give him a better sense of himself. Some inner peace. Alison discounted the idea at first, but it kept coming back to her on her long walks with Michael. Also, now Michael had arrived, Charlie's father had become a more important figure. He was her child's grandfather. He was attached to her, in that roundabout way, and if he was floating around out there, Michael had a right to meet him. So she decided to do something about it. She got the number of Cecilia's private investigator, the one who'd been checking out Sarah. It turned out that she'd been doing nothing out of the ordinary. Her secret and furtive air was caused by clandestine horse riding lessons. These had been forbidden by Adrian, who was afraid that horses were dangerous.

Cecilia had liked the private investigator and recommended him highly to Alison. Cecilia had some sisterly reservations about the plan, though.

'What if you find him and he turns out to be an ogre?'

This hadn't occurred to Alison. Long-lost fathers in her imaginary landscape were thoroughly decent types. Rough round the edges perhaps, but great nonetheless. They were people like Magwich from *Great Expectations*. Or Geppetto from *Pinnochio*. Poor, perhaps, down on their luck, but noble.

'I'll risk it. If he's an ogre, so be it.'

'Sometimes it's better not to stir things up, Ali. Genies can't be put back in boxes.'

'Lamps, Cici. Genies live in lamps.'

'And besides . . .'

'Besides what?'

'Surely the initiative should come from Charlie. It's not really up to you.'

Alison saw the logic of this but disagreed. The initiative was not hers. The initiative came from baby Michael.

Michael was seven weeks old now. The miracle of his first smile had occurred, and Alison and Charlie had marvelled at it. Alison spent hours trying to coax more smiles from him. And he frequently obliged. 'What did you do all day?' Charlie would ask. 'Smiled at the baby.' Sometimes she smiled so much her face hurt.

A beep on the intercom sounded. Cecilia and her mother had the code for the gate. Probably some hawker. Alison decided she'd better answer it. She lifted the receiver. Donna's voice.

'Alison. I'm glad you're there.'

'Hi, Donna.' Alison hadn't seen her for a few weeks, which was unusual, because they stayed in close touch.

'Are you alone?'

'Yes.'

'Can I come in? I need to talk to you.'

'Sure.'

Alison activated the gate and shortly Donna appeared in the front door. She looked peaky.

'Are you OK?' asked Alison.

'No,' said Donna, and followed Alison through to the kitchen. Alison put on the kettle and got down some teabags.

'What's wrong?' asked Alison.

'Could you turn that down?' The radio was blaring, and Alison had ceased to notice.

'It's Joe Duffy. Talk to Joe. Eighteen-fifty, seven-one-five, seven-one-five.'

Click.

'Thanks be to Jesus.'

The kettle boiled rapidly and Alison made two steaming mugs of tea. She brought them over to the table in the sun room. Donna still said nothing. Alison stared at her. She looked terrible. White and ill and distressed.

'What is it, Donna?'

Donna didn't reply.

'Is David all right?'

'David's fine,' she whispered. 'He's a beautiful, good baby.'

'James?' queried Alison.

Silence.

'It's James. He's had an accident.'

'No. No accident.'

'What? Please tell me, Donna. I'm not going to guess. He's having an affair?'

'Worse.'

'He's left you.'

'Worse.'

Silence. Tea drinking. Michael wailed. Alison got up and went to him where he slept through the arch in the dining room. She lifted him and he favoured her with one of his little apprentice smiles.

Donna took advantage of her distraction to blurt out her tale. 'He's got the au pair pregnant. Can you believe it? What kind of a fool did I marry?'

Alison was shocked. There had been developing tensions between Donna and James. She had sensed them. And she'd sensed that the au pair was a little on the frisky side.

'They've been having an affair. I didn't mind that. I'd be away overnight with clients, I knew stuff was going on. I sensed it. I'm not a fool, Ali. And Sylvie is twenty. She's not a child. But I thought he'd be careful.'

'You mean you knew something was going on?'

Donna nodded miserably.

'I never expected his love, Ali.'

Donna had an expression of pure hurt on her face. Alison remembered it from when they were schoolgirls. Donna's parents were always away on cruises, leaving her in the care of help of one sort or another. Her parents were devoted to one another, and Donna had always seemed an irritation in their ongoing besotted affair. She was always loveless.

'I've bribed her, Ali. I promised her ten grand if she fucks off and has an abortion. She went to London on a plane this morning with a bag full of money to pay for everything. She'll be back in two days. I've made out the bank draft for the balance, and I give it to her when she comes back.'

'And what does James think?'

'I haven't spoken to him. I just go white with anger when he appears, so I avoid him. But I'll get over that. I won't get over it if that French tart has a bastard half-brother to my son. That I won't get over.'

Alison put her arms around Donna.

'This is bad.'

'I'd have given her fifty grand if she'd asked for it. She wept on my shoulder. Thinks I'm her best friend for helping her out of this fix. Apparently her papa would go crazy if she came back pregnant.'

'And James?'

'Oh, Ali. I tried very hard to be right for him. I've been his slave. He fancied me at first because I'm young-looking. I knew that. So I go down to the gym and spend hours working out so I stay slim and petite and adequate to his tastes. But I can't compete with a real twenty-year-old. I get in a line on the treadmill, with a load of other women, and we all walk for miles, going nowhere. Slaves, all trying to stay beautiful so our men won't leave us. A line of women going nowhere on a treadmill. Sometimes I want to stop and shout, "We're going nowhere! Can you hear me? Nowhere!" Oh, and there's a few male slaves too. I sit on the balcony drinking juice and looking down at the weights room. Sometimes I see Charlie there with his pal – what's his name? His best-man pal. And I see that Charlie's a slave too. He's in the slave caste, just like me. Working away down there trying to keep himself beautiful for you, while James sits on the sofa swilling beer, watching the match, his disused rugby muscles turning to fat. He occasionally turns himself over to air his arse for a fart.'

'I don't think Charlie's keeping himself beautiful for me, Donna.'

'I think he is. I was so surprised, Ali, when you said you were going to marry Charlie. I was amazed. You'll forgive me for saying this, but my first impression of him was that he's a knacker. When we were kids hanging out on Killiney beach, there were always groups of knackers hanging round down there, drinking cider. Don't you remember? Charlie is like one of them. In fact, he probably was one of them. What is Ali doing marrying a knacker? That isn't the sort of boy girls like us marry. Girls like us marry boys like James. Who went to the right school, and played for the right club, and got the right jobs. Then I got to know Charlie, and like him of course. But it only made sense to me when I saw him down at the gym, in his shorts and singlet. He has a beautiful body. And he works hard at it. At maintaining it. And it all fell into place. How could you not fall for someone who worked so hard keeping themselves beautiful for you? And why didn't it work for me? Why didn't James stay fallen for me?'

Donna started to weep. Baby Michael stared at her, his head leaning to one side, mimicking an expression of pure astonishment.

The sleek lines of Charlie's BMW caught the eye of the kids playing on the verges of De Valera Park. They dropped their toys and stood frozen, a tableau of childish wonder, staring at the monument to success and prosperity which purred slowly along the road and stopped outside number 43. 'Uncle Charlie, Uncle Charlie,' called out two of the scruffy children who ran after the car and clustered round it. Charlie got out and ruffled their heads. 'Hello, Susan. Gimme five, Mark.' Mark delightedly slapped Charlie's outstretched hand. Then the kids ran up the path to their own front door. 'Ma, Ma, Uncle Charlie's here with the baby.' Alison swallowed her lack of greeting from the children. They were shy with her and, unused to youngsters, she was a little over-the-top with them. She was conscious of this, but didn't know how to fix it. And consequently they circled her in a suspicious fashion.

Alison got out of the car and looked around. It must have been strange growing up in a place like this. The little houses huddled so close together. The paint-chipped, unaffluent windows. Curtains and blinds not matching. The kids a bit bedraggled and wearing ill-fitting clothes. All the cars parked at the kerb at least ten years old. There was no advantage here, thought Alison, none whatsoever. She took the baby in the Carry-tot out of the back of the car and followed Charlie up the path.

The small front garden was an explosion of colour. Beautiful rose bushes elegant and abundant revelled in their full bloom. Mary and Brendan were both green-fingered and the roses were magnificent. Alison lingered on the path and inhaled the splendour. A patch of genuine glory. She followed Charlie through the front door and into the house.

The house was always chilly. Even on a warm summer's day, the angle of the windows was such that they never got the sun. Alison was happy to walk into the coolness. In the winter the house was freezing, apart from the kitchen, which had a fireplace. The rest of the house was heated – or rather not heated – by an inefficient back-boiler radiator system, which hardly worked at all, no matter how high the kitchen fire was. Alison followed Charlie down the corridor, past the rarely used front room and into the kitchen, which stretched the width of the narrow house at the rear. The kitchen was filthy. Alison stared around at the mess. Unwashed pots and pans littered the hob and worktops, mostly half full with the remains of what looked like porridge. The linoleum floor was grimy, and Alison felt her shoes stick to it in spots. An overflowing bin stood unashamedly in a corner, refusing to accept any more detritus and spilling it out onto the floor. Cobwebs lurked in the corners of the ceiling. The kitchen table was piled high with newspapers and bits of paper. Alison found the domestic chaos terrifying.

The double doors were open, and a curtain wafted in the gentle breeze. Because the house was at the bottom of a cul-de-sac, its front garden was particularly small, but the back garden opened up like a fan, about seventy feet long and nearly sixty feet wide at the end. It was spread out proudly with lines and lines of kitchen garden produce. Cabbages, lettuces, other unidentifiable vegetables. Strawberry plants ran in lines, modestly hiding their fruit under leaves. A nest of loganberry bushes stood straight to attention in a sunny corner. A quartet of hens picked about in a loose pen. The garden was as neat as a living room. It was tended with immaculate care. Brendan was down at one end, doing something mysterious with pots.

Alison followed Charlie through to the garden. Mary was lying down, sunning herself.

'Hi!' she said, and got to her bare feet. 'How's my favourite nephew?' She went over to Alison and looked in the Carry-tot at baby Michael.

'He's your only nephew, Ma,' pointed out Mark, a most logical child.

Brendan smiled and waved from the end of the garden, and continued with his task.

Charlie lifted baby Michael and handed him to Mary. She cradled him in her arms. 'Oh, I love the smell of new-born baby,' she said, and inhaled his scent. 'He's so cute. What a lovely outfit.' Baby Michael was wearing a little pale green outfit, a birth present from Donna.

'It's Ralph Lauren,' said Alison, the irony in her voice disappearing on the breeze.

'Oh, that must explain how nice it is so,' said Mary uncertainly.

Alison was sorry she'd said anything. Ralph Lauren baby clothes just weren't ironic here, in this garden, in this place.

Brendan, the gentle giant, rumbled up to them. 'How's the little man?' he said, and peered in to look at the baby.

'He's gorgeous,' said Mary. 'Look at him.'

Brendan looked at the child and then looked at his wife. 'Oh, no,' he said. 'She's getting broody. That means I won't get a

122

minute's peace and I'll be worn out.' He winked at Charlie. 'The sight of a new baby gets her blood up.' He threw back his head and laughed. Ha ha ha.

'You'd be so lucky,' retorted Mary with a gentle slap. 'Go in and get our guests a drink.'

'What'll you have, mate?'

'A beer,' said Charlie.

'White wine,' said Alison.

'Me too,' said Mary.

'Coming up,' said Brendan, and lumbered off into the house.

'I'm in right bad form,' said Mary.

'What's the matter?' asked Charlie.

'We have to get rid of the hens. I applied for planning permission for them and got turned down.'

'Planning permission? How can you need planning permission for a hen?' asked Alison. 'I thought they just grew.'

Brendan returned with a bottle of white wine, two glasses and two cans of beer.

'Oh, she's telling you the bad news. Desperate,' said Brendan as he uncorked the wine.

'The hencoop. You need planning permission for a hencoop in a suburban area. Noise pollution, apparently. One of the neighbours objected. Can you believe it? The O'Reillys in number 49. And they have four noisy, smoky cars that come and go at all hours. Talk about pollutants,' said Mary, a tiny edge in her voice in the comment directed at Alison.

She hadn't meant to be aggressive, it just came out that way. Her annoyance at officialdom was seeping out, and Alison was becoming the recipient. Mary had a bad gut instinct about Alison, which she tried unsuccessfully to conquer. There was something about Alison's indolence and self-possession that got on her nerves. Nothing Alison had said or done had ever annoyed Mary. She had no rational reason to dislike the girl. But there was some block to her acceptance of her. And it wasn't just that nobody would ever be good enough for her beloved younger brother, though that was certainly part of it. To her, Alison epitomized shallow materialism, the thing in the world she most despised.

'We live in a mad society. You don't need planning permission to run four cars in the one household, but you need planning permission to own a few harmless hens.'

'Not hens, Mammy, film stars,' said Susan.

'Yes, pet, film stars.'

The hens were named Marilyn, Rita, Meryl and Julia.

'I can't believe we'll have to get rid of them. They're like part of the family,' said Brendan.

'Maybe we should move to the country, Bren. We could bring the hens with us. Get some place civilized where hens are allowed.'

'Can't you appeal?' suggested Alison helpfully. She came from a mindset which believed in legal challenge. When in doubt, litigate. 'Counter-sue your noisy neighbours for noise pollution, then reach a compromise deal.'

'It would just cost us a ton and we'd lose. So we'd be poor and still have no hens. Worse off.'

'That's a bit defeatist,' said Alison combatively. Something in Mary's tone made her bristle a bit.

Marilyn, Rita, Meryl and Julia pecked away in their little chicken run, oblivious to the fact that their fate was being deliberated by giant beings on deckchairs.

'It's not like we've got a rooster. Now there'd be noise.'

'Our kids love the hens. And so do the other kids from round here. Most of them have never seen a hen before. They think eggs are made in the supermarket,' said Brendan.

Alison sipped her wine, trying not to notice that the glass was grimy. She looked at Mary and Brendan. Such a suitable couple. They belonged together. You couldn't imagine either of them with anybody else. They had the exact same values, exact same ambition – or lack of it, as Alison saw it. They wanted to grow their vegetables and live a healthy life and rear their children. And that was that. And they matched each other in a very obvious way. Alison's eye fell on Charlie, who was staring out into the middle distance, his eyes squinting against the sun. She was aware that she and Charlie weren't such an obvious couple. Not by a long shot. You wouldn't immediately pluck them from a crowd and put them together. But the differences were essentially super- ficial, she thought. They did match very well in a more understated way. They were on a twin upward curve, Charlie because he was ambitious, Alison because she had high expectations. Her sights were set high, because she knew no other place to set them.

'Well, we named the first one after Marilyn, because she's a white and when we got her Mary said that she waddled like Marilyn Monroe. I never saw it myself, mind you,' said Brendan, and laughed. Ha ha ha. 'Hens have a lot more personality than is immediately apparent.'

Brendan and Mary had met in London. He was a Londoner and worked for a painting and decorating business. Mary had come to London, originally to train as a nurse, but she got tired of that and took a casual job as a 'stripper'. 'No, not that kind of stripper. The kind that goes into a house and strips the old wallpaper and generally gets it ready for the painter,' Brendan would say as he revisited the worn tread of the story. Brendan had come back with Mary to Ireland, and had moved in to number 43. This was a few years after their mother had died. Charlie moved out and Mary's children started to arrive. Mary and Brendan took over the remains of the purchase agreement with the county council. Mary kept wanting to compensate Charlie for his half of the house – by rights it should have been shared between them – and Charlie couldn't get her to drop it. His business expanded and his wallet with it, and Mary still kept wanting to compensate him. Charlie had forbidden her from mentioning it again. Brendan continued to work as a painter. Mary devoted herself exclusively to the children.

'My wife used to be a stripper,' Brendan would often joke.

'I'm not your wife,' retorted Mary with good humour. Mary had always refused to get married. 'I have no need nor liking for pieces of paper,' she declared haughtily whenever Brendan pressed her, which he frequently did with company present. He wanted to be married because he felt it would be better for the children.

'Let's go inside and eat,' declared Mary.

They returned to the gloom of the kitchen. Brendan started to clear the table of the piles of papers, stacking them precariously in the corner on top of another pile. A leaning tower. They all sat around the table. Mary handed a bowl to Susan.

'Salad.'

Susan ran out into the garden. Mary stirred a huge cauldron-like pot, from which emanated an absolutely gorgeous smell. She put fresh-baked brown bread on a large breadboard in the middle of the table. Susan came in with a bowl of salad ingredients: lettuce, radishes, peas. Mary rinsed them quickly and put them in a big bowl.

'No scallions?' asked Mary.

'I don't like scallions,' said Susan.

Mary tossed the salad with a home-made dressing she had in the fridge, then dished out a very nice-smelling pasta into large bowls and sat down.

'Oh, sorry. I forgot the forks.' Mary handed out forks to everybody and they started to eat.

Alison thought the meal was delicious. Everything tasted really fine. It was strange, this house, with all its chaos, and high standards of food. She ate hungrily. Charlie's phone rang. He sighed and scrutinized the phone. 'That's the showroom. Now what?' He went out into the garden to take the call.

'Does the showroom open on a Saturday afternoon?' asked Mary. 'I thought it was only open Saturday morning.'

'Oh, it's open all the time, Mary. If somebody wants to buy a car at three a.m., Charlie will open up for them.' There was a narky edge to Alison's voice which she tried to smother.

Charlie came back in. 'I'm sorry, I'm going to have to nip down there. Jim needs some documents and they're in my desk and only I have a key. Jim is like an old woman, chasing fiddly cheques up and down columns of figures. It'd make you dizzy. And he's complaining about my petty cash not being petty enough.'

'What's your accountant doing working on a Saturday?' asked Mary.

'Oh, he's double-booked. He can't fit all his work into a five-day week. Honestly, I won't be long. Thirty minutes. Forty-five at the outside.'

He stood and finished his bowl of pasta, hopping from one foot to the other, then left. Alison shrugged. She was used to it. Always panic stations. Charlie always running round after his business.

She wasn't unhappy to see the back of Charlie, as she had an ulterior motive. She wanted to get Mary on her own. Brendan in his inoffensively unmannerly way put his gardening shoes back on and returned to the pots at the end of the garden. Mary was left staring at Alison. She was a bit uncomfortable with her.

'Have some more wine.'

Mary filled the two glasses.

'Mary, I wonder could I ask you about your father?'

'What do you want to know?' An air of suspicion in the set of Mary's chin.

'Well, anything really. Just anything.'

'What has Charlie told you?'

'Almost nothing.'

'Maybe you should ask him.'

'I don't want to bother him too much.'

'Well,' Mary sighed, 'I remember him only vaguely. I was five when he left, Charlie was three. I can't picture his face any more, but I remember the feel of him.'

'And what did he do?'

'Do?'

'For a living.'

'I don't know. Mam would never talk about him. She just clammed up on the subject.'

'And have you any idea why he left and never got in touch? Did your mother ever give any hint?'

Mary sighed and shook her head. 'Alison, I really don't want to talk about this. It's the past, a painful past, and dwelling on it ain't great. What's got you fired up about it?'

Alison shrugged. 'I suppose Charlie wanting the baby named after his father. It got me curious.'

'I knew naming the child Michael would cause trouble. I knew it.'

'Not necessarily trouble.'

Mary emptied the wine bottle into the two glasses.

'I was heartbroken when my daddy left and never came back. Charlie was too young to remember. And it left our mother in an awful state. Mam had to go out cleaning to make a few bob. She used to clean houses to keep us fed and clothed. She probably cleaned your neighbours' houses, up there on Military Road.

Perhaps she even cleaned yours. But the worst thing about it was that I was ashamed of her. I remember very clearly I used to stand at the crossroads with my mates waiting for the bus to go to school. I was about thirteen or that. I used to pray that the bus would come on time, because if it was late, we'd see them. The scrubbers. An army of women in those navy nylon pinafores left our area to go to the big houses up the hill. After they'd got their children out to school and straightened out their own homes, they went off to scrub other people's. My mother and Mrs MacCarthy from number 30 were among them. The rest of the women I didn't know, from further down the estate. They went by in ones and twos, like slaves. And me and Judith MacCarthy used to stand there mortified. We never let on to the other girls at the bus stop that they were our mothers in the nylon pinnies. "It's the scrubbers," one of the smart alecks would say, and the rest would laugh and me and Judith would go redder and redder and laugh a bit. Our mothers, Mam and Mrs MacCarthy, always kept to the far path, and faked a deep conversation as they passed, smoking intently, the two of them. And as I think about that now, as an adult, I don't know which was worse. How me and Judith pretended not to know them, or how they didn't salute us to save us the embarrassment of having them as mothers. I still blush when I see Judith MacCarthy down at the school. At the shame of it. At the shame of having been ashamed of them.' She gave a little rueful laugh. 'Judith MacCarthy married a drunk. So she's scrubbing now.'

Alison listened to Mary with mixed emotions. The story made her feel uncomfortable, and she thought it a little inconsiderate of Mary to tell it to her. She tried to steer Mary back to their father.

'I am talking about my father. I'm talking about what his absence meant.'

'And Charlie, how did he take it?'

'Charlie didn't mind things so much. He always had a proud streak. He was lucky in that he was never bothered what other people thought of him.'

Little Michael was snoring in his Carry-tot.

Mary gestured to Alison to follow her. She went up the stairs and into the front room, Mary and Brendan's bedroom. There was even more chaos here, piles of clothes and corners stacked high with jumble. Cobwebs and dust everywhere. The only thing that was orderly in the room was the bed. It was neatly made, with gleaming white sheets. Mary rooted in a biscuit tin and produced a key. She went to a corner of the room and took a pile of clothes off what turned out to be an old desk. She opened the desk with the key and the front panel folded down to create a writing space. The key was stiff and difficult to turn.

'It's the archive. I just dumped everything belonging to my mam in here. I haven't looked at it since.'

'May I?' asked Alison eagerly.

Mary shrugged, said 'You're family now,' and left the room. Alison smiled, grateful for the crumb of friendliness.

She sat in at the desk. It was a beautiful walnut desk with an intricate inlay. Probably very valuable. The house was full of this old, possibly valuable, unkempt antique furniture. The inside of the desk was stuffed with papers. Alison lifted a few documents. Bills. Electricity bills and gas bills. Probably stuff Charlie's mother was dealing with at the time of her sudden death. She rooted a little further. School reports. Charlie's reports from primary school. She scanned those. Very bright. Always got good grades. At the back of the desk there was a box tied up with pink ribbon. Alison opened it, her heart racing. Sure she was about to find something. The ribbon slipped off and inside the box were two parcels wrapped in tissue paper. She gently took the tissue off one package and inside was a hymnal. The stitching on the spine was beginning to fall apart, hence the careful packaging. Written on the inside of the hymnal was Deborah May Lennon, Second Year. Alison smiled. She opened the other parcel. An old and worn hardback book with a blue cover. The spine was missing and the book was utterly disintegrated into several pieces. She opened it. The title-page read *The Spirit of St Louis* by Charles Augustus Lindbergh. His autobiography. And it was signed by Lindbergh. A first edition. Could be valuable if it was in better condition. She shrugged. Funny what people treasured, she thought, and re-wrapped the books. She looked on through the papers. There was a menu for a dinner dance. Recipes torn from magazines and newspapers. More bills. A little tin of stray buttons and threads. The detritus of a life. Nothing very dramatic, and not a trace of Charlie's father. No wedding photograph. Nothing. Then, at the very back, there was an envelope. Photos. Alison opened it eagerly. A dark, serious-looking woman with a look of Mary. Must be Charlie's mother, she thought. Photos of her life, as a young woman, on a hot beach in a bikini. As a child. With other young women. But none of Charlie's dad. There was one with the children, cropped at one side. Charlie's dad exorcized? Cut from the record. Not a trace of him. There must have been a wedding album, thought Alison, and as she thought it she pictured the blaze as it got reduced to cinders in some fiery purge. Nothing. Then, casually, in a stack of bills, an engagement party invite. Deborah May Lennon and Michael John O'Brien. She filched it and put it in her pocket. It was something. Something to go on.

There was a little drawer at the back of the desk, unnoticeable at first as its seam fitted neatly into the inlay. It opened at a touch with a cute spring mechanism. This desk is definitely valuable, she thought. Inside the drawer was a little leather bag. Alison's heart raced again. Something important here, she was sure. She spilled the contents of the bag in front of her. A pair of diamond cluster earrings. A gold bracelet. A gold chain. A large diamond and perhaps emerald ring. An engagement ring perhaps? A brooch. All good stuff. And a powder compact. She opened the powder compact and little puffs of pink dust scattered into the air. The compact was hallmarked, again pretty valuable. Alison had stumbled on the family jewels. Not a huge collection, but all good pieces. They shouldn't be left lying around here, she thought. A burglar might get his hands on them.

She heard the little cries of baby Michael and gathered the jewellery into the leather bag and brought it downstairs. Mary had lifted Michael and was giving him a cuddle.

'Time for his bottle,' said Alison.

Mary put the kettle on and the bottle was duly heated. Alison put the leather bag on the table.

'There was some jewellery in a little drawer. It's valuable stuff.'

Mary opened the little leather bag and spilled the contents onto the table. 'I recognize these. Mam used to wear them.'

'You should use them.'

'I don't like jewellery. I find it uncomfortable.'

'They're too valuable to leave lying around up there. Susan might like them when she's older.'

Mary shrugged and put the leather pouch on the windowledge alongside a jar of pickled onions and a rolled-up pair of socks. Alison shook her head. 'I mean very valuable. You should get them valued and insured.'

Mary shrugged. 'Nobody is going to burgle us. The burglars know there's nothing in this house. We don't even have a video and the TV is ancient. You'd have to pay a fella to take it away.'

The doorbell rang. It would be Charlie returning.

8

Cormac stretched out on the large bed and bit into an apple, recently procured from the complimentary bowl of fruit on the sideboard.

'This reminds me of our honeymoon,' he said.

Marie Rose smiled, and looked at her husband reclining on the bed, reflected in the dressing-table mirror, as she applied colour to her lips and eyes. Not too much. Understated was best. She didn't want to look like a circus performer. She smiled at the result. It really lifted her face.

The annual *Garda* ball. A big dress dance in the Great Southern Hotel in Killarney, and Marie Rose and Cormac had taken a room because they'd have to stay overnight. Michael had gone protesting to stay with Kate for the night, but had been promised a donkey ride the next day as an inducement. It was the first night since he was born that Marie Rose was away from him and she felt the separation keenly. But it was also a thrill to be away. They had declined to go on each of the previous years, as Marie Rose felt she couldn't stay away overnight and Cormac wasn't bothered going without her. Also, it was expensive. The tickets to the dance and the train fare and the hotel. It all added up. And the dress. Marie Rose had to have a gown made up by Alice Sweeney, the dressmaker in Dingle. She got ten yards of beautiful old world floral chiffon sent down by her father, and Alice had made quite a magnificent dress with a dark green bodice. She had used a lot of expensive trimmings. The neckline was finished with a patterned edging of diamanté. Marie Rose had to go for three fittings because the bodice pattern was a complicated fit. Also a little jacket was made to go over the dress, as the occasion was in early March. But the end result was a vision to behold, as it hung on a hanger on the hotel wardrobe door.

'I'm keen to see you in that,' said Cormac. 'You'll look like a film star.'

'Oh, I'll be a sight for sore eyes,' giggled Marie Rose.

'It'll make a change from those old countrywoman skirts you go round in at home.'

She threw a hairbrush at him.

'I suppose you'd like me in satin, scrubbing out the range.'

'I expect to come home some day and find you shuffling about under a shawl like the aul ones.'

'You're hardly a dandy yourself.'

'I beg your pardon. I am always well turned out in my uniform.'

Marie Rose walked over to the wardrobe and took down the floating dress. Underneath it was Cormac's dress uniform. It had never been worn before, but Cormac was still lean and it had been a bit big for him when acquired. It had a high neck and intricate piping and stitching down the front. And the trousers had a fine dress cut. Marie Rose had pressed it carefully and now surveyed the creases. They were to her satisfaction.

'Your good shoes are a disgrace. I think I packed polish in the bag.'

'Already done. I sent the young lad off to do it. Gave him sixpence. He said he'd bring them back at five, which was an hour ago. No such thing as service any more.'

'Serves you right for giving him the tip before he'd done the job.'

'I'd better go find my shoes and give that young pup a clip round the ears.'

Cormac left and Marie Rose looked at herself in the full-length mirror. The slip was flattering and her figure still good. She was delighted to be away on an adventure. Maybe it would help.

She sat down at the dressing table. Michael was now five and no more babies had come. They had avoided it for a few years. Marie Rose felt that she didn't want to go again too soon. All that child-bearing wore a woman out. It had been the finish of her mother, who had never been right after the last baby. Marie Rose's mother had died two years ago, but her sisters said she was so low at the end, it was a merciful release. And these big families with a new-born every spring were very old-fashioned, she thought.

Nowadays, a small family of about four children was plenty. So she was determined to take her time. They had been very careful about dates and had not been caught out.

When Michael was about two and a half, they decided it was time to go again. And nothing happened. She'd tried to bring the subject up with Cormac, but he didn't want to talk about it. 'Talk, talk, that's all you want to do. You'll drive me to the grave, gabbing,' he said unkindly, to dismiss the subject. He was often quick with the cross word, but Marie Rose had got used to that. In black moments, she wondered if she had brought bad luck on herself, being so careful for so long. Maybe God was punishing her, telling her she had no right to thwart his plans. It was against Church teaching, she knew. You weren't supposed to interfere with the divine plan for your marriage. You weren't supposed to avoid having babies by being careful. It was a sin. She'd confessed it and been given absolution. Not to Father O'Keefe. She only told him the harmless sins. A bit of envy here, a bit of anger there. She sometimes went to confession in Dingle, when she'd anything big to get off her conscience. There, Father Moore, who had christened Michael, was always very sympathetic, no matter what you had done. He was a grand priest, very kind. Marie Rose really liked him, though she was never fully sure he knew what she was talking about. After she'd got the absolution, she was very hopeful that things would be right, but still nothing happened. Then it occurred to her that maybe Cormac should confess the matter as well. After all, he had done half the sin. Cormac just scoffed at her. 'Stuff and nonsense. Superstition. I'm not discussing the intimate details of my marriage with any of those fellows. Sure they're celibates. They wouldn't have a clue what you're talking about. They wouldn't know one end of a woman from the other.'

'That's vulgar,' she said, but she couldn't get him to go. In rational moments, she was sure it wasn't the problem anyway. She went to a doctor in Tralee, where nobody knew her, and sought his advice. He was kind, but couldn't come up with anything, except keep trying. He took her through the science of working out dates carefully, and advised her to concentrate on her fertile period, and abstain for a week beforehand. But she found she was getting stressed about it all, and the sex act was becoming fraught and losing some of its spontaneity and allure, as she marked and crossed dates on calendars, and pushed Cormac away when the time wasn't right. It was putting a strain on them.

Marie Rose flounced the dress over her head. The bodice hooked closed at the side, under the arm, so she could manage on her own. She then slipped on the little jacket and stood in the middle of the room. She twirled, admiring herself. A bit of romance and magic. Maybe that's what they needed. A bit of luck.

'I bet you'll be the most beautiful woman in the room.'

Marie Rose started. She hadn't heard him come in.

'They'll stand in snow staring at me.' She laughed.

'They might be standing in snow. It's freezing tonight.'

Cormac had the good shoes in his hand, freshly polished.

'The young lad was just about to bring them. You'll never guess, I'm after meeting Froggy down in the lobby, and he has a lady friend. Never said a word to me about it.'

'That's a surprise.'

'She's a fine-looking girl.'

'Is she now?'

Marie Rose was still wary of Froggy. She didn't trust his lack of industry. Thought it unhealthy. It wasn't right for a man to sit around doing nothing but reading books and papers. Froggy had bought his little cottage and he now appeared in Ballyferriter frequently during the winter months. Marie Rose had forgotten, but Cormac had mentioned that Froggy had purchased a pair of tickets to the *Garda* ball. Froggy had complained vociferously about the price. One pound ten shillings for a double. He was outraged. Rich men were great for complaining about money. It had started Cormac speculating as to the recipient of the other ticket, but it had gone out of his mind.

'Gearóidín de Paor is her name. A *gaelgóir* from Dublin. And she calls Froggy Proinnsías. It's the Irish for Frank. He told me, very proudly, that he met her at his advanced Irish conversation class in Dublin.'

Marie Rose was glad. It was dawning on her that she'd know nobody at the dance, and though she had reservations about

Froggy, he was at least familiar. And it might be nice to talk to his lady friend. She rarely met new people and at this moment she felt hungry for stimulation.

'Better get dressed, dear,' she said. 'We'll be late for the dinner.'

Mr James McGowan's Full Orchestral Band, all the way from Dublin, were in full swing. The atmosphere was marvellous, Marie Rose had had a few glasses of wine and was feeling very festive. Gearóidín was good company, if a bit brassy, and Marie Rose was slipping into a tipsy euphoria. The dance had started with a 'Walls of Limerick', and the crowd was well up for that. They liked their Irish dances down here, and no matter what jazz numbers were in fashion, they were hanging on to their own. Couples lined up for 'The Walls of Limerick' and the colours of the women's frocks flashed splendid as the dancers spun. The traditional music got the crowd warmed up nicely. Then a foxtrot, followed by a waltz. Then a one-step called 'I'm Flirting with You', along with which Gearóidín sang in an outrageous manner. She was very pretty, blonde hair cut in a bob and lots of make-up. Her dress was very smart, a long-waisted bodice fitted tight to the figure to below the hipline. There a deep frill and a cape of fishnet which gave an unusual and somewhat racy impression. It made Marie Rose feel her own gown was rather old-fashioned. Gearóidín smoked cigarettes almost incessantly.

'Terrible habit,' she remarked. 'It makes you cough so.'

'May I try one?'

Gearóidín offered her one from a silver case.

'I got into the habit when I was studying. It was the only thing I truly mastered at university, blowing smoke rings.'

She formed a pretty O with her painted mouth and blew delicate rings across the table at Froggy. He poked them with his finger in a rather suggestive manner and Marie Rose, despite herself, giggled. Gearóidín's presence was making her bolder. She lit up the cigarette and happily puffed it without inhaling.

'It must be so splendid to live in Ballyferriter. I've been dying to meet you. Proinnsías told me all about you. Your wonderful handsome husband who fought for Ireland and your beautiful young son. I feel I know you intimately. And there you are

136

perched on the edge of the Dingle peninsula, the most romantic place on earth. And you look just the picture, in your green dress. They should have put you on the pound note, rather than your woman, that tart. She's not even Irish. A Yank!'

Marie Rose was taken aback at this speech. It had never occurred to her that anybody would envy her.

'Like as though we haven't beauties of our own.'

'Have you been to Ballyferriter?'

'I was there for two weeks just after I left university to learn Irish. And I've visited the Blasket Islands. It must be great to live so near the islands. I bet you visit them all the time.'

Marie Rose had never gone over.

'I've no reason to go there. I don't know any of the people.'

Gearóidín smiled. 'It's like the Garden of Eden.'

'Maybe in the summer. But in the winter the wind would skin you.'

The band started a new tune. A foxtrot.

'Oooh,' squealed Gearóidín. 'It's "Red, Red Robin". I love this. May I borrow your husband?'

She steered Cormac off onto the floor, leaving Marie Rose alone with Froggy.

'She's nice, Froggy. How long have you known her?'

'A few months.'

'And is it going anywhere?' Marie Rose was emboldened by the wine. 'Might you be on the way to the altar?'

Froggy shook his head.

'Not because I wouldn't like to. She's already married, Marie Rose. Her husband ran off to America. Apparently he married again out there and has a squad of kids. They don't pay too much attention to people's past in America. But she's stuck in holy Ireland. Where there's no room for a divorcée.'

'Oh.'

Marie Rose looked out at the dancing. Gearóidín was a very able dancer, but Cormac wasn't making a fool of himself. He was keeping up. And to Marie Rose's eye, he was exceedingly hand-some in his dress uniform. The cut of it had a way of broadening the chest and shoulders. And Gearóidín was very pretty in her very modern dress and with her very modern manners. She had this way of making eye contact with Cormac as she executed the moves of the dance, and Marie Rose felt a little jealous. She never made eyes at him in that way. It had never occurred to her. Cormac was lapping it up.

'But at least she has money. Family money. Being rich and divorced is much better than being poor and divorced.'

'Oh.' Marie Rose had never met anybody divorced before. You didn't see too many divorcées wandering round Kerry.

'She wants to come and visit me in Ballyferriter, but I've told her she should stay in the hotel. I don't think the locals would take too kindly to me shacking up with a divorcée in Duntobbar Cottage. Next thing, I'd find myself not getting served in Sean's pub.'

'Sure they'd serve anybody there.'

'Or Father O'Keefe would be knocking on my door.'

'She should stay in the hotel. No point in drawing them on you.'

The dancers returned, breathless. Panting. Post-coital, thought Marie Rose. Cormac had that alertness about him that she generally only saw in bed. Or when under pressure in the barracks. Gearóidín was raising the temperature, sure enough. Marie Rose was mildly irritated, but couldn't bestir herself to serious jealousy. A waltz started.

'Froggy?' asked Marie Rose, a little boldly. He gallantly got to his feet. Froggy wasn't as good a figure of a man as Cormac, he was a bit heavy set, but he could waltz smoothly, and the rhythmic movement gave his corpulent body some grace. Marie Rose glided about the floor with him, holding her head high, and displaying her long and beautiful neck, her hair piled high on her head.

Gearóidín took out her cigarette holder from her purse and lit up. Cormac was entranced. She was a seductive package. Recklessly flirtatious, she behaved as though she had nothing to lose. She tipsily ordered champagne from a passing waiter and laughed at Cormac's slightly disapproving look. It wasn't that he disapproved as such, it was more that he was surprised at how commanding she was. It was unusual in a woman.

'You remind me of my husband,' she said. 'He always looked

disapprovingly at me. But he couldn't boss me around, because I had more money than he. A girl should always marry her financial inferior in order to have a conducive life.'

'Well, your marriage didn't last.'

'Oh, yes. I knew there was a flaw in my theory. My theory is fine in theory.'

Cormac laughed.

'My husband was in the seminary when I met him. The seminarians used to stand about on the steps outside number 86 St Stephen's Green, where the university was, looking splendidly unattainable in their dark suits. I was spoiled as a child, and have always wanted, as a matter of course, that which I cannot have.'

She smiled at Cormac here.

'He wasn't cut out to be a priest. I think he realized that, and I was his excuse to jump ship. I invited him for our first date, to a picture in the Grafton. It was only after we married that it became clear that we were utterly incompatible. How we made such a mistake, I'll never know. I suppose I can plead youth in my defence.'

'You don't have to plead anything.'

They both looked out at Froggy and Marie Rose.

'Proinnsías has great admiration for your wife. He sings her praises night and day. He thinks her the ideal Irish woman.'

'I think he's just jealous because he'd like to be married himself.'

Gearóidín shrugged. Across the room, Cormac could see Superintendent Geraghty making his way in their direction. An outgoing man, he stopped at many tables to chat. He finally appeared at Cormac's side and asked if he could be seated. Cormac pulled out a chair for him. They got on well, Cormac and the super. Gearóidín turned her shiny lightbeam on him.

'Superintendent Maurice Geraghty, Gearóidín de Paor, a friend of ours.'

'Charmed, charmed.' Gearóidín held out an arm and Geraghty kissed it. She poured some champagne for the superintendent and smiled lasciviously.

'I just love being surrounded by men in uniform. I must get Proinnsías to get one.'

'These aren't our uniforms. These are our dress suits. And rarely do they get an airing.'

Geraghty drank some champagne and smiled at Gearóidín. Really, this Dublin blonde had a way of perking up men, thought Cormac. She was like a honey pot. The dancers returned and Marie Rose greeted Superintendent Geraghty as an old friend. He had always been kind and avuncular with her, especially when they came first, when she really needed it.

'And how is your lovely little boy, Mrs O'Brien?'

Froggy and Geraghty shook hands. They knew each other slightly from Cumann na nGaedheal meetings in Dingle.

'Oh, he's the tops. Quite the prince. Gives us all our orders. And your boys?'

'The eldest is getting married next month. Agnes Quinn, that nice little girl from the chemist by the station. Mrs Geraghty thinks the world of her, and that, as they say, is the main thing. Joseph likes her well enough.' He chuckled. 'I jest. They are love's young dream.'

'Must go and powder my nose. Come on, Marie Rose.' Gearóidín got up and put her arm through Marie Rose's and steered her off to the ladies' room, leaving a silence in their wake.

'Bad business, the election.'

'I suppose so,' shrugged Cormac. The Republicans had done very well in the general election just passed and the new administration was settling into its offices. Fianna Fáil as a minority government, supported by Labour.

'That's the drawback to democracy,' said Froggy. 'The other crowd sometimes win. It's a fatal flaw in the system.'

'What bothers me,' said Geraghty, 'is that those bastards did their best to cripple this state only a few bloody years ago, and now we're going to have to take orders from them. Several Fianna Fáil election candidates have been behind bars in our barracks. Sure wasn't I combing the hills round Dingle with an arrest warrant for Dev at one stage? I'm a bit nervous, Cormac. And so should you be.'

'Have you heard something?'

'Only that the commissioner is for the chop. They're going to replace him with a Republican. And they'll be stacking the senior echelons of the force with Fianna Fáilers. It'll have an effect. I don't know how secure my position is.'

Cormac shook his head. 'I think the commissioner is for the chop anyway. Our crowd are agreed on that. It's not in their interests to open up those old wounds. They'll leave it well enough alone. If it isn't broke, don't fix it. They aren't going to fire you, Maurice.'

'They won't fire me, but I could find myself transferred to some miserable Limerick slum or a midlands bog, and Mrs Geraghty would not be pleased. And you, Cormac, I'd watch my back if I were you. You're known for having strong views.'

Cormac shrugged. He thought it most unlikely. There had been a lot of scaremongering about the change in administration. Everything would go on the same, he felt. The civil war was over, and the trick was to keep passions damped down. Let the bitterness get bred out by the next generation. Or certainly the generation after that. And if the new administration started stirring things up, you'd never know where it'd lead.

'De Valera is full of praise for the force. He's making very placating noises,' said Cormac. 'Even complimenting the outgoing administration on us. We're the shining light of the Free State.'

'You're an innocent abroad, Cormac,' said Geraghty.

'I was at a de Valera rally in Roscrea on my way down here. Shortly before the election, it was,' said Froggy. 'Dev was banging on about how he'd lower taxes if elected, buying the vote as usual. Full of sophistry and bombast. And a man broke from the crowd and yelled out, "Who is responsible for this onerous burden of taxation but de Valera himself for causing the split?" A bunch of bully boys burst forth to silence the objector. Dev himself appealed for the man to be allowed make his point, all sweet reasonableness, and then at inordinate length he demonstrated by mathematics how he hadn't caused the split. Until the audience was so tired and bored they wanted to go home. But the bully boys were still pushing and shoving the poor fella that made the point. And what I'm saying is, Dev is all sweet reasonableness, but there are those on his side who aren't. There's a thug element. And it hasn't gone away. And, Cormac, if you think it'll all go on as before, you are an innocent.'

Cormac shrugged. Maybe Froggy was right, but there was nothing that could be done about it. The election was lost. Fair and square.

'They're going to take the tax off the sugar and put it on the tea,' said Superintendent Geraghty. Froggy laughed and Geraghty continued. 'That's the height of their economic policy. Jiggling things around. They aren't good housekeepers, the Fianna Fáilers. Not used to keeping a tidy house.'

Marie Rose finished powdering her nose and left the ladies' room. Gearóidín had gone off to pee. She idly crossed the lobby and went into a sitting room where some people sat reading papers. The wireless was on. A crackly reception. Not as clear as her own, she mused. And you'd think they'd have plenty of money in this hotel to get the best wireless equipment. A lively jig was playing, and an elderly man in a great tall armchair was tapping out the beat with his two fingers, a dancing agility which had long left his legs. Marie Rose smiled to herself at the sight of the old man with the frisky digits. She hadn't seen her own father for almost two years. He was getting old now, and the sight of old men always brought him to her mind. The old man in the armchair smiled at her as the music ended. Somebody adjusted the tuning and a news programme came on. She stood stock still and listened.

'A small bed in the nursery of a New Jersey country house is empty, and the whole of America wants to know the reason why . . . The kidnapping of the nineteen-month-old son of Colonel Charles Lindbergh, idol of the nation since he made the first solo flight across the Atlantic in May 1927, has roused the American nation to anger as no other crime has done for years.

'The baby was kidnapped between seven thirty p.m. and ten p.m. last night from his nursery. A window near the baby's crib was found open when the nurse went into the room. The window is thirty feet from the ground and a three-piece ladder was found in a thicket near the house.

'President Hoover of the United States intervened as soon as the news reached the White House this morning. The president summoned the attorney-general for a conference about the kidnapping.

'A note was found on the windowsill demanding a ransom of fifty thousand dollars, that is ten thousand pounds at par, and threatening harm to the child if this sum was not paid. It is understood that Colonel Lindbergh is willing to pay the ransom.'

Marie Rose felt herself go a bit light-headed. Kidnapped. That's a terrible thing to happen. The little golden-haired boy. Marie Rose had seen photos of him in the magazines. She felt a pang as she thought about Michael. Suddenly she worried about having left him at Kate's, her maternal anxieties swamped round her. Gearóidín appeared at her side.

'Let's go back to the dancing. I'll die without a foxtrot,' she declared with drama, and some desperation.

Marie Rose stood on the strand and looked out to sea. Out there, in the middle of the cove, bobbed a creature which to a short-sighted eye might have seemed a seal, but she knew it was her husband. In the summer months, he took a swim almost every day, and she tasted it from his skin at night. He hadn't spotted her on the strand, and was still swimming to and fro, following an imaginary course with great concentration and determination. Kathleen, the new girl in service in Sean's pub, occasionally minded Michael for a few hours to make some extra money, and it gave Marie Rose a very welcome break. She had been getting thin and peaky-looking, and Cormac had encouraged her to take a bit more time for herself. As far as he could see, she never stopped. She was always washing clothes and scrubbing the house and baking and making and mending and stitching. It was he who suggested they get someone to mind Michael occasionally. They could afford it without difficulty. The idea simply never occurred to Marie Rose.

She walked to and fro on the beach for a while, and then decided that he either didn't see her or else saw her, but didn't fancy cutting his swim short. She cursed him and his damn contrariness. She wanted badly to talk to him, but not so badly that she was going to wave or otherwise gesture him in. She climbed up on the little headland at the edge of the strand and lay on her back, watching the clouds canter across the deep blue sky. It was unusually warm for May, but the sea nonetheless looked blue and icy. Marie Rose shivered at the thought of it. Shed no cloth till May be out. That's what they said, but Cormac wasn't inclined to take advice from anyone, and definitely not a man to follow folk wisdom. The talk was that they were going to have a good summer. Something about the jellyfish arriving early, or the frogs spawning deeply, or a lot of tourists being seen in the hotel. There was talk anyway; whether there'd be temperatures to back up the talk was a different matter. Marie Rose had lived six summers here on this peninsula, and every year the optimism about the summer prospects was boundless. She thought she'd go out of her mind if she had another conversation about the weather. It was compulsory to have views. Getting warm now. Grand stretch in the evening. Red sky at night, shepherds' delight. Red sky in the morning, shepherds' warning. This last winter's the worst we ever had. The summer coming is set to be just grand.

She sat up and pulled at some grass, feeling the dampness of the earth underneath her. She got up and sat on a rock, and looked on out at the determined head cutting through the water. She had just heard on the news that the Lindbergh baby had been found. Dead. And she wanted to tell Cormac. She was terribly shocked, but somehow not surprised. It hadn't looked good. No word for so long, and it's hard to hide a noisy toddler. She wasn't as upset as she thought she would have been. She had faced it, she supposed, and imagined it so many times, that she was in fact prepared for it. She heard the news on the wireless.

She had been in the kitchen, getting things ready for Kathleen. Just idly tidying away some loose ends and listening to the wireless.

'A wave of fury has swept America. Colonel Lindbergh's baby, who was kidnapped from his New Jersey home on 1 March has been found dead near the Lindberghs' estate. Somebody had tried to bury the body, face downwards, and it was in a bad state of decomposition. The spot is approximately five miles by road from

144

he Lindbergh estate and four miles in a direct line across the ourland mountains . . .'

Marie Rose immediately went out into the back garden to check on Michael. There he was, sturdy in his short cotton trousers, contentedly playing with his aeroplane. It had been put away on a shelf for some time, but perhaps the buzz about Lindbergh and the kidnapping had rekindled his interest in the toy, and it was now enjoying a revival in his affections. He was full of difficult questions. What is a kidnapping? Why would someone do that? What'll happen to the little baby? Who will make him his bottle?

She stroked his silky black hair and gave him a big hug, kissing him on the top of his head. He pushed her away.

'Leave me alone, Mama. I don't like being kissed on the head.'

She cuddled him a little longer, before releasing him to run along the garden, holding his plane aloft in his right hand and creating an engine noise, a high-pitched drone. Then, sputters, and a crash-land into the flowerbed. Always high drama.

'Be careful of the plane, *a stór*.'

'It's only a toy, Mama,' retorted Michael, with childish scorn.

'It's a special toy.'

To Marie Rose it was a lot more than a toy.

Kathleen arrived, breathless and delighted as always. Marie Rose knew that Kathleen liked coming here. Her family home was a remote sheep farm way up in the hills and there wasn't much spare there, so she was sent into service. Marie Rose was inclined to mother the girl, who was only fifteen and out bravely making her way in the world at such a tender age. Her surplus mothering instincts found an outlet here. They were fine and honourable over in the pub, and treated her generally well, but there was no one there who would have much time to chat and a girl that age needed to be able to chat a bit, especially to a woman. Kathleen was a maid of all work, run off her feet from early morning to late at night, but she had free time in the middle of the day. This was when she minded Michael. Marie Rose always left a big lunch for the girl, and a pot with Cross and Blackwell soup on the stove. And she brought down the cake tin.

She went to the post office and posted a few items. A letter to her father. An order for stockings and underwear from a big drapery in Dublin called Pim Brothers of South Great George's Street. She was too self-conscious to buy such items in Dingle. Everybody seemed to know her and the woman in the drapery was very overfamiliar. And besides, she liked the adventure of sending away for parcels. She had done it before for some garments for Michael and it had worked very well. So she was happy to try it for herself.

She responded to an advertisement in the *Iris an Garda*, the monthly *Garda* magazine. It was a big special-value promotion week at Pim's on corsets and undergarments which promised to mould and perfect the figure. She could happily buy such things with discretion by post. And it didn't cost any extra. And the colours were entrancing. Sky, Sahara, apple, cream, dusk. What lovely colours. And it was all very good value.

In the night she would lie awake and think about her letter on its journey. Stacked in a mailbag with lots of other letters, getting sorted and put on a train to Dublin, and finally landing on an order desk in South Great George's Street in Dublin. Then a package being made up and piled up with lots of other packages. Then posted back. Perhaps catching the early train and speeding down to Kerry in a rush of excitement. Sitting around in a siding for a while, then being put on the little train to Dingle. Then a car out here, with all the other exciting mail, from Dublin, from England, from America, even from Australia. Then Mick O'Reilly, the postman, would knock on her door and cheerfully cry, 'A parcel for Mrs O'Brien.' And she would take the package with girlish thrill.

The post office was unusually busy and Síle, the girl behind the desk, unusually slow. Marie Rose was in no hurry. In fact, she was at a loss what to do after the posting. While waiting in the post office, the weather chorus started. Soft day, thank God. Seems softer. Do you think the summer's finally here? Maybe is, maybe isn't. After she'd finished her business, she strolled out the road aimlessly for a relaxing walk. She didn't know where she was going, just ambled along, thinking about the poor Lindberghs. It was a terrible blow. Her own son was so precious, even the thought of him being lost for an hour was enough to give her a tight feeling in her chest. It would be the end of her.

She pulled a long stalk of grass from the hedgerow and walked along, heading north. Poor Anne Lindbergh. She must have been so proud to marry such a great man, she must have thought him such a catch. But then the very thing that made him so great was the thing responsible for this hideous thing happening to her first-born son. If she was plain old Anne O'Reilly, married to a postman or a fisherman round here, nobody would be bothered kidnapping her baby. The thing that was so great about her life was also the thing that was so awful. There was something to be said for being a nobody and leading a nothing life.

Marie Rose had followed the story of Lindbergh's romance and wedding closely. She had been disappointed in Anne Morrow Lindbergh, didn't think her half beautiful enough to marry this great sky hero, but she was impressed by the way she flew the aeroplanes with him. Maybe a prettier woman wouldn't have had the guts to do that. Marie Rose kept a scrapbook on Lindbergh, on the pretence that Michael might be interested in it when he was older. She cut out items from the paper and magazines with meticulous care and pasted them into a big book. She followed his career like a hawk. She had a beautiful portrait of Lindbergh pasted on the cover, cut from a magazine. Pictures and accounts of the historic transatlantic flight. Pictures from Paris of the landing. Then the ticker-tape parade in New York. She often gazed at the picture of New York with longing. It sounded like the most exciting place she could ever imagine. His life thus far was contained neatly in the pages of this green book, the ongoing chronicle continuing into the remaining blank pages. It had been a golden life of marvellous achievement and glamour, until this nightmare, just horribly concluded, had begun. And what was it all worth? All the glamour and achievement? When with all your wealth and privilege, you couldn't keep your baby safe? What was all the money in the world compared to the value of your child's precious head? She felt guilty about the envy she felt for Anne Morrow Lindbergh. Guilty, because she didn't envy her now, and guilty because she shouldn't have envied her in the first place. It was disloyal to Cormac, and she was slightly ashamed.

It was her little secret, her imaginary trysts with Lindbergh. In one of these daydreams, Lindbergh's plane got into difficulty and he crash-landed in Kerry, just up the hill behind the barracks. And she, Marie Rose Bourke O'Brien, bravely dragged him from the burning wreckage, which soon after burst into flames. But Lindy would survive to fly again. Disaster averted. She would have interceded in world events; her own story line and history would have intersected and flared briefly and gloriously. And he would fall madly in love with her, his saviour. But she would turn him down. Because she was married and had a baby son, and nothing was more important than that. But there would be fine high emotions felt by everybody. And Cormac would be proud of her and look up to her. And maybe Lindbergh would teach her how to fly. Like Amelia Earhart. It was such a silly dream, but it passed the time in the evenings after the radio went off, as she sat darning by the fire, Cormac often working late.

She walked on aimlessly, thinking. The air was warm, but the road and fields were still damp from the winter. It would be a while yet before they dried out. The familiar curls of the road and contours of the hills, once so alien and frightening to her, now seemed friendly. She had come to accept this place and begun to feel almost part of it.

She got to the turning that led down to Whitestrand and followed it. Cormac might be down there. He mentioned he was going for his swim this morning. She wanted to see him. To tell him the terrible news about the baby. She strolled down toward the strand.

Sitting on the headland, she watched as her husband worked the water. She began to get annoyed with him. She'd been there almost half an hour and he really should have come in when he saw her. She was about to get up and march off home, when she saw the figure turn in the water and head for shore. He stood up once he got to the shallows and shook his head in the manner of a dog, spraying water from side to side. He was unaware of her presence. He wasn't ignoring her. She watched him as he continued on up the shore to a rock, and behind the rock he pulled out a little bundle, his stashed clothes.

He dried himself quickly with a towel and pulled on his clothes, oblivious to his observer. He looked very happy after his swim.

flushed with the exertion. Cormac made his own adventures, out there in the bay, pushed himself against his own barriers. Got a thrill of heroism at his own efforts. Why couldn't she emulate him and make her own adventures in life? But just as she formulated the thought, she knew the answer. She'd never swim out that far, because if something happened to her, who'd mind Michael? It didn't stop Cormac, but men were different. Femininity and heroism didn't go together. She had to get used to that idea.

She climbed down the rocks to the strand and started walking towards him. He saw her and smiled, and his face creased in that way it did when he was in good humour. She smiled at him, glad to recognize the uncomplicated pleasure with which he was greeting her. Because sometimes he looked at her without joy. And she feared that.

'Have you been here long?' he asked.

'A little while. A half-hour. You are quite a fish.'

'I love that swim. I always feel great after it. You must come in yourself.'

Marie Rose shook her head.

'Oh,' she said. 'There was bad news on the radio. They found the poor baby. Dead.'

'What baby?' he asked.

9

Charlie pored over the figures on the computer printout and tried to concentrate, but the numbers all slid in a jumble to the bottom of the page. Like some computer virus had invaded his brain. He went back to the beginning and attempted to focus on the matter, but halfway down the first page of the document, kind of headache set in at the base of his head and he lost the thread. He wasn't a genius at figures normally, but he was competent, and it worried him that he wasn't able to follow this. A sneaking suspicion raised itself in his mind that he didn't want to follow this because it all led inexorably the one way: up queer street. A merry dance into the red. He had to trade out of this. He didn't want to follow the document to the conclusion, because he wanted business to pick up and the conclusion to change before he got to it. But deep down, he knew this was a pipe dream. The headache started at the base of his neck and sent feelers up the sides of his head, along his ears. Then it throbbed malignantly about his temples. Throb, throb, throb.

The business was in trouble. He had a drawer stuffed full of signed cheques which hadn't been sent out yet because there was no cash in the bank to meet them. Charlie had been at a loss. He had always run his business without reference to anyone else, but after the expansion he now felt the lack of some sort of financial or business adviser who could help him with the overall financial view. He had called in Jim Dolan, his accountant, to have a look at everything and give him some advice. Honest Jim had taken him through the figures and pointed out the problems. 'Auto dealerships are a high cash turnover business, blah blah. There can seem to be loads of money sloshing around in the accounts, blah blah. But, but, the margins are slim. Last year you sold two hundred and fifty new cars and about half that number in second hand cars. The average price of the new cars was twenty-one K representing a turnover of five million, two hundred and fifty K. The average price of the second-hand cars was seven K. Representing a turnover of eight hundred and seventy-five K approximately. The second-hand turnover is somewhat set against the primary business turnover. These look like vast sums, but you've got to remember that the margin is small. Minuscule in some cases, where you give deals that are too advantageous to the customer. Salary costs are soaring. Repayments on the building development are pretty steep, and frankly a bit of a millstone round the business's neck. Maybe the repayments could be rescheduled to a slower timescale? That might return the company to profitability.' Honest Jim's voice droned away in Charlie's ear, an internal and infernal loop of fiscal rectitude. 'The separate accounts for Charles O'Brien Repairs are fine. That remains profitable, marginally, but solidly profitable nonetheless. But the building repayments have all been yoked to the main business, so that's a little unrealistic. And what's this figure?'

Charlie held up the printout and examined the figure up close, in the forlorn hope that it might diminish if closely scrutinized, or preferably disappear altogether.

'That's a mortgage payment on Ashleigh Court.'

'And why is it coming out of this account? Shouldn't it be coming out of your personal account?'

'Yes, it normally does, but I didn't draw any salary that month. I thought I could manage, but when the time came, I needed to do that.'

'Tut tut tut,' said Jim. 'This is all a bit of a mess. The revenue commissioners go stark raving mad if they see any financial jiggery-pokery like this in the books, and they go through everything with a fine comb, looking for nits. And what's that cheque?'

'That's the clinic payment for Alison's hospital stay.'

'Charlie, Charlie. This won't do at all. Burying a personal mortgage repayment is one thing, but a cheque clearly marked Taney Maternity Clinic is never going to pass an audit.'

Jim's bottom-line advice was for Charlie to go to the bank and ask for a rescheduling of the loan repayments, a general slowdown, and that could give him a chance to trade out of hot water. Jim was essentially optimistic about his prospects. He felt that

Charlie had a viable business. Very strong customer loyalty. Valuable premises in the perfect location. 'Go for it,' he urged.

Charlie was now trying to get his head round the figures in order to make the call to the bank manager. There was a new bank manager in his branch, Stuart Sharpe. The old guy, Alan Cox, had retired, and Charlie had no particular liking for the replacement. He and Alan had had a good rapport. Alan had nursed him and his business along. Been very supportive. He had that old-world banker way about him. A gent. Loved to get into a bit of a chat. Horses were his thing. Liked a bit of a flutter. Charlie now saw him often out walking the seafront with his dog, retired and cheerful-looking, scrutinizing the racing results in the evening paper.

The new guy was all business. No small talk out of him. Never even bothered with the pretence of asking you how you were. Charlie had taken an instant dislike to him. And that didn't make the phone call any easier. He was afraid to draw Sharpe on him. Feared inviting too much attention. He fingered the business card. Stuart Sharpe, Bank Manager. He would have to make that call. He had no choice. It started to rain. Heavily. You could hear the rain loudly on the roof, which was made of corrugated iron. And it suddenly made the building feel insubstantial. Tinny.

Just as he'd steeled himself, and reached out his hand to pick up the receiver, the phone rang. Sondra's voice. 'Your sister to see you.'

Unusual. He couldn't think when Mary had ever come down to the showroom. She'd been there at the champagne reception to open the new building. That was the last time. He opened his office door and went out onto the crow's nest. Mary, accompanied by young Mark, made her way up the stairs. He watched their progress. Mary in her loose purple dress and flat hippie sandals, her dark hair plaited down her back. He was glad to see her. He was always glad to see her. There was something so reassuringly moral about Mary. It was comforting to meet such moral surety, and know that it existed in the world. Mark, now six years old, trotted after his mother and thought he was in heaven. All these gorgeous cars!

'It's amazing. I tried to rear them without gender bias, but Mark loves cars and Linda is inseparable from her dolls.'

'I loved cars when I was his age. All I ever wanted to do was play in or around cars.'

'And look at you now,' smiled Mary. 'Still playing with cars.'

'Wow,' said Mark. 'Are all these cars yours, Uncle Charlie?'

'Yes,' said Charlie. 'I own a hundred cars. Do you want to go down to the basement to look at the rest of them?'

'Wow, yes.'

Mark was amazed that his mother hadn't brought him to this paradise before now. Charlie was glad to put away his figures. Mark went to the stairs to go down.

'No, no, this way.'

Charlie led Mary and Mark to the rear of his office, where there was a discreetly placed elevator.

'This is my escape hatch. I can avoid somebody on the shop floor if I want to by taking the elevator to the basement and leaving by the basement ramp.'

The three of them stood in the little lift.

'Beam us down, Scottie,' said Charlie, pressing the button.

'When I was about your age, Mark, Santa Claus brought me a garage. It was my first premises. It had a little wind-up lift to transport cars from the first floor to the third. This lift is based on it.'

'Wow. When you were my age, you started your first garage.'

The basement was dark and gloomy, but Mark was thrilled by it. Lines and lines of cars. All shiny and ready for sale. Some so new they didn't have number plates. There was a fleet of BMWs he'd imported for an information technology company which was stalling on the purchase. Emerald Blue Technologies. Fred Roper was the MD. They were lined up against the far wall, pristine and new and accusatory. He hoped against hope that the deal would go through. It would make a big difference to him right now. He needed some luck. He willed Fred Roper to call him and put the deal back on track. Fred was a bit of a wideboy. Thought big. Was all talk about expansion and vision. He had seemed solid enough, but now Charlie suspected he was a fantasist. And there was a lemon-coloured VW Beetle which had been ordered for a lady who had lost her job as a production manager at a mobile phone factory. It sat there now, unsold, frivolous and mocking in the

153

shadows by the ramp. It looked like a hat you'd wear to a spring wedding. A rare taste, that lemon colour. Bitter. He mustered a smile for his nephew.

'Would you like to sit in one?'

'That one,' said Mark. 'The blue one. You must be the richest man in the world to have so many cars.'

Charlie got the key and let the young fella sit in. He happily turned on all the lights and beeped the horn.

'What brings you down to visit me?' he asked Mary.

'I just wanted to see you. There's something I want to give you. I hadn't realized what a thrill the visit would be for Mark, though.' Mary smiled at her young son's delight.

They went back up to the shop-floor level, and the din of the rain on the roof was loud again. Sondra had some chocolate cars in her desk and Mark happily tucked into one.

'We bribe our customers' children with chocolate VW Beetles.'

A glass case contained a display of BMW merchandising. A T-shirt and golf hat with the BMW logo, and a couple of miniature cars. Mark's eyes strayed to them. Charlie got out a merchandising packet from Sondra's desk and put the T-shirt and cap on the child. The T-shirt was too big, but it added to the cute effect. There was a silver BMW 3-series coupé parked in the middle of the front window which Mark was eyeing enviously. Charlie was way ahead of him.

'When you've finished your chocolate, you can hop in.'

Mark guzzled down the chocolate car. Charlie opened the coupé and let the child in. Mark happily sat behind the wheel, thrilled with himself. Charlie turned on the turntable under the car, which started to rotate slowly, the movement barely perceptible. Mark shrieked with glee. 'From the house of BMW, a lusty son is born,' said Charlie in a mid-Atlantic accent. Mary laughed.

'Now if anyone comes in, Mark, you're to sell them that car. It's called a BMW 3-series coupé. And it goes very fast. And they have to have lots of money to buy it.' He smiled at Mary. 'We could make a salesman out of him.'

Mary followed Charlie back up to the office. She took a faded leather pouch from her handbag.

'Charlie, you know the way I've always been unhappy that I got

154

the house and you got nothing. Well, I wondered, maybe, would Alison like these?'

Mary spilled the contents of the bag onto his desk. It was some old jewellery. A brooch he remembered his mother wearing. A ring. A string of pearls. Diamond earrings. All tarnished with age.

'I think that they might be valuable, but in any case, if they were cleaned up, they'd be nice to wear for Alison. She likes that kind of thing.'

It just looked like a pile of junk to Charlie. But he'd happily take the stuff. Ali might well like it. She always wore jewellery. And he knew it would make Mary happy.

A noise. Charlie could hear a drip-like noise.

'Can you hear that?'

'What?'

'A drip.'

'No.'

'There.'

They both strained to listen past the rain thudding on the roof.

'Oh yes. I heard that.'

'Sssh. There again.'

Charlie's attention fell on a pool of water on the floor in the corner. He looked down at the pool and then up at the roof. A series of water drops clung to the ceiling of the office, until one of them became too heavy and fell to the ground. Mary stared at the pool. Charlie came and stood over it. A damn drip. The ship was getting leaky. Mary got a basin from the sink in the corner and placed it underneath and it started to fill.

'This building isn't a year old. It shouldn't be springing leaks,' said Charlie, very down-hearted. It was a bad omen, this leak. Just as he was trying to get the courage up to make that appointment with the bank manager, he didn't need this. The builder had been a bit shifty. Charlie had to chase him for lots of finishes, and the snag list was endless. The builder had only just finished rectifying the snag list a month ago and got his final payment. Damn. Damn. The architecture was getting sinister.

He picked up the phone and barked at Sondra. 'We've got a goddamn leak up here. Will you get that cowboy of a builder down here as soon as you can?'

Mary looked around at the palace that Charlie had built. It was really quite something, this monument to ambition and hubris, yet it was so far removed from her own value system. She looked at Charlie, his face now a little strained. Was it making him happy? All this money achievement. She knew it was essential to him, but right now he looked tense.

'You look a bit off form, Charlie. Everything OK?'

Charlie turned to her and smiled.

'Sure, sis. Everything in the garden is rosy.'

'How's the little man?'

Charlie smiled.

'He's the king of hearts.'

Charlie put the little faded leather bag on the table.

'These are for you, sweetheart.'

Alison immediately recognized the bag. She opened it and its contents spilled on the table.

'Where did you get it?'

'Mary gave it to me. She's always felt guilty that she got the house and I didn't. I keep telling her it doesn't matter a rattling damn to me, but you know what she's like. Everything has to be right and proper. She has a horror of injustice. So she was mad for giving me these bits and bobs. They're just a few old trinkets belonging to my mother. She wanted you to have them.'

Alison lined up the items on the table.

'They're not just a few old trinkets. These are fairly valuable.'

'Would you like them?' asked Charlie.

'Sure, but are you certain Mary realizes how valuable they are? I mean, it's probably not sensible of her to give them away.'

Alison slipped the diamond and sapphire ring on her middle finger. 'I couldn't say how much this is worth, I'd have to get it valued, but it's good stuff.'

'She just appeared in the office with it. I didn't argue. She seemed very sure. It'll make her happy if you take them.'

Alison shrugged. It was better than having them tucked away at the back of a drawer. Sparklers should be given an opportunity to sparkle. She made Charlie a cup of tea and he sat down at the table, fingering the jewellery.

'I remember this,' said Charlie, picking up an emerald and diamond brooch. 'My mother used to wear it to Mass. She'd close the top button of her blouse, pin this on there, at the throat, then off to Mass.'

'It's beautiful. I'm delighted to have the stuff. It's thoughtful of Mary.'

Alison was still reeling with the shock of having returned to work after her slightly extended maternity leave. First of all there was the wholly unexpected wrench she felt every morning, leaving little Michael at the nursery. Then there was the sense of being a different person, in the same clothes and sitting at the same desk, but a different person underneath. She felt uncomfortable in her suit. Despite all her dieting and tummy exercises, her favourite suit was tight at her waist. She refused point blank to buy a bigger size, and resolved to slim back into her size twelve clothes. Size fourteen would be the end.

'I've just got to slim down, Charlie. I've got this great big bulge that flops over my waistband. And my breasts are starting to sag. I'm beginning to look like my own granny.'

Charlie looked over at Alison. He shook his head. All he saw was perfection.

'Now that I'm back at work, I feel I'm getting visually inadequate. Advertising is all about image. It's important that I look right. I've told you about the cute young one called Sam who's been taken on. I'm showing her the ropes. Yes, I was overrun, and there's work for two people, but it's making me insecure.'

'That's all in your head. You'd been saying for ages that you needed an assistant.'

'That's just it. Sam isn't my assistant. She's been given separate jobs. She's junior to me, sure, but not my assistant.'

Alison had come into the office on her first day back to find Sam sitting at her desk, in Alison's custom-made candy-striped chair. Sam had cheerily vacated the spot when Alison stood over her with a 'Sorry, weren't expecting you till Monday!' but it had been an omen. Maternity leave creates a vacuum. And matter rushes to fill it. Sam was perky. A mop of curly brown hair and a bare midriff. Twenty-five or so. Full of go.

Alison arrived in at nine o'clock every morning, and Sam would be on a coffee break, always giving the air of having been in since seven thirty. When Alison left at quarter to five to get Michael from the nursery, Sam was stuck in to some work and looked like she'd be there for the night. Very cosy-looking. Alison's immediate boss, Jeremy, was leaning over her, dangling his tie onto her sketchbook. Jeremy used to trail his tie across her work. She remembered the intimacy of it. The smell of his aftershave and shower gel. And she was a little jealous. Unreasonable, she knew, but jealous nonetheless. She had liked the way they were so dependent on her in the office. The way they treated her more as a partner than an employee. And she felt that now they treated her differently. A touch of the cold shoulder. They no longer asked her to do unreasonable things, like stay on late and drop things across the city. It was just as well, because she had to pick up Michael and couldn't have agreed, but she missed the sense of everybody being under obligation to her because she worked so hard and loyally for them. It was contradictory, she knew, but it still made her feel unhappy and uncertain. They were no longer grateful to her. It was as though having a baby was an act of unfaithfulness. As though she had been committed to the office and now she was having an affair with her baby. And was being punished. Not in any obvious way. Not in any legally actionable way. But nonetheless. And the flab she felt around her midriff seemed to encapsulate all the insecurity.

'Appearance is important in my job,' she said.

'Yes.'

'I'm not going to pretend that I've been promoted according to a scale other than fuckability. Sure, I'm good at my job, but that's only half the story.'

'What do you mean?'

'The top brass in the company like to be seen with fuckable women.'

'You mean they fancy the female employees? Want to sleep with them?'

'No, no. These guys are very happily married. They like to be seen doing lunch with fuckable women. They don't want to have sex with you. They want other people to imagine they are having sex with you. It's like a modern version of a harem. These business brass surround themselves with beautiful girls because they like to imagine that other people are imagining that they are having sex with them. It's vanity.'

'It's all imaginary. Imaginary sex,' said Charlie, trying to understand what she was saying.

'Except the raise. That wasn't imaginary. That was ten K.'

Charlie was a bit bewildered. He was sure Alison was underestimating people.

'Sondra is very nice-looking,' said Alison. 'But I'm sure you hired her for her book-keeping skills.'

I wish, thought Charlie. Guilty as charged. Sondra had been somewhat hired for her looks, but he was in the glamour end of the car market. And he needed a good-looking bird out front. Also she was hired for her class. Sondra made rich people feel good when she brought them a coffee, because she was one of them. She didn't bring the coffee with the style of a waitress, she brought it with the style of a lady of the manor making you more comfortable. It was a question of presentation. Teams of designers were hired to get the cars looking right. They had to be sold right.

'Don't worry, Ali. It's strange to be back at work. Of course you'll feel weird. Mary says it takes her a year to feel normal after having a baby.'

'Let's go and look at Michael.'

They went into the dining room and peered into the pram. Michael slept, his fists still curled up to his chin, like a boxer.

'He looks like he's spoiling for a fight.'

He was getting bigger. Had lost that new-born look and filled out the pram. He could barely fit in it now.

The intercom rang.

'That'll be dinner.' It was Friday night and dinner had been ordered. Alison never cooked on a Friday night. Charlie never cooked at all.

Charlie went to the front door and received the bags. Indian takeaway. He brought them into the kitchen and reached in for a poppadum. Alison set the table in the sun room. She was starving now and wanting food. She'd skipped lunch, as a dieting measure, and hunger gnawed at her insides. She poured some wine, and immediately started to feel light-headed. Charlie took off his jacket and hung it on the back of a chair. He too sipped his wine. She distributed the curry dishes onto plates and put the packaging out of sight.

'I hate looking at the cartons while I'm eating. It puts me off.'

As she ate, Alison fingered the jewellery. It was kind of Mary to give it to her. She always felt uncomfortable with her sister-in-law. Felt a glow of mild dislike from her. She felt judged. Mary seemed to judge her and find her wanting. There was a hard, unforgiving streak in her.

'I wonder, does Mary like me?' asked Alison.

'What makes you wonder that?'

'Well, I don't know. Just a feeling I get.'

'She's never said, Alison. I'm sure she does like you. You wouldn't have much in common, though. I like Brendan well enough, but I don't have a lot to say to him. I don't get excited about seedlings. And when he sees a motor car he just shudders about the ozone layer. So, you know, we ain't ever going to be best mates.'

'I saw this stuff up in Mary's house one time. I did say it was valuable, but I wasn't dropping hints that I wanted them. I thought Susan or Linda might like them.'

Alison picked up the powder compact and turned it over to show Charlie the hallmark.

'This is 24-carat gold. And there's a lot of gold in it.'

Charlie took the compact and opened it and some pink dust scattered out. Ancient pink cosmetic dust. It was like a little puffy ghost of his mother. He snapped it shut and turned it over.

'There's a hinge at the back.' His mechanic's eye spotted the anomaly in the metal design.

Sure enough, tucked into the rear of the main front hinge was a little ornamental one that Alison hadn't noticed. Charlie slid his fingernail into the seam and opened a rear compartment. He gave a little shriek and dropped the compact. Alison snatched it up. Inside the rear compartment was a photograph of Charlie's father. He was the spit of him. A handsome man in a pilot's uniform, standing in front of the nose of a plane. The uniform looked civilian rather than military. His eyes were crinkled against the light in exactly the same manner as Charlie's eyes crinkled.

'Your father,' said Alison, staring at the picture.

'I thought my mother got rid of all the photographs. Because they upset Mary too much. She used to go hysterical. I've never seen a picture of him. And Ma died so young. She left a lot of loose ends.'

I've found him, thought Alison. I knew I'd find him. Once I started to stir things up, I knew he'd rise to the surface.

Alison woke from sleep to hear a funny rasping sound. She flopped her arm out and checked the bed beside her. It was empty. Just the smell of Charlie and the creases made by him in the sheet. She had fallen into a deep sleep after lovemaking. She always dropped off immediately after sex. She was like the type of man her friends complained of. She turned on her bedside light. Four a.m. Where could Charlie be? Watching TV? Gone for a run?

She got out of bed, pulled on a light dressing gown and went into the baby's room across the hall. Little Michael slept soundly in his cot. She padded along the hall and down the stairs. The rasping sound got louder. There was a light in the kitchen. She went in. He wasn't there, but she could smell cigarette smoke. Unusual. He almost never smoked at home now. She followed the trail of the smoke smell out to the sun room. Charlie was standing on the table in his pyjama bottoms, with a saw in his hand. He was sawing at the crossbeam, which, to Alison's eye, was holding up the sun-room roof. He was intent on his task and didn't see her. The muscles in his right arm were tense and alert, and the saw made a rasping sound as bits of sawdust fell down across Charlie's jacket which was still on the back of the chair. Alison stared in wonder at him. What was he doing? Was he sleep-walking?

He stopped sawing for a moment and surveyed his progress. He had cut right through the right-hand side and the portion he was working on, the left, was about three-quarters done, and beginning to crack with the strain. He was just about to start up again when . . .

'Darling, what are you doing?'

He spun around and saw her and was momentarily afraid. Like he had been caught doing something very bad. He put the saw down and got off the table.

'Charlie, are you OK?'

Charlie shook his head. He wanted to tell her what he was doing, but he was afraid she'd think he was crazy.

'Charlie, why are you sawing through the crossbeam? I think that holds the roof up.'

Charlie went into the kitchen and made some tea. He carefully poured two steaming mugs.

'Charlie, what's going on?' she asked, a note of panic in her voice.

He sighed. 'I couldn't sleep. I needed to do something vigorous to keep myself feeling OK.'

'So you decided to chop down the roof?'

He lit another cigarette.

'I hate that crossbeam, Alison. It spooks me. I keep seeing myself hanging from it. I have to get rid of it.'

'Jesus, Charlie. That's bad.'

'Don't worry, Ali. I'm not suicidal or anything.'

'You get flashes of yourself hanging from the roof, but you're not suicidal?' Panic rose in Alison.

'It's hard to explain. It's like pressure building up. I feel tense inside, and then this flash comes of me dangling from the crossbeam, and I feel OK again. But now I'm getting spooked by it. The flash doesn't relieve me so much.'

Alison tried to follow what he was saying. She didn't like the sound of it one bit. He pushed the tea over to her and urged her to drink.

'When I was a teenager, about seventeen or eighteen, me and Declan used to go to Mondello Park every weekend to do stock-car racing. Basically, racing scrap cars which are made up of bits and pieces of wreckage. It's a great sport. Very popular. We were the only people from our area that used to go. You reinforce the cabin of the car with scaffolding, add extra reinforced seat belts and wear a helmet, but it's not that safe. You can do a lot to protect yourself, but there was always a risk. I used to feel the tension building in me all week, and then at the weekend we'd go racing. I'd always do up the cars, but Declan would help with the non-mechanical bits. He was the better driver. Very sharp manoeuvres. We were famous out there, the two of us. The Ballybrack Boys. When Declan got Shelley knocked up, she stopped him coming. And I started the repair business, so my energy got sucked in there. Do you see what I'm talking about?'

Alison was utterly bewildered. She'd heard before about the Mondello glory days, a welter of dust and broken wrists. She'd always thought it a bit eccentric. She shook her head.

'It's like every week we went out there and we faced up to death. And now that happens with the flashes, but they're beginning to spook me. In a bad way. So I wanted to get rid of the beam of wood, because I can't have flashes of myself hanging from it if it isn't there. Look, I'd better finish it now. It's half done and it's dangerous.'

'But won't the roof fall down?'

'No. The crossbeam is ornamental, not structural. The walls are holding up the sun-room roof, not this silly beam.'

Charlie went back out to the sun room, got up on the table again and resumed sawing. Alison looked on in bewilderment. Was he crazy?

'I'm sorry, Ali. I just hate this crossbeam. I don't like this house. I think the architecture is sinister.'

'I'd ordered an indoor vine from the Plant Store to grow up along the pillar and across the crossbeam. It's due to be delivered next week. I'll have to cancel that,' she said futilely.

Charlie was almost through cutting the beam and, with an almighty crack, it came away. He caught it and lowered it gently onto the table. It lay there, like a severed limb. Alison stared at it. She stared at the ceiling, half expecting the roof to fall in. Half expecting the sky to fall on her head.

'Honestly, it's not structural,' said Charlie. 'It was just put there for effect.'

Alison got a cold clammy feeling. Panic was growing inside her. Charlie was off the script here. He was displaying symptoms of utter dysfunction. Much worse than she had suspected before. The photo of his dad must have upset him, she thought, though he doesn't realize it. It has caught him on the hop and un-balanced him.

'Come back to bed,' she said, stretching out her hand and drawing him back to her. 'It's chilly here.'

10

Cormac stood on a bank overlooking the village, his binoculars in hand. The village was alive. Dev's visit had provoked a new civil war over where he was to stop for tea. Who would have the pleasure of brewing the presidential cup? Father O'Keefe was claiming the honour, on behalf of the people and God. A man named Daly who emerged from a hovel claimed to have hidden Dev for three nights during the civil war before Dev went out to the islands as a much welcomed fugitive. 'Me cuppa tea was good enough for him then, it's good enough for him now.' The two publicans insisted that hospitality was their professional business and amateurs should butt out. It looked like everybody in the village was a Dev supporter. And those who weren't kept quiet about it. Keeping your head down was often the wisest move, if your own flag didn't flutter to the prevailing winds. Cormac sighed. He wasn't surprised by the attitudes of the villagers, but it was annoying to have it flaunted.

The general election a few years back had given Dev and Fianna Fáil their overall majority and this was a much postponed victory lap. And despite all of Cormac's good intentions, it irked him. An elected statesman now, installed in power by the very institutions that he violently resisted. Everybody knew he wasn't directly behind the assassination of Michael Collins, but everybody knew he had fanned those particular flames. Thrown petrol on them. In Cormac's eyes he was more guilty than whatever young scut had pulled the trigger. These big men who led the gullible astray. People need leadership. Little people need leadership. And the Irish were good to follow a leader, given half a chance. Dev had opposed the treaty because Michael Collins had negotiated it. And now he reaped the rewards of a civil society and free and democratic elections that Michael Collins had died for. He enjoyed the protection of the *Garda Síochána*, many of whom were slaughtered in the early days by his very supporters. Dev was now doing his victory parade on Michael Collins's grave, and despite all his efforts to cool himself down, it made Cormac's blood boil. In theory it hadn't bothered him. If you'd asked him a few months ago would a Dev victory lap bother him, he would've said no. He'd take it in his stride. But now that it was upon him, he found it hard to swallow.

The village was gay with bunting. People had hung out flags and streamers and a big banner was made from flour sacks. The children were all dressed in their Sunday best. Cormac put the binoculars to his eyes and looked closely at the crowd. Women were smiling and waving as Dev did an impromptu walkabout. He spoke in his schooled Irish and the people were thrilled. He was wearing a cream-coloured *báinín* sweater fashioned and knitted in the local style. Almost a figure in a fantasy. As though he had imagined himself into being. Like he believed he had imagined Ireland into being. To Cormac he looked a fool in his *báinín* jumper and his green socks.

Young girls were flirting with him. Old women kissed his hands as though he was the Pope. Grisly old veterans shook his hand and muttered, 'Up the Republic.' The entourage consisted of Dev's secretary, the local Fianna Fáil leader, a couple of officially invited press people. A few tame journalists with their teeth pulled, thought Cormac. Dev was always good at the public relations. They knew the value of the press, the Fianna Fáilers, and no mistake. Dev had his two personal bodyguards. Cormac stationed two of his own men to be beside him, guarding him at all times. O'Donnell and young Slattery. It would have been more normal procedure for the sergeant to have kept that honour for himself, but Cormac felt he could forgo it. He spat in the grass. The whole caper left him with a bad taste in his mouth.

He looked through his binoculars again. There he spotted the distinctive figure of Marie Rose in the crowd. She too was waving at Dev. He stopped and greeted her. And she held up young Michael's hand to be shaken. Michael was tall for his seven years and mature-looking. Dev leaned down and straightened the boy's cap. Damn it. Cormac was very irritated by this. He hadn't expressly forbidden Marie Rose to attend the celebrations, but he thought she'd have the wit to stay away, or at least hang back if she wanted to be there. She knew how he felt about it. And as for presenting Michael to him, this particularly annoyed Cormac. He continued to look through the binoculars. She was chatting away to him. Probably introducing herself as the sergeant's wife. Liked to indicate that for a bit of status. Cormac was very annoyed. He started to get into a boil. He was going to have words with her later. Marie Rose had this weakness. She always liked to be in the thick of things. Socially, she had no independence. Not any more. Not since she'd married. One of the things he'd been attracted to that first day was her aloofness. He softened a little. Marie Rose just wasn't political. Never was and never would be. She judged people according to a scale of pleasantness. If someone was pleasant, she would like them and deal with them. If they weren't she'd avoid them. It was as simple as that. He felt a hand on his shoulder. It was Froggy Duignan.

'Give us a smoke there, Sergeant.'

Cormac took out two cigarettes and lit them carefully in the breeze.

'A fine showing,' said Froggy. 'This village is Fianna Fáil to the bone and no mistake.'

'Sure is.'

'Old beaky is having the time of his life down there. The women are crawling all over him. You'd swear he was Rudolph Valentino.'

'He sure is.'

'O'Brien, I want to play a trick on him. Would you let me? I've just got to get close to him. I have this bunch of flowers which squirts water. I'd just love to give him a squirt with it. Wipe a bit of the smugness off his face.'

Froggy produced the bunch of flowers from under his coat. He held them under Cormac's nose. Cormac sniffed and Froggy squirted. He got a blast of water in the face. Cormac laughed.

'I bought this in a joke shop in Paris.'

'It'd be a good one all right. But it's more than my job's worth. People like you and I, Froggy, we just have to swallow this. Like they swallowed us. Though it sticks in my throat. Like the oath stuck in theirs.'

'Jaysus, O'Brien. He should just know that though everybody is smiling at him there's a few of us out here on the edge of the Dingle peninsula that don't think he's God almighty. He'll go away from here in a fit of messianic megalomania if we don't manage to puncture him some little bit. Sure, even your missus has been in a cuddle with him.'

'I know, Froggy. But we just have to swallow it. Offer it up.'

Froggy had a good few whiskies on. He had become more and more of a drunk over the years, and when Gearóidín de Paor abandoned him and went to live in America, he took it very hard and seemed to hit the bottle earlier and earlier in the day. Cormac never knew how seriously to take this broken heart. Gearóidín and Froggy couldn't realistically have set up house together, though she had come down and stayed in the hotel for a month. They had been toying with each other. Gearóidín had become slowly colder as the month wore on and the weather turned on one of its finer displays of wretchedness. She realized just how dull it was in the countryside. Marie Rose had turned against her, as she found her far too flirtatious. She wasn't judgemental about this, just thought it silly. Flirting with Sean the landlord? She must be out of her mind. Gearóidín claimed to like the south-west of Ireland, but it was a fairy-tale version she had in her head that she liked. She had gone back to Dublin, and a few weeks later Froggy got a letter saying she was off to New York. He had shown it, crestfallen, to Cormac in the pub. Froggy seemed to take it well initially, but as time went by it emerged she had left a legacy of recklessness that surfaced occasionally in him. The drink, always on his tail, was catching up with him.

A band had been rustled up from somewhere and their quasi-military tunes lifted the atmosphere to a slightly more strident pitch. The presence of Dev had rewoken some of the old passions and a bunch of drink-fuelled old men were already plotting to march on the ports, to take them back from the English. A lot of the men had had a few drinks by now and things were getting a bit rowdy. Drunken revolutionaries. The same old tomfoolery. It was all so tiresome. A few pints of porter and people loved shaking out the old battles for a re-run. Move on, thought

Cormac. Move on. He said it as much to himself as to anyone else. He made his way down to the village.

Marie Rose and Michael appeared at his side.

'Daddy, Daddy, I'm after shaking his hand.'

'I know, son. I saw you.'

'Mammy said I wasn't to tell you.'

Marie Rose looked a bit guilty. She knew Cormac wouldn't be too pleased with her.

'Sorry. It's just we were in the thick of the crowd, and I turned round and he was just there, so I thought it would be rude not to say hello.'

'That's all right.'

'And I know you're set against him, but he is popular locally. Michael wants to be able to boast to the other boys in school that he shook Dev's hand.'

Cormac nodded in resignation.

'I've a chicken ready. I'm going to go above and put it in the oven. We'll have a fine fancy tea tonight.'

Marie Rose loved festivities. They lifted her spirits. She made her way up the barracks drive, the boy skipping at her side. Cormac watched them go. At least they had enjoyed it. That was something. It was approaching four o'clock, the time that the motor cars were scheduled to depart. Cormac joined O'Donnell, who was guarding the cars which had just been driven into position in front of the church.

'Sergeant, could I be excused please?'

Cormac stared at him.

'I need to go to the bathroom, sir.'

'You can go for the day, O'Donnell,' said Cormac. 'I'll see him off.'

O'Donnell was very glad to be replaced. He'd been dying for a pee for the last hour and was only barely holding it in. He hobbled off. Dev made his way to the rear car, a crowd moving with him like a huge, many-legged animal of which he was the nucleus. He smiled and continued to shake hands and pat children's heads. He began to get Cormac's goat again, and Cormac had to swallow hard. Froggy appeared in the line for hand-shaking and Cormac for a moment wondered about the trick bunch of flowers. But Froggy displayed his hands to Cormac, showing them innocent and empty. Cormac for a moment regretted this. It would have been nice to wipe the smile off Dev's face.

The cars were both open-topped and Dev, rather than have the door opened, stood on the running board to hop over the side. He perched there for a moment and waved at the people, smiling all the while. Cormac smiled stiffly at him. Dev turned to climb over the door into the back seat. He hesitated one more moment to wave at the people clamouring opposite. Then Froggy rushed forward. Cormac, a little bit dazed, momentarily considered stopping him, but in the moment of consideration the opportunity was lost.

Froggy kicked Dev right square in the rear and Dev went flying, head first, into the back of the open-topped car. His rear end hovered in the air for a moment and then his long legs dangled in the air, kicking and dancing, displaying pale green socks to the world. Then he landed square on the back seat. There was pandemonium. Dev's two bodyguards jumped on top of him to protect him from further assault, thereby squashing the breath out of him. He was awkwardly trapped beneath one of them, and his legs continued to kick in the air. Garda Slattery jumped on the man standing beside Froggy in an identical cap, thinking him the culprit. Panic infected the crowd. 'What's happened? What's happened?' Dev pulled himself up and sat again in the back seat of the motor car. Composed once again, he turned to the crowd and smiled and waved. Reassured, the crowd responded with a huge cheer. Dev turned and smiled and waved at the crowd in Cormac's direction. Cormac couldn't help it, but a smile was twitching at the corners of his mouth and a huge laugh was trying to escape from his belly. His whole frame shook. Dev looked directly at Cormac, and fleetingly the politician's smile disappeared and a cold accusatory stare replaced it. Then his eye moved on to the rest of the crowd and the smile and wave returned. The cars started up and in a cloud of dust they were gone. The scuffle at the end was so minuscule and so rapidly covered over, most people never knew it happened.

Cormac went over to Slattery and pulled him off the innocent he was sitting on.

'Slattery, get up. It wasn't him. It was Frank Duignan.'

'Oh.' Slattery got off the man and helped him up. The man was dazed and didn't know what hit him. He wandered off to the pub.

'Will I arrest Duignan, sir?'

Cormac considered for a moment. Froggy was swaying over by a ditch and drinking from a hip flask. Out of his mind with drink.

'No,' said Cormac. 'I'll see what orders there are from Dingle. We know where he's to be found and we can always pick him up whenever we want.'

Cormac went up to the barracks, thinking happily of the roast chicken for his tea. His frame still shook with the unindulged laughter. He had enjoyed the spectacle so much. Enjoyed it as much as if he'd planted the boot himself. In that single swipe, Cormac felt he'd personally avenged Collins. Nothing could be done to bring him back, obviously, but to have for once wiped the smile off his arch enemy's face was a triumph and a joy. Collins was twice the man Dev was. When his country needed a gunman, he was that. When it needed a statesman, he was that. And when it needed a big enough man to compromise, he could do that. Had his patriotic duty required of him to be a cabbage, he would have endeavoured to become that too. Cormac chuckled. And to kick Dev in his vanity, that was the real joy of it. To give him that humiliating shove just at the moment of his greatest vanity.

Cormac let himself in the door of the married quarters and finally he allowed himself to laugh. Great bellyaches of mirth. He had to sit down.

'What is it?' asked Marie Rose.

'Oh, it was so funny,' said Cormac.

'What? What?'

The tears were flowing down Cormac's face now. And he was convulsed with laughter. He slid helplessly off the chair and onto the floor. Marie Rose stood looking at him, holding up a saucepan of onion gravy she was stirring.

'Dev fell head first into the car. It was the funniest thing I ever saw in my life.'

171

'What? How did it happen?' asked Marie Rose, joining in the laughter, which was infectious.

'Froggy gave him a boot in the arse.'

'Oh, God, Cormac, that's bad,' said Marie Rose, her face worried.

Cormac was lying on the floor now, rolling over and over, clutching his tummy. He laughed so much he got a stitch. Young Michael shrieked in glee at the mirth of his father.

That night in bed, Cormac couldn't sleep. He kept convulsing with helpless laughter. The boldness of Froggy. His quick move. And what presented most clearly to his mind's eye was the sight of the presidential arse in the air. And the pale green socks. And the chicken legs kicking and jerking. The ballerinas of imperial Russia couldn't have performed a dance more eloquent than this one moment of supreme and exquisite comedy.

The telegram lay on the table between them, untouchable and unlucky. Marie Rose was white. The telegram was from Superintendent Geraghty, informing Cormac that he was to be transferred to an as yet unspecified destination. They were to leave the barracks without delay and would be accommodated in the first instance in married quarters in the big barracks in Kildare. A replacement sergeant was arriving on the train the next day and would stay in Dingle for a few days but was expected to take up residency in the Ballyferriter barracks as soon as possible.

It didn't come completely out of the blue. Geraghty had warned him a few days earlier that this was in the offing, but he'd kept it from Marie Rose as long as he could.

After the incident, Cormac had expected that he'd get some instructions from Geraghty regarding how to proceed. On hearing nothing, a few days later he had gone over to Dingle, called at Geraghty's home and related the story. He asked whether or not Duignan should be arrested. For drunk and disorderly behaviour, or assault, or whatever. It was the first Geraghty had heard of the incident. The Dev party had hushed it up. Didn't want it generally known. The two journalists covering the tour had never mentioned it in their reports. All had gone glowingly well on the travels, according to the press. The plain people of Ireland were delighted to finally have their right and proper leader in his right and proper place, and de Valera was fêted wherever he went. Dev's people hushed it up because it showed him in an undignified light. And they didn't want to invite copycats. So there'd been no formal complaint.

'That's good,' said Cormac.

Geraghty, a wiser and more experienced owl, shook his head. 'No, that's bad. An official complaint is always above board. And easy to deal with at a certain level.'

'Oh,' said Cormac.

'You can defend yourself from an official complaint. I don't like the smell of this one bit, O'Brien.'

Superintendent Geraghty was annoyed with Cormac. The incident put the Ballyferriter barracks under suspicion, and in turn a bad light was cast on the Dingle office.

'Duignan is your friend, isn't he? What did he do such a stupid thing for?'

'Drunk, sir. The whole parish was rotten with drink.'

'It's a serious business, O'Brien. An assault on the president of the executive of the Irish Free State is a serious business, no matter what way you look at it. And they're very nervous up in Dublin. The new administration isn't sure they can depend on the *Garda Síochána* or the army. They've recruited all these half-trained Republicans to bulk out the loyalty factor. There's guards in Dublin working side by side with fellas they spent years arresting. An "incident" like this will make them very nervous. They're terrified of a *coup d'état*.'

'Are you serious?' This all sounded a bit far-fetched and hysterical to Cormac.

'They're jittery. The whole of Europe is jittery. There's talk of army takeovers everywhere. Between the Bolsheviks and the fascists, democratic governments are getting very nervous. Especially here, where there's so much blood on everyone's hands.'

Superintendent Geraghty took down the bottle of whiskey, and Cormac was glad of the old pattern of friendliness. He poured out two glasses.

'Should I arrest Froggy?' asked Cormac.

'Well, there's nothing to charge him with since there's been no complaint. I don't know what you should do. But I'd say your goose might well be cooked, my friend. And maybe mine as well. Cheers!'

Geraghty clinked Cormac's glass.

'How exactly did it happen?'

Cormac drained his glass and Geraghty refilled it.

'The visit had gone splendidly and Dev was just about to leave. Well, Duignan was in a line to shake his hand, and this happened without incident. And then Dev was up on the side of the car, about to hop over the door. The car was open-topped. He was like a fine Olympic athlete and Froggy . . .'

The laughter started up again in Cormac. The scene was so vivid in front of his eyes. The jaunty hop of Dev onto the running board of the car. The crowd so full of cheers and enthusiasm. The day was warm and bright and ideal for walkabouts. Birds sang in the trees.

'. . . and Froggy swung high with his leg and gave him . . .'

The laughter became uncontrollable. Tears came to Cormac's eyes. He saw Dev executing the nifty pirouette which positioned him to wave at the cheering crowd on the other side of the car.

'. . . and Froggy gave him . . .'

Geraghty refilled the whiskey glasses in a gesture of encouragement.

'. . . and Froggy, he gave him . . .'

Cormac tried to steady himself so he could speak. He coughed and straightened his face. He tapped his cheeks.

'Froggy gave him a boot in the arse and he went flying into the car and, to make matters worse, the two bodyguards he had, great hunks of fellas built like oak trees, they jumped in on top of him and flattened him.'

The laughter was infectious. Geraghty started to laugh as well.

'And his skinny legs, with the pale green patriotic socks, were kicking in the air.'

Superintendent Geraghty shook with laughter.

'Kicking like chickens' legs,' Cormac managed to say between guffaws. Then he straightened himself up and managed to proceed with his account. 'And Dev pulled himself together and waved, as though nothing had happened. Waved, like royalty, like the king of England.'

'Ah, Cormac, we'll pay for this.'

Cormac sipped his whiskey. He knew it was the last one he would have here, in the Geraghtys' parlour. Its heavy old furniture and cigarette-smoke-stained wallpaper. Its small heavily curtained window which admitted very little light. He knew that trouble loomed.

Marie Rose stood up, irate.

'But what about Michael's schooling? We'll have to take him out of school. They can't do that to us, Cormac. They can't just shove us around like that.'

'I'm afraid they can, Marie Rose.'

Marie Rose shook her head.

'A big man like Dev. He wouldn't be bothered being vindictive about a little man like you.' The merest hint of marital contempt in her voice.

'He doesn't have to be bothered. People do things on his behalf. He didn't hand down a big order parchment from Dublin. He hasn't said anything. All the Republicans that have crept in like termites, they'll do it on his behalf. Dev never leaves fingerprints. He doesn't give orders. People look into his heart and act accordingly.'

Waves of anger rose up in Marie Rose.

'Why? Cormac, why? Why couldn't you have apologized? Why couldn't you have locked Froggy up straight away and attempted to right the situation? Instead, you had your laugh. And your stupid pride.'

'Don't you get thick with me, Marie Rose.'

'You fool, Cormac. What about the child? You have no right to indulge yourself in your stupid jaded politics, because you have no right to ruin Michael's life. Forget about me. What about the child? Get over there to Dingle, right this minute, and get down on your knees and start apologizing.'

'I'm not going to apologize. I didn't do anything wrong.'

'Oh, I know it was Froggy, but you have to apologize.'

'I've nothing to apologize for. If I apologize, it looks like I did something wrong. Which I didn't.'

Marie Rose couldn't believe her ears.

'I didn't do anything wrong, except laugh in the privacy of my own home.'

'Cormac, Cormac, how can you be so stupid? I've never asked you for anything. All our married life I've given you your head and supported you. Eight years now. I've made the best out of everything. I've never asked you for a single thing. But I'm begging you now. They'll take away your sergeant stripes. They'll fire you. We'll be ruined. Arrest Froggy and apologize.'

'I can't arrest Froggy. No complaint has been made. I can't arrest Froggy for nothing. The incident didn't happen. Officially.'

11

'**M**aybe you'll think about it and get back to me in the next few days,' said Sharpe, as he picked up his folder, placed it under his arm, turned on his heel and left.

Charlie put his head in his hands. This was it. This was the end of the road. He watched Stuart Sharpe and his fat sidekick Cusack exit his premises like some gruesome and malign Laurel and Hardy. He couldn't bear Sharpe. His manner infuriated him. Once the business had started experiencing difficulties, Sharpe had developed this false intimacy which enraged Charlie. Sharpe touched Charlie on the shoulder. He spoke to him with an ex-aggerated sympathetic tone, stared in an overintimate fashion into his eyes. Cusack took his cue from his boss and indulged the same routine of mannerisms. A great big fat replica. They did this macabre dance. They finished each other's sentences, as they stuck to their duet of ruin.

Maybe it would have been hard to take it from anybody. Maybe even good old Alan Cox's form might have been challenged. Charlie was conscious of this and did his best to control his feelings towards the duo, who were now crossing his forecourt to Sharpe's car, a VW Golf GTi, which Charlie had sold him last year. For a tough price. His instincts had stopped him giving Sharpe a good deal, and he was glad of that now.

The bank had appointed an examining accountant to Charles O'Brien Motors. He had been on the premises for three days, a silent navy-suited man named Roger Cooke, who moved about like a dark cloud. Cooke had sat in Charlie's office and looked through everything. He had been cold and clinical to Charlie. Charlie didn't resent this. Cooke was only doing his job. Couldn't be getting matey with all the poor fools whose businesses were in trouble. Charlie had tried to get Cooke to tell him what he thought, but Cooke was tight-lipped. The only thing he did let slip, as he went out the door after thanking Charlie for his cooperation, was, 'It could go either way.'

Charlie had fussed over this scrap of information for the last two nights. At least he didn't say you were up shit creek, he thought. But 'It could go either way' was hardly comforting, was it? He hadn't slept a wink. Alison kept asking him if he was all right. He kept nodding and making an effort to be brighter.

He was supposed to go into the bank to see Sharpe that morning, but Sharpe cancelled. He was double-booked. Charlie was relieved. He couldn't face it. But he knew the encounter was just being put off and sat nervously waiting for the phone call which would resummon him. He was mildly surprised when he looked up and saw Sharpe's car pull up outside the front window. He briefly considered making a run for it via his elevator, but decided he'd better face the music. His mind was in a fog of confusion.

Sharpe came in with his false bonhomie.

'The investigating accountant has given me a mixed report,' he said. 'It looks like you could trade out of current difficulties, but you'd need a sizeable injection to meet current expenses. And I have to decide if it's wise to do that.'

Charlie nodded.

'It's not just my decision, you know. I have a responsibility to my shareholders. I can't refloat you without complete confidence that it'll work.'

Charlie nodded. Sharpe laid out some papers and sat down. Cusack remained standing and surveyed the vista.

'Nice view.'

'Cooke identified the fatal flaw in your operation. He criticized some of the accountancy practices and business procedures, but mainly the building and site are too big and the repayments too costly for this to ever be a profitable automobile showroom. He has suggested that you lease part of the building, say the top bit with the nautical theme, to a restaurant. Let's face it, the views are fantastic. You don't need all that grandiose space to sell cars. That was his suggestion. Or a fitness club. Something that would give you more revenue.'

Sharpe continued in the same vein. He resketched the business

178

and Charlie could see the sense in it. He had originally rented the ground under the showroom. His little repair business was in a garage next door, and when he'd started dealing in second-hand cars, he'd rented the yard space. It was a quarter of an acre. Then the owner put it on the market in two lots and he had to buy both, in order to remain adjacent to the repairs garage. He had perhaps been a little ambitious in his designs, got a bit carried away, but there were all sorts of pressures on him at the time. There was a danger that he might lose his distributorship of BMW if his showroom wasn't impressive enough. There was another guy snapping at his heels in this area, and in order to renew the distributorship he had to have a very competitive showroom. So he had built the Taj Mahal. It had gone along fine while they were super busy in the boom years, but now things had slowed a little, it was proving problematic.

'And what makes you decide you can advance the money to let me trade out?' asked Charlie.

Sharpe smiled.

'Well, you would have to employ the services of a business manager, somebody like Mr Cusack here, who would be on site looking out for the bank's interests and your interests, which would be one and the same really. Profitability.'

'And if I agreed to that?'

'Well, then, it's a matter of security. Security is the name of the game.'

'You have a fixed charge on the site and the building,' said Charlie, 'and a floating charge on everything else.'

'I notice we don't have a cross-charge on Charles O'Brien Repairs, building or business. I see in the file that documents were prepared by my predecessor, Mr Alan Cox, to include a cross-charge on Charles O'Brien Repairs, but they seem to have never been signed.'

Sharpe looked up at Charlie, mildly accusatory. He wafted the unsigned documents in the air.

Hmmn. Charlie couldn't remember this detail. He couldn't remember if he'd agreed to that or not. Cox had been very laid back. He just looked at his business plan, waxed lyrical at his architect's drawings and gave him a glass of sherry and a cheque.

'We would need that signed.'

Charlie thought about this.

'And we would need a personal guarantee from you for all outstanding bank debts, so that in the event of the business collapsing, you personally would be liable to us. In other words, a limit on your limited.'

Charlie's head started to spin.

'And that would include a charge on your home.'

'My home already has a mortgage.'

'Yes, but you have a substantial amount of equity in it, and we could arrange for a second charge to be put on it.'

Charlie began to feel there was no oxygen in his lungs.

'Alternatively, we will have to appoint a receiver, probably as early as next week. As soon as the legal structures can be put in place. We'll change the locks, wind down the company and satisfy the creditors.'

Sharpe got up. Cusack turned away from the window.

'Fabulous, fabulous view.'

'I'm sorry, Charlie. This is not a pleasant task and I don't do it lightly.'

Sharpe and Cusack left. Charlie put his head in his hands. Going into receivership. Everything he'd built up would be gone. His beautiful building, his client base. Even his name, Charles O'Brien Motors. They would take that. And he'd have no salary. No income. No car. It'd be back to square one. Ashleigh Court would have to go. The mortgage couldn't be kept up. His thoughts went to Alison and despair set in. How would he break it to her? It was all right for him at a certain level, he was used to nothing. But it would come as a shock to her. She wouldn't be able for it at all. Alison wasn't meant for poverty. Every bone in her body required comfort and luxury.

He sensed a presence and looked up. Sondra stood there, with a coffee in her hand. She put it on his desk. He stared helplessly up at her.

'Charlie,' she said, 'I'm afraid this isn't the best time to tell you, but I'm giving in my notice. I've got another job.'

Charlie stared at Sondra. The sun was shining through the glass and glinting on her highlights. Her long, almost pretty face wore an expression of concern. He understood her position. She'd sniffed the way things were going and reckoned the future for Charles O'Brien Motors was lacking in that essential brightness. And she needed her job. Sondra had married some ne'er-do-well squandering husband when very young and before she had much sense. He'd run off, his pockets bulging with the contents of her bank account, leaving her as sole breadwinner with two children. Despite appearances, she didn't have the luxury of hanging round to play dominoes on the deck of sinking ships. Charlie nodded.

'I'm sorry,' she said with genuine regret.

Charlie knew that Sondra was one of the good people. He didn't mind her abdication at all.

'That's OK. I understand. Thanks for everything, Sondra.'

'I'll work out my notice, if you want.'

'Please do.'

'What did they say?' Sondra was breaking boundaries here. She wouldn't normally ask a question like that.

'I've messed up, Sondra. Big time. And things don't look good. I'm going to have to have a long hard think.'

Guys like me, he thought, shouldn't get ideas above our station. Guys like me should have stayed in our little garage fixing dead-beat cars for other dead-beat guys like me. Guys like me shouldn't think it is our right to do whatever we want in life, to build up glamorous businesses from scratch. Guys like me should know our place. His thoughts drifted to the lovely Alison, whom he pictured now as she had been last night, lounging on the sofa watching TV in a pure silk pyjama set, laughing at some American sitcom. He had aimed high with Alison. And she wouldn't be capable of understanding this development. She wouldn't be able to deal with his business collapsing. She shouldn't have to. For the first time in his life, Charlie felt a sting of inadequacy.

Alison arrived home with baby Michael, exhausted after the day. Michael was teething, and the nights were broken, and she was in the middle of a big project at work so it was all go in the office. How to make stamps sexy? This was the latest task she was working on. The postal service was reacting against the term 'snail mail'. Wanted to be rebranded. Everything wanted to be sexy nowadays. Nothing was content to be merely useful.

She let herself into the empty house and sat Michael in his high chair. She warmed a beaker of milk in the microwave, and gave it to him. She went round the house switching things on. Warming the place up. She picked up the post from the hallway floor. Loads of junk. A credit card bill. Her mobile phone bill. One letter addressed to her caught her eye because it had no identifying marks. She emptied a jar of babyfood into a bowl and put it in the microwave. Michael's tea. She'd get it into him before Charlie came home and then get on with preparing their food. Charlie usually came in around seven.

Michael was in great chirp. No hint of the wailing of last night, the cheeks no longer the fevered red of teething. It was great to see him back in form. He smiled and gurgled as she fed him and kept trying to snatch the spoon. Playing with Michael was a tonic, because it made her smile all the time. No matter how tired she was, he always made her cheerful. She spooned the food into his wide-open mouth. He was like a little bird, beak wide open eagerly awaiting worms from mama bird. We must be genetically programmed to enjoy getting food into babies, she thought. She left him chewing a biscuit in the high chair while she prepared their own food. Some lamb and onions fried in a pan, and a jar of goulash sauce she got in a smart deli near the office in Donny-brook. She put a pot of water on to boil for rice. It would be a fine Tuesday dinner. Quick but tasty. She opened the post.

The credit card bill was a narrative of profligacy. Clothes shop, hairdresser, baby shop, restaurant, beauty salon, clothes shop, restaurant, designer baby shop, gift shop and on and on. The itinerary of Alison's spending for the month. Pages of it. She was faintly amazed at the figure at the bottom. It didn't really matter, she and Charlie had loads of dough, but this month seemed particularly fantastic. Then the mobile phone bill. This too was very high. She scanned the calls. Long chatty calls to Donna or Cecilia at lunch time, which was a peak time. Alison had become much more careless about money since she'd married. When on her own, she managed perfectly well on her fairly hefty salary. No matter how much your income, you needed to make sure it wasn't dwarfed by your outgoings, and you had to keep an eye on things when you had tastes like Alison's. And she'd had a mortgage on her apartment and general bills and expenses to look after. But after moving in with Charlie, she'd sort of relinquished responsibility for her spending. He looked after the mortgage and paid the household bills, and she just forgot to bother about the matter. Her head had been astray after the baby anyway, and so tired, she didn't really have time to scrutinize bank statements. She just produced cards in retail outlets where necessary and ceased to worry about them. She never looked at the price of anything. If she liked it, she bought it.

Then she opened the unidentified letter. It was from Ray Cunningham, the private detective. It indicated that he'd located a man in a nursing home in London whom he believed to be Charlie's father. A Michael John O'Brien, born in Ballyferriter, County Kerry, in 1926. Alison couldn't believe it. She'd only engaged Cunningham a month previously and had heard nothing since. She was just getting round to thinking about sending him a perky e-mail to speed him up a bit. And here was a letter. Cunningham believed he'd found the right man, but hadn't spoken to him directly. He'd got his information from an Irish nun who worked in the nursing home. He hadn't expected to make such rapid progress and wanted instructions on how to proceed. 'The man is in poor health. Something wrong with him. My nun informant wasn't fully specific. Would I make an approach? Please advise.'

The letter also contained an invoice for a huge sum of money. Alison was amazed. All so fast. So easy to find. She'd thought that Cunningham would have to comb the whole of Britain and possibly further afield. And here he was. Found. She hadn't told Charlie what she was up to, just hadn't got round to it. Didn't want Charlie to get too worked up about it, especially if she didn't have any luck in finding the man. Alison was partly thrilled, but also wary. Charlie had been funny lately. He may not take the news well. No matter, it could proceed no further. If Charlie didn't want to go and see the old man, well, that was that. At least she'd tried. Her mind went back to the night she'd found Charlie sawing down the beam in the sun room. The butts of the beam stuck out from the slopes of the ceiling on each side, a constant reminder of its curious end. Part of Alison didn't want to put him under any more pressure, but part of her believed that if he could somehow make some connection with his father, it would help him generally to sort out the tensions in his life.

Where was he? It was late now. The timer sounded, and Alison drained the rice. Michael was yawning and beginning to whimper, tired little sounds, so Alison brought him upstairs and bathed him quickly before putting him down in his cot. He whimpered a little more, before tiredness won the battle with the life-force and gentle breathy snores emanated from the nursery. Alison smiled and went back downstairs. She divided the rice and goulash onto two plates and started to eat her own. Charlie's could be reheated in the microwave when he got in. It wasn't like him to be this late without letting her know. She phoned the showroom. Just the answering machine. She phoned his mobile. Switched off. She ate her meal.

It was sort of glutinous. Sticky. Almost marmalady in taste. Not great, but she was hungry and it did the job. Her mind went to wondering how best to break the news about Charlie's father to him. She took out the powder compact belonging to Charlie's mother which she had stashed in a drawer and opened the rear photograph compartment, hoping to get some inspiration. There he was, sort of frozen in time. A fine-looking man. Fairly dishy in his uniform. Charlie's mother must have thought she'd landed a catch. Alison wondered how it had gone wrong. Then she shrugged. Things often went wrong. Marriage was a tricky business. And it could go disastrously wrong sometimes. It must have been quite a disappointment for his mother, to be left alone with the children. Or maybe it was a relief. Maybe she was glad to see the back of him. Alison scrutinized the man in the black and white photo, looking for answers to questions. Was it your fault? Were you a bastard? Come on now, tell me. Am I going to send Charlie to London to be greeted by a ghoul? But the man in the photograph stared back at her, grinning, his fringe falling across his forehead, exercising his own inscrutable and frozen charm.

At about half past nine, Alison heard the key in the door. At last. She was annoyed with Charlie. Why hadn't he called to say he was delayed? They rarely quarrelled, but she was very cross by now. She decided to suppress the annoyance, because the middle of a row wouldn't be a good time to bring up everything about Ray Cunningham and the London nun and his father. She heard Charlie's case thud to the ground in the hall, then he came down into the kitchen.

'Will I put your dinner in the microwave?' she asked.

He dropped his car keys on the counter, walked across the kitchen and went into the sun room, where he half sat down, half collapsed in a wickerwork armchair. She followed him. She could smell drink. Something strong, like whiskey.

'You've been drinking?' she exclaimed. 'Did you drive home?'

He nodded.

'Where have you been?'

'I just went for a walk on Dun Laoghaire pier. I got a naggin of whiskey in the off-licence. Did you know that the guy who designed Dun Laoghaire harbour, or was it the guy who built it –' his words were slurred – 'one of them, or maybe it was the engineer, well, one of them, they got it wrong by so many feet, or yards or something, that they jumped off the end of it? A sobering thought. Failure leaves a bitter taste.'

The microwave pinged. Alison went back into the kitchen to get the plate of food. She'd never seen Charlie like this before. He wasn't a drinker generally. She wondered if she should wait for him to sober up before she mentioned his father. She decided she'd launch right in. He was so off balance at this moment that it might in fact be a good time.

She put the dinner and a glass of water on a small table beside him, carefully arranging a knife and fork and a napkin.

'Honey, I've something to tell . . .' she started

'I've something to tell you, darling . . .' he blurted.

'You go,' she said.

'No, you go first,' he said.

Charlie picked up the fork and started to eat. 'I'll eat, you talk.' He was glad to put it off, even for a few minutes. He chewed and swallowed, and the food immediately started to steady him up. He slurped the water gratefully. He listened to what Alison was saying, but it was only half going into his head. Something about

185

a nun and his father being in a London nursing home. A sick man. But his father was gone. Had left years ago. Something about a private detective. What could she be talking about?

'So what do you think?' she asked brightly. 'Will you go and see him?'

Charlie nodded vacantly. This was too much for him to take in.

'I think sooner rather than later on account of his health. I can get you a flight at a moment's notice.'

Bewildered, he ate the last of the goulash, which shuddered down his throat like sticky cardboard.

'So what were you going to tell me?' asked Alison.

Charlie paused for a moment.

'Are you pleased?' she asked anxiously.

There was silence for a moment.

'I'm in trouble, Ali.'

'What kind of trouble?'

Panic rose in her. Fear had been in the back of her mind since the night of the sawing down of the crossbeam. She'd tried to suppress it, but dread lurked there.

'I've lost Charles O'Brien Motors. I've driven it into the ground.'

'What?'

The news should have shocked Alison, but it didn't. When he said it, she realized she'd known it was coming. Not with her conscious brain, but subconsciously she'd sniffed something. It was part of the fear and dread in the back of her mind. She hadn't asked any questions about her hunch because there wasn't the time in her life now, between work and the baby, to dwell on anything. And besides, she always avoided confronting the unpleasant. But she wasn't shocked. Annoyance rose in her.

'Tell me all.'

'Well, there's been cashflow difficulties for quite some time and the bank appointed an accountant to look at the business, and, basically, they're more or less going to appoint a receiver.'

'What do you mean, more or less?'

'Well, they've offered to refloat me, but the terms are too bad.'

'What are they?'

Charlie took out a cigarette and lit it. He fiddled with nervous violence with the cigarette pack.

'They want me to put up the house.'

'You can't do that. Much of the capital in the house is mine. I know we jointly own it, but all the cash from my apartment is in it.'

'That's what I mean. The terms are too bad.'

Alison immediately regretted what she'd said. The word 'mine' hung in the air. It was a repugnant word now. 'Mine' no longer existed. 'Ours' had superseded it. So it rang there strangely, from some alien lexicon. Mine, mine, mine.

'Charlie, why didn't you tell me things were going badly? I could have got some help, some advice.'

'Shame, Ali. I am ashamed. It is hard to face the fact that things are going belly up. And it's been difficult for you, managing the baby and your return to work. I didn't want to bother you. But I'm sorry, we should have talked.'

'The house. They can't take the house.'

'The house'll have to go anyway. We'll never be able to keep up the mortgage. Ali, I'm broke.'

His voice cracked. She couldn't bear that.

'Everything will have to go. My company car, I've defaulted on the HP. Without a bail out from the bank, it's gone. The house will have to go anyway.'

Alison got annoyed now.

'They can't just do this. It's your business, Charlie. They can't just send in a receiver against your wishes. We'll talk to a lawyer.'

'I know it has my name above the door, Alison, but the bank owns it. The banks own most businesses really. They'll change the locks and I'll be locked out.'

Alison got up and made some coffee. She needed to think straight. She poured them both a mug and brought them out to the sun room. Charlie still sat slumped on the chair. He seemed to have sobered up a bit. The food. The coffee would help him further. She looked around at the house and knew it would have to go. Though she had dislocated herself from the money side of things, she knew that the mortgage on Ashleigh Court was very

187

high. She stood there, in her beautiful life, watching its bricks and masonry collapse around her.

'So it makes no difference about the house. It goes anyway,' she said.

He nodded.

All at once she had a vision of a small house in some dreary lower-middle-class housing estate, where there were rows and rows of vin-ordinaire dwellings. They'd be able to afford something small if they sold Ashleigh. They had enough capital in the house. And if need be, they could live on her salary. If she destroyed her credit cards. And stopped living. And never went anywhere. She looked at Charlie, his body slung in the wickerwork chair, limp and defeated. It was a big blow. An unfathomable loss. Unimaginable. Whatever daydreams she'd ever had about the future, this was beyond even her worst fears.

'And my name,' he said, 'my name is finished.'

'Oh, Jesus,' she said.

'It looks like I might be able to hang on to Charles O'Brien Repairs. But it'll be rough going, 'cos I'll have to take up some slack on creditors from the main business. But at least I'll have a position.'

'You mean, back to being a mechanic?'

'Yes.'

A flash. Alison in a scruffy lower-middle-class housing estate. And Charlie coming home from work, in blue overalls, covered from head to toe in engine oil.

'And what about if we consider putting the house up as security? What then? Would it be worth the gamble?'

'And they want the repairs business put up as well.'

'What I'm asking is, could you trade out of the problems?'

'I don't know. They'd want to appoint their own people to stick their oar in and put a restaurant in the attic or something. And if it didn't work, their business plan, we'd be up even worse shit creek.'

'But there'd be no receiver next week.'

It was tempting.

'Are you agreeing to it, Alison?' he asked.

'Are you asking me to agree?'

He shook his head.

'No,' he said. 'I'm going down but I couldn't use the house, which is essentially your money . . .' and his voice trailed away. 'Leave me the foundations of my pride. At least I'll have that. I can sustain myself on that,' he said bitterly.

Suddenly she felt overwhelmingly sorry for him. He was so proud of his business. He loved standing on his crow's nest and looking out to sea, master of all he surveyed. And now he looked so vulnerable. She'd never seen any vulnerability in him before. He was always such a working-class hero. And he would be ashamed. His self-worth was tied up in the business. Charlie without his business. She could hardly imagine it. She looked calmly at him, at the slightly collapsed version of her husband who now sat before her.

'Say something, Ali. I really need you to say something.'

She didn't know what to say. She leaned over and touched his face. A tear started in his eye, and she couldn't bear that, so she pulled him to her and kissed him. He was like lead. No energy in him at all. But she persisted and opened his shirt and unbuttoned his trousers. Soon her deft touch and hot breath got him going and he responded to her. They made love there, on the cold tiled floor, and Alison looked up at the severed wooden butts that jutted out from the ceiling at both ends of the sun room, like wounds.

She came quite quickly, in a half-hearted way, but it took him ages. He was going for such a long time, that Alison began to feel sore. He pumped away in a desperation to get there, somewhere. Straining grunts every now and then indicated his struggle. She began to feel bruising on her lower back from the hard tiles, and thought she couldn't take him any longer when finally, with a roar, he came.

'Jesus,' he said. 'That was mind-blowing. Are you OK?'

'Fine,' she lied.

'Sorry it took me so long, but when it happened, it blew my head off. I didn't want to stop. I couldn't bear to fail at that too.'

She ran her fingers though his hair. She knew he would feel that with his business collapsing, his masculinity would also be under threat. Charlie was old-fashioned in that way. He presented

189

himself handsome, no doubt, and virile. But rich. That was part of what he felt he had to offer. Part of what he felt was his essential worth. Would he have wanted Alison without her beauty? Probably not. It was her beauty that led him to her. And would she want him without his money?

She followed him upstairs to bed, his semen trickling down her inner thigh. She was thinking of having a shower, but he took her by the wrist and pulled her to the bed.

'Don't shower, I want to be able to smell you.'

She lay down in the bed and he lay by her side, still holding her wrist in one hand. He ran his fingers along the Caesarean scar, then placed his hand possessively on her still-flabby tummy.

'I'm weary,' he said, and in moments he was asleep.

Alison lay there awake for many hours. She was sore, and she knew that the stiffness in her lower back would be bruising by tomorrow. In the darkness, the fear came again. She looked at his sleeping face. She knew she had taken some of his devastation from him, literally absorbed it into her body. And at least he was now asleep. But the fear and dread were there with her in the bedroom. She feared they were losing their touch.

12

Marie Rose put the biscuit tin containing her sewing things in the back of the van and slammed the door. The van now contained all the accoutrements of their life. Everything they owned apart from the contents of a few overnight bags. She had worked to get the van loaded in a blaze of fury. The van man had told her not to be lifting heavy things, but she wanted to load it herself. Wanted the physical exercise of it. Wanted to handle every precious object of their life with her own two hands.

She hid her fury from Michael, who thought they were on a big adventure. His father had always told him that they would move on from Ballyferriter eventually, stressed that they didn't belong there, so he was happy enough at the move. 'Home' to him was Glenmore, as his father spoke of it. Or Carrig, as his mother did. His mother would say things like, 'We used to have one of those at home,' or his father, 'The water isn't as good as it is at home.' Not there, not Ballyferriter. It had never been referred to as home. He had his pals from the village that he ran around the fields with, but he knew he was different. When he was in a fight with any of the other boys, they often taunted him with being an informer. The biggest insult, though the children barely understood what it meant. The next minute they'd be running about, great friends again. But Michael knew that his destiny would take him away from there to other, more splendid places.

Marie Rose sighed as she looked about at the splendour of the countryside. It vibrated in the June sunshine. She had settled in here, made it her own. She belonged here now and felt a huge wrench leaving it behind. Her mind drifted back to the early days, to how frightened she had been of everything. What a young one she had been. How strange she had found the local people, with their strong accents and use of Irish. But she had got used to it. And the local people had been very kind to her. They were sorry to see her go. And the sincerity of that touched her. Even Father O'Keefe had been very warm and kind to her. It was only now, leaving, that she realized that people in the community had liked her. Her natural friendliness had endeared her to almost everybody.

The new sergeant, a man called Feeney from Galway, had arrived a few days previously, and Cormac left to go up to Kildare and see what was in store for them there. Feeney was hatchet-faced and very unpleasant. Politically, he was a Republican, and a vocal member of Fianna Fáil, but that didn't really come as a surprise. He had a wife and three children who would be following on in due course, and he was fussing about the married quarters, barely giving Marie Rose time to vacate them. Every time she turned around, he was there beside her. He questioned every item she removed: 'Are you sure that's not barracks property?' Marie Rose became enraged at him, and he became the focus for her anger. She had originally intended leaving the range as a legacy to the next barracks wife, though it had been bought and installed by her with her dowry money. Instead she had it removed and carted over to Kate as a present. Kate was thrilled to accept it. She knew the workings of it intimately as she'd done plenty of cooking in Marie Rose's kitchen over the years.

'I'll call it Marie Rose. I'll talk to it, in fact, because I'm going to miss you so much. Who else can I talk to here? You're my only friend.'

'I'm sure Mrs Sergeant Feeney will be a delight to all,' said Marie Rose with a wicked gleam. 'You'll be having tea and talk with her in no time.'

Kate shook her head. 'You're one in a million, Marie Rose. There's no replacing you.'

When Feeney came into Marie Rose's kitchen later in the day and saw the bare hearth, he started to splutter.

'Where's the stove? I've explicitly written to Mrs Feeney telling her there's a stove.'

'The range was mine. And I've taken it. There was nothing here when we moved in, not a stick except that ugly hallstand in the front hall. The whole place was damp and dirty and unused. There hadn't been a woman living here in years before I came.'

'I would've bought the range off you, Mrs O'Brien, if you'd mentioned it to me.'

'Too late. I've disposed of it.' Marie Rose was very happy with where the range had gone. It fitted snugly into Kate's hearth. A man would come over from Dingle later and install it.

Feeney sighed.

'It might have suited you better to have made an effort to be a bit more pleasant, and you might have got things to go your way a bit more,' she said.

'Bitch,' he muttered.

'Ignoramus,' she returned.

Marie Rose shrugged. This would have upset her a lot in previous times, but her circumstances were such at that moment that she didn't care. Let him have his dirty mouth.

Cormac had instructed her to get everything packed and follow on up to the big barracks in Kildare. But after he left, she formed her own plan. She wasn't arriving in an unknown place with a van full of belongings there may be no space for. And she didn't want Michael to be exposed to whatever humiliations might be waiting for them. She wired her father in Carrig that herself and Michael would be along and a vanload would arrive later. She tried to word the telegram in such a way as not to arouse worry or suspicion. 'Cormac being transferred' was how she put it. There was plenty of warehouse space in Carrig attached to the shop to put their stuff in. She could leave Michael at home with her family in Carrig and go and inspect Kildare. She decided all this unilaterally, didn't consult Cormac, because she knew he wouldn't approve of the plan. His stupid pride wouldn't let them depend on his in-laws for help. Marie Rose knew he would be furious at her for disobeying him, but she didn't care. She was furious too. Let them both have their furies.

She put on her light coat and scarf, and put a jacket on Michael before they set off in a car for Dingle to catch the train. Michael sat beside her, thrilled with the adventure. Marie Rose had forbidden her friends to come and see her off. They specialized in emotionally draining farewells round here, as person after person went off to live in America.

'I don't want an American wake,' said Marie Rose to Kate, who

193

was insisting on seeing them to the train. Marie Rose knew that Kate would only start wailing if she let her come.

They were tight for time and only barely caught the train. Marie Rose saw Mrs Holohan from the chemist getting into the first carriage, so she made her way to the second. She didn't want to talk to anybody. Or explain her business. She had been vague to everybody about their move.

Young Michael was beside himself with excitement. It was only the second time he'd been on the train. He had gone once with her to Tralee the previous summer. He thought it the most exciting thing he'd ever witnessed. He inspected everything – the seats, the windows. He peered out to look at the wheels and coupling. When the engine let off steam and whistled loudly, he bounced giddily on his chair, and when the train groaned and started up slowly, heaving to bring its heavy carriages with it, he yelped with excitement. 'I've forgotten, Mama, how does the steam work again?' She had shown him the steam lifting the lid on the kettle on the range at the barracks to explain this phenomenon to him. He had a memory of some demonstration, but couldn't remember quite what. She smiled at him. His giddiness and enthusiasm dented her gloom.

As the train pulled slowly up the slight incline out of Dingle, Marie Rose's tears flowed. Typical of the place to look so beautiful on the day she was leaving. Typical of this contrary place. Often so grey and windswept and unforgiving. So unwelcoming it had been for their first while there. But now, as she left the place behind her, mile by mile, it had turned on its bewitching charms. The smell of the earth cast spells to left and right. The contours of the hills, the glinting sea, and the patchy shadows of a few small clouds which fell on the hills and valleys. A field of cows stood and chewed and stared at the train as it passed, like an attentive audience waiting for a political speech. The colours of the fields were vibrant and ecstatic. She cast her mind forward to what awaited her when she eventually made it to Kildare. Cormac would be there, enduring whatever petty humiliations they had in store for him with typical stoicism. He had a strong and disdainful character. The opinions of others never bothered him much. Not even the opinion of his wife, she thought sadly. Marie

Rose couldn't bear the thought of it. The hot shame she would feel, as other more powerful people moved them about like minute pawns in some deluded chess game. As the engine climbed, the view to the south of Dingle Bay grew more expansive. The sea glistened and glinted unmercifully. In a moment or two, the train would cross the first peak and the view of Dingle Bay would be gone, and Marie Rose knew she would never see it again. She looked back over her shoulder for a final glimpse of the dazzling vista and felt her heart turn to stone.

13

Charlie walked down the corridor, a strong smell of disinfectant wafting about. The nun leading him along was tiny. Under five foot. The place was full of holy pictures. Sacred Hearts, Virgin Marys, Infant of Pragues. Charlie always found that kind of thing creepy. His practical mind liked things to be what they were, and not infused with unfathomable significance. The nun, Sister Catherine, smiled at him in a very friendly fashion. She was youngish, about fifty perhaps, but she wore a brown old-fashioned habit and a pair of rosary beads which swished from her waist.

Charlie didn't fully know what he was doing here. He had been in a daze and somehow Alison had shovelled him onto a plane. A budget plane. And now he was here. Against his will, it had to be said. He hadn't arranged to be here. He didn't want to be here. But he was here. He had an idea in his head, possibly incorrect, that coming here and doing this was the price that Alison demanded in exchange for accepting the business collapse with such good grace. He had the two things tangled up in his head. He wasn't dreading meeting his father. He just didn't want to do it. His overriding sensation was one of numbness.

Suddenly he was in a room, and the nun was saying kind things and he was standing in front of a very thin old man sitting in a chair beside a bed. There were four other beds in the ward. This bed was beside a window which looked out on a brick wall. Not really a view. The window was stocked with potted plants. The nun disappeared, soundlessly, on rubber soles. The old man stared at Charlie, not shocked, because he had been forewarned of the arrival, but faintly surprised. He stared in an inscrutable fashion. Charlie didn't know what to say. The old man didn't know what to say. Charlie put out his hand to shake and the old man took it. He shook it with warmth, but without strength.

Then there was silence again. Stray thoughts fluttered through Charlie's head. Questions. Where did you go? Why did you leave? Some anger suddenly from nowhere. He'd never been angry about his absent father. That had been Mary's role. The silence stretched. He took out his wallet and produced a photo of Alison and baby Michael. It was a glossy posed shot they'd had done in a specialist studio when Michael was six months old. Charlie loved the picture. It was like something from a magazine.

'My wife and son,' he said with pride.

The old man took the picture in his bony hand and looked at it with great care and attention.

'She's very beautiful. Like a goddess.'

Charlie smiled. Alison didn't look entirely real in the picture.

'And the boy. What age is he?'

'A year and a bit now. He's about six months there in the photo,' said Charlie.

A young woman arrived with a squeaky tea trolley. She poured out tea and left a plate of biscuits on the bedside trolley. She put a straw in the old man's cup. Charlie was glad of the tea. He hadn't bothered with breakfast as he'd departed the house so early. He had intended to eat at the airport, but when he saw the groaning trestles of rashers and sausages, his stomach had started to heave, and he'd avoided all intake. But his system had settled on the flight and now the tea looked very inviting.

'What is this place?' asked Charlie.

'It's a small hospice attached to the Convent of Mercy. They're mainly priests and religious folk here, on the way out, but they took me in because I worked for them for so many years. The religious look after their own and that's for sure.'

'Work?'

'Well, I was the caretaker over in the school. For twenty years.'

The questions started to bubble up again in Charlie's mind. Why didn't you come back? Why didn't you get in touch? I thought you were a pilot? He confined himself to one question.

'Weren't you a pilot?'

There was a long silence from the old man. Followed by, 'Yes, I was.' Then more silence. Charlie wanted to get the old man to talk. He tried another tack.

'Mary lived in London for a while. She studied nursing here.'

The old man nodded him to continue.

'She's married now, with three children. Her husband's English. They're happy.'

Then he remonstrated with himself for not bringing a photo of Mary and family. It had never occurred to him. He hadn't exactly prepared for this trip. Either mentally or practically. It was as though he had suddenly woken up and found himself here. A bright and chirpy nurse arrived with some pills in a little paper cup and a glass of water.

'Now, Michael, here's your medication. Your son might help you with the water.' She turned to Charlie. 'His hand shakes a bit.'

Charlie was shocked at this stranger so casually calling him the son of this old man.

'The pills make me a little woozy and unfocused, but they keep me from feeling the pain, and pain must be avoided at all costs.'

He swallowed the contents of the paper cup and picked up the glass of water. His hand shook. Charlie put out his own hand and steadied his father's as the glass went to his old and cracked lips. Charlie had a momentary flash of spooning food into baby Michael, and felt some spark of emotion. He steadied himself. Emotion, this kind of emotion, was ruthless and unsettling.

'What do you do for a living, Charles?' asked the old man.

'I have a car dealership. I specialize in BMW and Volkswagen.' He didn't want to go into the recent collapse of the business. Pride. Even here, in front of this old man, he had his pride. 'I started as a mechanic and built the business up from scratch. I have a big new showroom, overlooking Dun Laoghaire harbour. I sold two hundred and fifty new cars and about half that number in used cars last year.' Charlie heard himself boasting and was a bit ashamed. He wanted to show this old man that he had done fine without him. The old man nodded.

'I was a mechanic,' said the old man. 'I joined the air force as a mechanic. And eventually I trained as a pilot.'

'You were in the army?'

'I was trained by the army. I moved afterwards to Aer Lingus.'

'I saw a photo of you in a civilian pilot's uniform.'

The old man nodded.

'That would've been when I was in Aer Lingus,' he said. 'How did you find me here?' he asked.

'My wife found you. Some way or other. I don't fully know how, to be honest.'

The old man's eyes fell back to the photo of Alison and the baby, which he held tightly in his hand.

'What's her name?'

'Alison.'

'And the boy's name?'

Charlie hesitated. 'I called him Michael.'

Michael O'Brien sat forward in his chair. He was startled by this fact. This stranger, this stranger-son, had taken his name and given it to a child.

'Why did you do that?'

Charlie didn't know what to say. The reasons had been clear to him at the time, but now he had forgotten.

'I think I wanted to give Michael O'Brien another chance.'

When the words came out, they clarified one thing for Charlie. He wasn't going to remonstrate with the old man. He wasn't going to blame him. He would accuse him of nothing further. But he would get him to talk. Michael O'Brien nodded. He took the insult. Guilty as charged. He nodded some more.

'I named you Charles for Charles Augustus Lindbergh. He was my hero.'

Charlie hadn't known that. His mother had never told him. It had never occurred to him to be curious about why he was called Charles. As a fact, it pleased him. It had a good feel to it.

'When I was a baby, around the age of your little fellow there in the picture, my mother lifted me up and showed me Lindbergh as he flew overhead on his way to Paris. We lived in Kerry, on the end of the Dingle peninsula, and my father was famous for being the first to spot Lindbergh. He wired Dublin about it, and was given a prize of a five-pound note by the government. The whole of Europe was waiting for the plane. Do you know much about him?'

Charlie shook his head. 'Well, I know he was the first to fly the Atlantic single-handed. I wouldn't know too much detail.'

'I kept a scrapbook about Lindbergh. Every item of information that was in the papers or a magazine, I cut out. My mother helped me. I wanted to do something great. Like Lindbergh. I wanted to be brave and achieve something marvellous. I remember those days in Kerry as a small child. We left when I was about eight, and I remember a paradise. A wet paradise. It rained all the time. But we were so happy there. And it was never the same after.'

The old man had started to talk and now seemed glad to do it. He talked as though he might not stop. Charlie took off his coat and scarf and settled deeply into his chair. And listened.

'Have you ever seen a picture of Charles Lindbergh in his heyday?'

Charlie nodded his head. He must've read something or seen a documentary, because he had a clear picture in his mind of what the aviator looked like.

'He was like a matinée idol. The perfect hero. When I was growing up, air travel was a complete novelty. Nowadays people hop on and off planes like buses, but then it was the outer frontier. For a small boy, an aeroplane was the most exciting thing. It was like magic. I had a toy, a wooden model of Lindbergh's plane, and it was my favourite toy in the whole world. I still remember playing with it so vividly.

'He came to Ireland in the 1930s to locate an airstrip for Pan American Airlines, when they were planning their first transatlantic passenger services. He brought Eamon de Valera on his first flight. Did you know that?'

Charlie shook his head.

'I used to have a first edition of his autobiography. It had a blue cover. I read it maybe forty times. When I was a young man, it was my inspiration. I don't know what became of it. I suppose it must have fallen apart at some stage. You should read it. It's a good book for a young man.'

'What's it called?' asked Charlie.

'The Spirit of St Louis.'

Charlie wrote it down.

'It was terrible what happened to Lindbergh. His reputation was shattered, you know. They called him a Nazi. But he wasn't a Nazi. He visited Nazi Germany to see their air force, but he reported everything he saw to the American air force. It was said at the time that the Germans fooled Lindbergh about their air power by shifting the same twenty planes from aerodrome to aerodrome while he was shunted the long way round by car. But Lindbergh was no fool. He didn't have the skills to navigate the Atlantic single-handed just to be codded by a bunch of Nazis. He would have been wise to a trick like that. And he really wasn't a Nazi. It was all very well for everybody to be wise after the event, but it wasn't immediately obvious at the time what skunks the Nazis were. It wasn't obvious what people should think. He didn't want America to enter the war. He opposed it, for reasons, as he saw it, of patriotism. When the Americans finally did enter the war, Lindbergh dropped his opposition and signed up because he was a patriot, yet the US army wouldn't officially let him fly for them. He did fly a few missions in the Pacific, but unaccredited.

'But overall I think it's mostly forgotten now. The war thing. Mostly now he's remembered for flying the Atlantic. He was my hero. And I always thought that if I had a son, I'd call him Charles.'

The old man looked very tired now. The nun came along and suggested to Charlie that he leave.

'He usually has a nap in the late morning. If you want, you can come back in the afternoon, after lunch, or tomorrow.'

Charlie wandered off into the centre of London. Alison had booked him into a cheap hotel in Bloomsbury. He went into a pizzeria and ordered a big feed of pizza and coleslaw and garlic bread. He used to love pizza, but Ali had something against it, so he hadn't seen one since he was married. He ate without appetite. All his limbs felt like lead and his skin felt too tight. He wondered if maybe he was in shock. Seeing his father after all this time was quite unsettling. It had perhaps nudged some of the business trauma to one side. He felt doubly shocked.

He wondered what to do next. He decided he would go back to the nursing home later on and visit again the following morning. His flight wasn't until the late morning. Now that he was here, he was eager to get the old man to talk.

He strolled aimlessly along the street, enjoying the anonymity of being in a strange place. Nobody knew him here. Nobody would come up to him and ask how business was. It was a comfort to disappear in this way. Like his father had disappeared. He stopped walking and looked around. He was on Charing Cross Road and found himself surrounded by bookshops. He knew what he wanted to do.

A young man behind a desk consulted a computer about his query.

'No, we don't have it, and it's out of print, so I can't order it for you. It says here that it was reprinted in 1997, so there's probably a few copies around. You'll find it somewhere, in some other shop.'

Charlie strolled down the road and, in the fourth shop he tried, he found it. *The Spirit of St Louis* by Charles Augustus Lindbergh.

When next he walked the length of the corridor with Sister Catherine, he felt more comfortable. She was even kinder to him than before.

'Your father was in very good form after your visit,' she said. 'You are a brave and kind man, because I know a little of the history and it must be difficult.'

Charlie wasn't used to compliments, and this one had an authentic feel, coming as it did from a nun. He smiled in gratitude at her. When they reached the ward and were about to go in, the nun stopped him.

'Oh, he's with Father Reilly. He does confession on Saturdays. We'll just wait a moment until they finish.'

She sat on a bench in the corridor and patted the seat beside her. 'The old men are never very long with confession, because there isn't much opportunity for sin in here. But they like the confession all the same. It's a comfort to them.'

'I'm not very religious,' blurted out Charlie for no particular reason.

Sister Catherine shrugged. 'It's better nowadays. In the old days everybody was religious. All the scoundrels. Now people find their own way to God. It's better.'

Charlie nodded and felt uncomfortable. His eyes strayed to the walls and all the pictures. Copies of old masters. Jesus as a shepherd with sheep. A copy of Leonardo da Vinci's last supper. Various gold-leaf Madonna and childs. Cherubic baby Jesuses and John the Baptists lined up like Christmas cards.

'Did you know my father when he worked in the school?'

Sister Catherine shook her head.

'No. I was in Africa until last year. I'm only here a few months. But I know his story.'

That was it. That was what Charlie wanted. His story. It emerged from the muddle of Charlie's brain that he was after his father's story.

Father Reilly, pink-cheeked and cherubic, came out of the ward and smiled at them.

'All the souls are in excellent order within, Catherine,' he twinkled. 'I've never seen better for scrubbed souls.'

'Father Reilly, this is Charles O'Brien, Mr O'Brien's son.'

'Ah, a pleasure.' He held out his hand to be shaken.

Charlie shook it. He found himself wondering if his prodigal father had been confessing all his sins of neglect towards his children, and if he had been forgiven. It was a handy system, he thought. You could be a great wretch, but so long as you were sorry after, it was fine.

Sister Catherine escorted him over to his father's bed. She checked the old man was all right, plumped up his pillows for him and left. Tea arrived soon after and cake. Charlie realized that he'd forgotten to take away the picture of Alison and Michael, and it stood now, propped against a little vase on the bedside locker. Here, surrounded by all the religious imagery, Alison looked like a gleaming blonde Madonna with the infant on her lap.

'I told Father Reilly that that was my grandson, named Michael like me, and he was very impressed.'

203

Charlie nodded. He took the paperback copy of *The Spirit of St Louis* from his pocket.

'I've started reading it,' he said.

The old man was very touched. He took the paperback in his shaking hand and caressed it.

'I'm sorry,' the old man said. 'I am sorry, and if it wasn't so late, I could think of making it up to you and to little Mary. I'll try and think of some way to make amends.'

Charlie shook his head.

'It doesn't matter. Truly. We are where we are.'

'Your mother, is she still alive?' Michael O'Brien asked.

'She died of a brain haemorrhage about fifteen years ago. Just suddenly.'

The old man nodded.

'I don't want to put the blame on her, but she was a hard woman, Charlie. She never forgave me.'

'Forgave you for what?'

The old man smiled ruefully.

'I lost my job in Aer Lingus. For a stupid reason. Pride. I wouldn't accept a co-pilot I hadn't chosen and I thought I'd be able to insist if I threatened them with resignation. It was a petty row over nothing. They called my bluff. And I had to resign. And Deborah never forgave me. I thought there'd be other jobs, but in those days there weren't. We had a beautiful house in Howth, which we had to sell, and we moved to a tiny flat in the centre of Dublin. It was shortly after you were born and Deborah never forgave me. She couldn't understand how I had put what she termed my "foolish pride" before herself and the children.'

Charlie nodded. His own current troubles spun about in his brain.

'It wasn't a good match. Deborah and I weren't made for each other. We weren't soul mates. I think we just got on each other's nerves. We hadn't the right feel for each other. It is so disappointing, to marry the wrong person. It dismantles you from within, Charles. If your judgement is flawed in that, how can you depend on it in any other area of your life? I did try to keep in touch for the first while, but my letters were returned unopened, and, to my eternal shame, I stopped trying. I failed at that too. And my sense of failure overwhelmed me and sapped out my energy. A failed marriage is a curse, Charles.'

Charlie looked at the glowing collagen-enhanced Madonna propped against the vase on the sideboard.

Charlie stayed on for over two hours and listened to his father talk. About his young days in Kerry, about his parents, Marie Rose Bourke and *Garda* sergeant Cormac O'Brien. About the civil war and its aftermath. The old man talked and talked and Charlie listened with a voracious curiosity. Now that his interest had been awakened, he wanted every little scrap of information, every little detail. The old man was happy to reminisce, but strangely it was the early part of his life, his young boyhood in Kerry until the age of about eight, which seemed most vivid to him.

'It's the drugs,' said the old man. 'I forget yesterday, but I remember long, long ago.'

Charlie returned to his miserable little hotel room. Five star no longer. He would have to get used to this. Have to get used to a one-star life. It was early evening when he went out to a phone box to call Alison. His mobile had been surrendered.

'Ali?'

'Darling, I'm talking in a low voice because I've just got Michael off for his nap. How's it going?'

'Fine.'

'Did you meet him?'

'Yes.'

'And . . .'

'It's going well.'

'You're brave, Charlie.'

'Thank you, Ali, for sending me here.'

Alison sighed with relief after she hung up the phone. Charlie seemed in reasonable shape. She wasn't 100 per cent sure about him going over to London now, at this moment, with everything in such turmoil, but on balance she thought it was the best thing to do. It'd take his mind off things. Also, it sounded like the old guy was in bad shape, and she didn't want him to die before she had called him to account. That'd be the end.

Since she'd received Charlie's news last week, she'd taken over the management of their domestic expenditure. Charlie had obviously been in utter denial, and there was a drawer of unpaid utility bills. She sat down with a notebook and worked out all the details of their expenditure. Really, they just had to get organized. They could live on her salary for the time being, once the crippling mortgage was unloaded. They just had to adapt. She regretted having handed over the management of domestic finances to Charlie while in a postnatal oestrogen fog. That had been a bad move. She now took back charge of all these details with gusto, and was sorting out bills and bank statements into tidy files. When she put her mind to it, she could be very businesslike. The crisis was forcing her to be disciplined. Her thoughts became lean and concentrated, and the stress was slimming her down. She could feel the tension tightening her tummy. This pleased her. She hadn't been able to shed the extra weight after the baby. Weight loss – the upside of bankruptcy, she thought.

Today was her mother's birthday and Cecilia had organized a surprise party at her house that evening. Alison knew that her mother would be tormented by the fact that she hadn't rung her to wish her a happy birthday, but it was an elaborately planned charade. Miriam would think everybody had forgotten her birthday and be in misery over it. Then she'd be overjoyed when Adrian went to fetch her and she found her twelve closest friends and two daughters waiting for her in party glee. Alison smiled at the mischief of it. She hadn't yet told her mother about the change in Charlie's fortunes. She'd leave it for another day, knowing the hysteria it would provoke. The receiver notice would probably be in the paper in the coming week. She was glad that Charlie was missing the party, because her mother would keep asking him about his business. It was the only thing she ever asked him about.

Miriam was sixty-five. There would be much lamenting about how old she had become. And what a marvellous surprise it all was. She would become emotionally overwhelmed. Alison was looking forward to it, to the drama of it all.

The intercom sounded. It was Mary. Alison opened the security gates and went out to the front door. Unusual. Mary rarely visited and never arrived unannounced. Mary pulled her battered, unwashed old car into one of the parking spaces. It looked terrifically incongruous there, lined up with all the gleaming machines.

'Hi, Alison, I'm just back and I've heard the news. Brendan told me.' She glanced up at the 'For Sale' sign, which was embedded in the flowerbed.

Mary had been away on some organic course for the week. Charlie had gone over to see her during the week to tell her about the business collapse, but she wasn't there. So he had related his tale to Brendan. Mary followed Alison into the house.

'We'll go out to the sun room. Michael's asleep in the sitting room.' Mary followed her out.

'Tea?'

Mary nodded.

'The house is on the market already? That's pretty fast.'

'Nothing to be gained from delaying.' Alison carried in the tea. 'To be honest Mary, we were never really happy in this house.'

'The market has slowed,' said Mary.

'Not really for a house like this. This house is geared for an exclusive market, and no matter how much the economy slows down, the rich always manage to stay rich. Except us, of course. We are the exception. This house will get a good price. And though the mortgage is large, there's a lot of equity in the house.'

Alison stared at Mary. She was fine-looking, or at least could be if she made a bit of an effort. Her dramatic dark hair was greying at the temples and peppering throughout. She really ought to dye it. She was only thirty-seven. Too early for grey. Her skin was beginning to look a bit raw and dry; certainly she needed some good facecream. And her eyebrows would be lovely and full if they were plucked into some kind of decent shape. She had a very good figure. All that good food and exercise. But her clothes were hopeless. Alison had an instinct that she wanted to take Mary upstairs and fix her. Bring her up and dress her in something really decent.

'Where is Charlie?'

Alison hesitated. She wasn't sure what to tell her. Whether

Charlie would like her to know where he was and what he was doing. She decided to kick for touch.

'Eh, he's in London, I think. Some business thing.'

'I tried to get him on his mobile.'

'The network has switched him off. The phone belonged to the business.'

'Where did you say Charlie is?'

'London, I think.'

Mary was becoming suspicious. She knew Alison was being evasive.

'What's he doing in London?'

'Eh, I don't know.'

Alison tried to change the subject.

'How are the kids?'

'Fine.'

The phone rang. Alison picked it up. It was Cecilia fussing. She'd been on three times before about the party. Once about the soup having curdled. Once about the balloons, whether they should be single-colour or multicoloured. What now, thought Alison. This time she was fussing about where Michael was to sleep as they were staying overnight. Alison shook her head.

'Cici, in the spare room with me. He's only two foot long, and he'll be grand in the big bed with me. I'll have the baby monitor so we can keep an ear on him. Fine, fine. I'll be over there at about six o'clock.'

Cecilia was getting more and more like their mother, neurotically fussing about nothing.

Mary's eye fell on the half-packed travel case which lay open on the wickerwork sofa.

'I suppose I'm not surprised really,' said Mary.

'What?' asked Alison.

'I'm not surprised that you're leaving him. But he deserves better.'

'What are you talking about, Mary?'

Then it all fell into place. The half-packed case on the sofa. The house so rapidly on the market. The discussion with Cecilia about staying over. Mary had got the wrong impression.

'I'm very sorry,' said Mary. 'I'm sure Charlie's heartbroken. And on top of the business trouble, it might destroy him.'

'Whoa, whoa,' said Alison. 'You think I'm leaving him?'

'Aren't you?'

'No.'

'But Brendan said . . .'

'What did Brendan say?'

'Well, something, I can't quite remember.'

'He must have the wrong end of the stick so.'

'What was that about staying in your sister's?'

'Michael and I are staying overnight at Cici's because it's Mummy's birthday party and I want to have lots of champagne and not drive home.'

'Oh.' Mary blushed crimson.

Alison became annoyed. Mary had obviously come along with her mind already made up that Alison would scarper now that Charlie was in trouble, and a few stray irrelevant details had confirmed her prejudices.

'You've never liked me, Mary. I've always known that. You think that just because I've had privilege, I've no character. Only people who have suffered as much as you have character.'

Alison was furious now. Really angry. Mary had always looked down on her and she had no right to. Mary had always prejudged her, never given her a chance.

A conversation she'd had with Mary in the early days came into her mind. Alison had been talking about hanging out in Dun Laoghaire when she was a teenager and laughingly discussed a flasher who used to lurk in the People's Park. Herself and Donna used to follow him around to get a glimpse, because he had a blue ribbon tied around his prick. And they would collapse with virginal giggles, thinking it the funniest thing on earth. A childish teenagerish prank. Mary had sat stony-faced through what Alison thought was an amusing anecdote from her childhood. But Mary too remembered that self-same flasher in the People's Park, with his distinctive blue ribbon. She was a little older than Alison, and she and her friends had been terrorized by him. She remembered the occasion when the flasher appeared in front of her. She stood stock still, petrified. It had been a lonely evening and there were very few people about. Finally, she broke the trance, and turned and ran and didn't stop running for about a mile. She had been terrified and terrorized by the incident. It had haunted her for years. She said to Alison, 'It must have been nice to be so secure that something like that didn't bother you. You must have always felt good about yourself.'

Alison had shrugged.

'I remember that same flasher, Alison. I was terrified by him. But I was terrified by my own shadow. All my friends were. We had no sense of entitlement. Didn't much feel we were entitled to the air we breathed.'

'Oh,' said Alison, realizing that her story hadn't gone down very well at all.

'A privileged child thinks in a privileged way.'

Now, here in the present, Alison contemplated Mary. It must be sad to be so miserable, she thought.

'Of course I'm not leaving Charlie.'

Mary flushed deeply. She was amazed at herself for getting the whole thing so wrong.

'Yes, I am pampered and privileged,' said Alison. 'But I will always remain so. Privilege is a state of mind, not of circumstance. I have known girls grow up with everything money can buy and be so poor.'

Poor scrawny unhappy Donna was in her mind.

'I'm sorry,' said Mary.

'I'm not saying it's not a problem about Charlie's business. We're going to have to readjust, of course. But we're OK. The principal loss he's sustained is not financial. Part of his heart was down there, Mary, looking out to sea.'

Mary nodded in agreement.

'Remember, I have a very good salary of my own. Most normal people could live on that without any trouble.'

Mary stared at the floor.

'You think I married Charlie for his money?' said Alison. 'Despite appearances, I have very little interest in money. That should be obvious from the way I spend it.'

'I'm sorry,' said Mary again. 'I've misunderstood you.'

'You sure have, Mary.'

'I'm sorry.'

'I wouldn't put such a low price on myself as money.'

Charlie tossed and turned all night, and drifted in and out of sleep, thinking about his father. And what the absence had meant. He'd always shrugged it off as a young man, but he felt it now. And he thought of Mary. She was the casualty really. It was a pity she wasn't here now. It would do her some good. He would try and persuade her to come over when he went back.

He went to the nursing home and was greeted once more by Sister Catherine.

'You do know your father hasn't long, Charles? It's only a matter of weeks or months.'

Charlie nodded. What did she expect him to say?

'He may feel he can go now. After you've come. Sometimes the dying hang on when something is unresolved.'

Charlie nodded.

'I'm just preparing you, that's all. The news will come sooner rather than later.'

Charlie smiled at her. He knew what she was saying.

The old man sat on the bedside chair, looking at the door, keen to see his visitor. He knew that Charlie would be off to get his plane and would have only a short time. He had prepared a story to tell him and was eagerly awaiting his audience.

Charlie arrived and sat down in the other chair. His father smiled at him.

'Did you sleep well, son?'

The use of the affectionate term startled Charlie somewhat.

'I tossed a bit.'

The tea and biscuits arrived like magic once more, and cups and saucers were clacked and distributed in the same ritual as before. The old man slurped his tea through the straw and spoke.

'I remember, my father took me to visit the old home place in Glenmore, West Cork. I have no idea what age I was on this occasion, I imagine I was ten or eleven. My grandmother always made a right fuss out of me and I loved it. I always remember it being sunny there. Unlikely, as it's one of the wettest places in

Ireland. In Europe. The house at Glenmore was built to face the sun. It had its back to the road. Like the great Huguenot houses in the midlands. They built their houses with their back to the road. Very un-Irish. The Irish like to have their lintel to the road, so the eye can be kept on other men's affairs. Outside the front of the house in Glenmore, round the back from the road, was an orchard and down a slope was the well the family used. The sun fell on that front step all day.

'One day my father and I went on a big long hike. My grandmother packed us sandwiches and a bottle of milk, and we climbed high up the hills and got to a place where you have a grand view of the whole of Bantry Bay. Vaughan's Pass it was called, and I presume it still is. I remember it clear as if it was yesterday. The sun shone and the sea sparkled like diamonds and, really, it was the most magnificent sight I have ever seen. Bantry town was below with its busy streets and buildings and over across you could see Glengarriff Cove. Whiddy lay to the fore, looking flat as a pancake and stretching out to the south was Mizen. There were many boats in the bay, commercial and pleasure, as it was summer and the area was popular with holidaymakers and excursionists. I sat on a wall with my father and drank my milk. And he told me a story: "It is the book of Genesis. Your great-great-great-great-great-grandfather was alive and well and living a good life in the townland of Glenmore. This ancestor, named Tim O'Brien, well he was a fine man altogether, and some would say the finest in the whole of West Cork. God became angry with the people of Ireland, for the general wickedness and for voting Fianna Fáil and giving them the overall majority. He sent a deluge to punish them. So it rained for forty days and forty nights. And the seas rose and flooded Bantry town and covered the island of Whiddy. It drowned the lobster fishermen of Castletownbere and the fine diners of Garinish. It drowned the palatial houses of the rich and the meagre dwellings of the poor, because when it came to wickedness, there was little to choose between them, or so God thought at the time. So anyway, this ancestor, Tim O'Brien, he was up here, at Vaughan's Pass one day, surveying the rising water and trying to form an opinion whether or not the floods would reach the townland of

Glenmore. And who should heave into view, but Noah on his ark. And Noah called out to Tim O'Brien.

' " 'Lo, there, are you Tim O'Brien?'

' " 'Yes,' answered this great-great-great-great-grandfather.

' " 'God said I'd find you here,' said Noah. 'I'm come to save you. Yourself and your wife are to come aboard and be saved from the deluge.'

' "And Tim O'Brien looked around at the rising water and at the angry sky and Mrs Noah held up a very tempting pot of stew, wafting its aromas towards him. Then she held up a lovely apple pie, and jug of cream from the cow they had on board.

' " 'You're on my list,' said Noah, 'because you are very righteous. God gave me the instructions himself.'

' "And Tim O'Brien was a proud man and stood up to his full height, as he was seven foot tall.

' " 'Thank you kindly,' he said, 'but I'll decline. The O'Briens have their own boats.' " '

The old man leaned forward and drank a little more tea through the straw.

'I remember my father telling me that story as clearly as though it were yesterday. My father laughed at the story and shook his head. And in that shake of the head there was a lot of regret. And at the time I didn't know but he was describing to me his downfall. He was describing to me the streak in him that lost him his job and lost my mother her dwelling place and poisoned their marriage. And later, of course, I could see that streak in myself. But at the time I was only a little lad and that didn't occur to me at all then. All I saw was a fine man who himself stood very tall on top of a mountain on a sunny day and all I felt was wonder if there was ever a boy who loved his father as much as I.'

Charlie found himself shocked at the story. It startled him. It made an eerie sense to him.

'In my memory,' the old man said, 'the sun always shone in my grandparents' house in West Cork. It shines there still.'

Charlie sat and looked at the old man. A tear trickled down his father's face. But there was no other sign of emotion. Just one lone glistening tear making its progress across gnarled and

213

mottled skin, before dangling a moment and dropping to the ground. A diminutive emblem of the described flood.

'I'm glad you found me, son.'

14

Number 144 Cherry Park. A snug, three-bedroomed, end of terrace, former local authority house on a corner site. Room to extend subject to planning permission. Gas-fired central heating. Double-glazed windows. South-westerly rear garden. Not overlooked.

'We may be living in the ghetto, but we're still on the sunny side of the street,' remarked Alison to Donna with a wry smile, as they sat on the newly installed wooden deck in the rear garden, drinking champagne from tall crystal flutes. The weather was beautiful and Alison's olive skin was lapping up the May sunshine. Alison and Charlie were having a house-warming party, at Alison's insistence. Charlie wasn't in the mood for parties. He found himself dreading seeing Alison's cronies. The good weather was a godsend, as the house was too small for their old dining table, and they hadn't got a new one. The garden was strewn with Michael's toys. The child was delighted to get outside.

'I've news,' said Donna.

Alison raised her eyebrow, slightly fearful of what was to come.

'We're expecting again.'

'That's great news, Donna. I'm just thrilled.'

Alison got up and hugged Donna. 'So is everything OK, then?'

'Well, in an act of contrition, and diligent and persistent love-making, the second in line to the throne of Keating Transport has been conceived.'

'And have you forgiven him?'

'Yes. I have.'

Donna had forgiven James his dalliance with the au pair. It was easy to forgive, once he came back to her. She didn't mind him straying, just as long as he came back. And paid.

Charlie was toiling at the side of the garden, getting the barbecue to the correct temperature.

215

'How's Charlie?' asked Donna.

'OK-ish,' said Alison.

'He's looking a bit thin.'

'He's had a bit of stuffing knocked out of him. That's all.'

Charlie, as though aware he was being discussed, turned. 'I'm afraid it's going to peak too soon,' he called out. 'I really should be putting the food on now.'

'It'll be another half-hour at least,' called back Alison.

Gemma and Harry Sinnott arrived round the side.

'Sorry we're so late. The baby-sitter was late because her mother was late coming home from work with the car. And I couldn't find the remote control for the TV and the kids were going barmy. And we got lost coming here. It's a bit of a warren.'

Silence. The hint of rudeness hung in the air.

'Oh, well, I don't mean warren, as in warren warren, rabbits, I mean lots of roads, twisting, er.'

'Champagne, darling?' asked Alison, gracefully smoothing every wrinkle with the golden bubbled liquid.

'Lovely.'

Alison poured two glasses of champagne and topped up herself and Donna. Charlie came up from the barbecue. He was embarrassed now. He hadn't seen any of them since the business collapsed. Of Alison's friends, Harry was the one he knew best. He had sold him four cars over the years.

'Hello, mate!' said Harry, with a false cheeriness.

'Harry, Gemma,' said Charlie, and nodded at them both.

'It's great to see you,' said Gemma, a little overenthusiastically.

He went past them into the kitchen and got a beer from the fridge. He felt as though they were afraid of him. Like he had some disease and they might catch it off him. People rarely mentioned the business collapse. Everybody pretended it hadn't happened. That which isn't referred to doesn't exist. Charlie was grateful for this, but resentful at the same time. The great unspoken. He had endured the humiliation of the receivership. It had been hard on him. But he'd managed to lose himself under cars. He seemed for a time to only be happy when he was under a car, twiddling something. His face had a pained look for ages, but it was beginning to ease.

Alison had taken on the practicalities of selling Ashleigh Court and buying Cherry Park. He hadn't even viewed the new house. She had disposed of all the excess furniture down in Buckley's auction room, and bought new things, smaller things, for the new house. She had got the house painted, the downstairs a cheerful yellow to lift his spirits, and pale wooden floors installed to cushion their bare feet. By the time they moved in, the place was very cosy. Charlie immediately liked it. He didn't dare say it to Alison, but he was glad to see the back of Ashleigh Court. It had been an unlucky house. And she had made Cherry Park so lovely, as she transformed it by waving a magic wand, asserting her indomitable privilege.

A week ago, a letter had arrived from Sister Catherine, describing a peaceful and prayerful death. He's gone to God, she said. To Alison's surprise, Charlie had taken it quite badly. It was as though all the depression of the business collapse had become focused onto his lately found father. When he read the letter, his face had crumbled, and she felt for him. She felt that component of love which is called pity.

James Keating now arrived round the side of the house. He had come directly from work.

'Hi, folks. I'm sorry I'm so late. I got lost on the way, must've taken a wrong turning, because I ended up back at the roundabout where I started. It's like a maze in here, and the streets all look the same.'

Silence.

Oblivious, he continued, 'It's great to see you all.' He went over to Donna and gave her a hug. 'How are you?'

'Fine,' she said, and smiled.

'It's great news, isn't it?'

'Congratulations,' said Alison.

'What?' asked Gemma.

'She's pregnant again,' said James, immensely proudly.

Alison couldn't get over the change in him. He appeared a man transformed. And so kind to Donna. And Donna lapped it up like a grateful cat.

Charlie emerged from the kitchen with a tray of chicken legs, which he brought over to the barbecue. They greeted the grille

217

with an almighty sizzle and soon filled the garden with delicious smells.

'This is quite a treat,' said Gemma.

'You haven't tasted it yet,' said Charlie.

James came down to Charlie at the barbecue and inspected the coals.

'That looks great. The glow looks just right.'

Charlie nodded.

'You've got to make sure the flame isn't too high.'

'Hey, man. I'm very sorry at what happened to you.'

'Thank you,' said Charlie.

'If there's ever anything I can do.'

'There wasn't really anything anybody could do.' Charlie nodded. He was glad it was mentioned, out in the open. But he didn't want it elaborated on.

'I always admired you, Charlie.' James put an arm round him.

Charlie was touched. 'Look, are we going to start weeping down here, like a pair of women?'

The chicken legs were cooked, and he brought them over to the table. Everybody tucked in, eating with their fingers. Everything tasted so well in the fresh air.

He put on the salmon.

'I see Charlie is adept at cooking, Alison. You must have him well trained,' said Gemma.

'All men like to cook outdoors. It fulfils an atavistic urge,' said Alison. 'They just close their eyes and it's the campfire and bison.'

Charlie was very quiet, but the rest of them were a talkative bunch. He scuttled off happily to baste the fish. He was relieved this gathering was happening, more for Ali's sake than his own. He wanted her life to continue with some semblance of normality.

He served up the fish, and salads were dispensed from containers.

A thin woman came round the side of the house.

'Hello, I'm sorry to disturb you, but is Charles O'Brien here?'

Charlie went over to her.

'My name's Eithne. I'm from number 102 across the road. The

postman left this with me 'cos there was no one here.' She held up a big brown parcel.

Charlie shook her hand.

'Hi, I'm Alison,' said Alison, coming over to greet her.

'Well, youse are very welcome to the neighbourhood. It's nice round here, nice for kids,' she said, eyeing the children's toys scattered about. 'If you need anything, just come over.'

'Would you like to stay and have a glass of wine?'

'Thank you but I won't. I've just put the dinner on across.' She left.

Charlie put the parcel on the table.

'Who's it from?' asked Alison.

'London, Sister Catherine.'

'Open it,' said Alison.

Charlie just stared at the package. Frozen.

'You open it, Ali.'

Alison was a bit tipsy. 'I love parcels,' she declared as she ripped the brown paper off. Inside was a box marked 'Diffney's Undertakers', and a sealed note taped to the top. She pulled that off and gave it to Charlie. It was a note from his father, written in a weak and spidery hand. Charlie went down the end of the garden.

Dear Charles
You are a living saint to have come to see me. I cannot describe what good it did me. I am so sorry I was no use to you or Mary. And there is no time for me to make amends.

   I am asking you one favour, and I will fully understand if you don't feel you have time to grant it. I would like you to scatter my ashes in the sea one mile off the coast of Ballyferriter, at the end of the Dingle peninsula in County Kerry. It was where I came from, and I feel I would like to return there.

   I go now. Blessing on you,
    Your father,
      Michael O'Brien

Alison joined him at the end of the garden. Charlie handed the note to her. She read it. It was a little disappointing. No grand statement. No family jewels. She was momentarily frightened of how Charlie would react. She feared the sight of his face crumpling once again. But he shrugged. The party had lifted his spirits. They rejoined the others at the table.

'What is it?' asked Donna.

'That's Charlie's father's ashes.'

'Ah.'

Everybody went silent.

'Let's get them off the dining table.' Alison smiled as she picked them up and took them inside, putting them first in a cupboard and then on the mantelpiece. She went back outside.

'More wine, anyone?'

After everyone had left, Alison checked Michael and came back downstairs.

'I'm so sorry about making you open the parcel. I thought it'd be just some mementoes or something.'

'S'OK.'

'What do you think?' she asked.

'I suppose I should do it. One should respond to dying wishes, as a general rule.'

Alison had given the matter a bit of thought over the evening. Two months ago, she had cancelled their five-star holiday in a resort hotel in Corfu, as they couldn't now afford it, and the travel agent had promised her she could put the deposit against some other holiday as she'd cancelled with plenty of notice. She had browsed through the Irish cottage rentals on their books and said she'd come back another day. She hadn't a clue where in Ireland to go.

'Look. Let's go down there for our holidays. I'll see if the travel agent can set us up with a cottage or something.'

'Fine.'

Charlie was still so very punched-looking. And undynamic. He would do as he was told. Like a broken dog. Her worries for their relationship had disappeared. It was stronger than ever now, she thought. The financial crisis had strengthened them. Charlie's repairs business was ticking over fine. And the receivership had been bloody, but it could have been worse. The

220

building had sold at a substantially higher price than expected and the creditors weren't as badly stung as originally feared. So Charlie had preserved some dignity, even if he was now back in overalls. And Alison was proud of how she'd reacted. She fancied herself a hero, and relished her own sense of virtue. Rarely did she have an opportunity to admire herself so thoroughly. And they would be rich again. She was quite confident about that.

They drove to Kerry in the yellow Mini Cooper. Alison watched Charlie's spirits lift as they left Dublin behind them. With every mile of road some of his cares dropped away. A break from everything. That was what was needed. Little Michael sat happily in the back of the car, and dropped off for a long nap. Everybody's humour was good. Alison had booked a cottage near Ballyferriter for two weeks. It was a fine four star cottage at the edge of the strand. It was a bargain, as they had had a cancellation, and Alison slotted neatly into the vacancy. They stopped in the village to get directions. Charlie went into a shop to ask, and emerged with two ice-cream cones and an empty cone. He made a mini ice-cream for Michael from the spare cone, who happily slopped it about his face, gurgling with glee.

'We're on holidays,' said Charlie. 'Ice-creams are a necessity.'

For the first time, Alison felt the return of his old spirit.

They reached the cottage which was startlingly pink on the outside, but very nice inside. It had that stripped down feel, easy to clean and maintain. Tiles everywhere. The beach was just down the road. Not a hundred yards away.

'This'll do the business,' approved Alison after they'd had a look around.

The next day Alison phoned Kerry Airport to make arrangements for the hire of a plane with pilot to take Charlie on a sightseeing trip. She put it delicately.

'What kind of aircraft might it be?'

'Well, I think Patrick O'Shea has a Cessna.'

'Could something be thrown out of it?'

'What might that be, ma'am?'

'Well, ashes,' she said a little awkwardly.

221

'That's fine, no problem, we do a lot of that. We've scattered ashes all over Kerry.'

Alison was relieved. She had thought her request would be received a little more suspiciously. She went into the sitting room to tell Charlie. He was watching a football match. It was something he hadn't done in ages, sat still and calmly in front of the TV. A normal thing. Michael nestled by his side, sucking his thumb.

'I've booked you in for Tuesday. You'll have to get to the airport very early. Eight a.m. And it's a solid hour and a quarter drive from here.'

'Fine,' he said. 'Yes, boss.'

Charlie climbed aboard the little Cessna two-seater, clutching the cardboard box of ashes with tight fists and thought of Mary. He had invited her to come and she'd declined. 'I was never very sentimental, Charlie. You go. You don't need me.'

'I know I don't need you, Mary, but I thought it might do you good.'

'Do me good? What are you talking about? I'm not in need of good,' she replied, banging pots around the kitchen in a culinary hysteria.

'Well, closure. It might give you some closure.'

'I don't know what you're talking about.'

Brendan shrugged and sat at the table. He shook his head resignedly and signalled Charlie to drop the subject.

'Our father took no interest in us when he was alive, so I've got no compunction to take any interest in him now that he's dead. The contents of that box are not interesting to me. Apart from finding them a little bit ghoulish and wanting them off the kitchen table before I serve the dinner.'

Charlie duly removed the box. His dead father had the knack of becoming a dining centrepiece. He went outside and put it in the boot of the car.

The little plane taxied along the runway in the early-morning light and Charlie was surprised at the ease with which it lifted itself up into the air. He stared around at the surrounding countryside, which receded, cows and sheep becoming little specks, toylike as the distance increased. They looked like Michael's little plastic farm animals. On this trip, Charlie wanted to introduce the child to the real thing. He wanted him to meet a real cow.

The plane flew into a cloud and Charlie could see nothing for a while.

'Just a little bit of cloud,' said Patrick the pilot. 'It's mainly clear, though, and weather conditions are fine. We'll have a perfect view of everything.'

'How long will it take us to get there?'

'Twenty minutes, roughly.'

The cloud cleared, and the world returned to its previous splendid sparkle. Charlie felt very exposed in the little plane and his nerves were getting a bit jittery. He had flown a fair bit for work, but somehow it was easier to forget you were up in the air while seated in business class sipping a G&T and reading *Car Weekly*. Here, wind leaking in through the door of the little plane, which felt every wind current like so many aerial potholes, it was impossible to forget you were in the air.

'A funny request,' said Patrick. Patrick had a thick Kerry accent, and Charlie had to really concentrate to be able to decipher his speech.

'Yes,' said Charlie.

'He couldn't have picked a more awkward place to have himself scattered than a mile off the end of the Dingle peninsula. But it's amazing what comforts the dying.'

'He was born down here. I think he wanted to go back to where he was born.'

'Did he die in Dublin?'

'No, England.'

Charlie fell silent again. He wanted to savour everything about the experience, to observe it meticulously, so he could relate it to Alison later in all its detail. He wanted to both perform and witness the act. They continued along in silence for ten minutes, and Charlie looked out along the Dingle peninsula as it fingered in a humpbacked fashion out into the sea. He had already done the trip from Tralee to the end of the peninsula a number of times

223

by car, and it was dramatic enough that way, full of hairpin bends and startling vistas. But the world looked different from up here. Cleaner. Simpler. This was where his grandparents had journeyed to begin their life, to give birth to his father. Out here onto the edge of Europe. It was a beautiful spot.

'There's the Blaskets up ahead,' said Patrick. 'That little one to the left is Inishvickillaun, Charlie Haughey's island.'

Charlie roused himself from the reverie he had fallen into. The Blaskets looked astounding all right. Great gobbets of land that had been left behind when the tide went out. The sun shone and the water shone, and the islands looked at their most hospitable.

'I'd say that's Ballyferriter,' said Patrick, pointing to a cluster of houses beneath them on the coast. 'And that there is Whitestrand beach.'

Charlie looked down at the beach he had been lying on for the previous few days. It looked smaller and more curved from here. The beach was empty now, too early in the morning, but would fill later in the day as it was going to be hot. He searched for the pink house they were staying in, but he lost his bearings and couldn't find it, and then they were past.

'This is the best summer we've had in years.'

Patrick curved the little plane and headed out to sea. He proceeded for about five minutes.

'You know, anytime now I'll turn back. We'd be a good few miles off the coast now.'

'We'll go a little bit further,' said Charlie.

They now could see no land, just a vast expanse of sky and sea stretching endlessly in all directions. It was very peaceful, the drone of the engine becoming part of the ambient noise.

'We'll turn now,' said Charlie, feeling they'd gone far enough and were surrounded enough by nothingness.

The plane banked a little sharply and jolted the occupants.

'Sorry,' said Patrick. 'I hit a bit of a wind current there. It's a little choppier out here.'

Charlie opened the cardboard box for the first time. He had expected to find the ashes loose, or in a plastic bag, but they were contained in a plain little wooden box. He carefully took this out and removed the lid. There was dust. He opened the window and carefully emptied the box out. A light film of ashes blew back in and covered him. Patrick made the sign of the cross.

'God rest him, your father.'

Charlie wanted to do something, to bless himself or mark the occasion with some sort of holy invocation, but he was mute in the language of the spirit. Yet his heart seemed to need some tool of expression. He looked at the beauty surrounding him and felt something stir. The little wooden box lay on his lap, the remains of the remains of his father. Land was visible far ahead, a thin strip becoming thicker. This was what Lindbergh would have seen. Charlie's heart began to beat faster. After twenty-eight hours' flight, this was Lindbergh's first sight of land. He must have been almost destroyed with tiredness, seeing hallucinatory demons, but this was the holy grail appearing for him. He had flown the Atlantic single-handed. The land grew more substantial as they got closer. Yes, this was it. The phantoms in the fuse-lage receded. The leaden tiredness fell from his eyes. This was definitely land, not a mirage. Even if he crashed now, this was the most westerly part of Europe and he had made it. He was exhausted and weak and badly needing food. All the years delivering mail, performing death-defying stunts for the bored householders of America, all the phenomenal hubris now added up to achievement and endurance of the highest order. The world had shrunk. History had been made.

This was why Charlie had been sent on this bizarre mission with the ashes. Rather than just happily curling up in the English earth, his father had sent him on this odd mission. In order that, for once in his sorry life, he could do something sublime for his son. His father had wanted Charlie to fly like Lindbergh.

'Can you fly in low over Whitestrand beach?'

'Sure,' and Patrick lowered the altitude steadily as they approached the land.

'There it is. That's the house we're staying in. The pink one.'

It stood out very distinctively, its cheeky colour an audacious taunt to the countryside.

'Can you circle here?'

Charlie hoped that the drone of the aircraft would entice Alison out of the holiday house, but she was out already. She was standing on the beach, holding Michael up in the air, and Michael's arms and legs were kicking in excitement at the sight of the aircraft. She stood tall, golden-haired and long-limbed, a turquoise blue light dress flattering her figure. She was a sight to behold, standing goddess-like, now cradling the child on her hip. She ran along the beach, waving at the plane, pointing at it and displaying it to little Michael. The plane headed off, back to Kerry Airport.

Charlie closed his eyes and lay back in the seat for the return journey. In his mind's eye he saw the nothingness. The sea and the sky stretching on to infinity in all directions. And then he saw the thin strip of land, getting bigger all the time. And then he saw the sight of a woman waving her infant son at the excitement of a plane. And the woman and child were so beautiful down there, and he as a father felt his heart was fit to burst with everything.

15

The sun shone on Whitestrand beach and Charlie worked diligently at making a fort to amuse Michael, who was now having a nap in his buggy, an elaborate white parasol shading him from the sun. Charlie built a central fort and a number of satellites, and linked them all with a complicated moat which twisted about the buildings. He worked quietly and carefully, and his ambitious engineering was a spectacle which impressed the passers-by. He created quite a palace and attracted the attention of young boys dripping water from the sea who marvelled at the creation. To one side, he built a Sphinx out of the sand, a mimic of the sorry premises of Charles O'Brien Motors. Considering the paucity of his materials, it was a very good likeness. It crouched, solid and silly-looking, staring out to sea. Charlie put the finishing touches to the fort, some flags made from bits of driftwood, and sounded a little fanfare. Alison duly admired the creation.

'The tide will be high in another hour and it comes to just about here,' he said, pointing to the tidemark in front of their patch. 'I'll dig a moat from the fort down to the edge and fill it with water. It'll look great. Michael will love it when he wakes.'

Charlie slumped beside Alison on the sand and lay down in the happy sun. He drifted off into a little doze, calm and peaceful and feeling somewhat resolved, deep in his core. Michael woke up cheery and happy after his nap and Alison gave him some lunch, which he wolfed down with eager appetite. She then covered him in suncream, a process which he resigned himself to with quiet grumbles. She put a sunhat on his head and the little lad happily chirped, thrilled with the huge fort his daddy had made, and started ineptly on a satellite fort of his own with his bucket and spade. He was delighted with the expanse of sand and sea and played merrily, tearing the sunhat off and casting it away.

Alison shrugged. 'He doesn't like the hat. And he won't tolerate anything he doesn't like. Here.' Alison handed Charlie a bottle of her own suncream and lay on her tummy.

Charlie started to apply it.

'The weather is great, Charlie, it's unbelievably good. I was looking at the weather in Corfu and it's not at all good. We've been very lucky. It's always supposed to rain in Kerry. All you ever hear from anyone who's holidayed here is tales of deluges. And we haven't had a bad day all week.'

Charlie smiled and rubbed the cream into his wife's soft olive flesh.

'I'll tell you a tale of a deluge. The old man told me this. It is the book of Genesis, and it had rained for forty days and forty nights. And my great-great-great-great-great-great-grandfather, who was called Tim O'Brien, he was farming his land and tilling his fields in the townland of Glenmore in West Cork. And the floods were rising all the time and every day he went up to the top of Vaughan's Pass behind the farm and surveyed the devastation of Bantry Bay, which was frightening to behold. Scores of people were fleeing the floods and herds of sheep and cows were drowned and God was full of vengeance.'

Alison turned over onto her back and Charlie continued rubbing in the cream on her tummy and thighs.

'Mmmmn. Thanks, love. This is heaven.'

'And this ancestor, Tim O'Brien, made his way up Vaughan's Pass each day and he could see the town of Bantry, which was disappearing little by little as the waters rose slowly but surely. The last thing to be seen were the spires of the churches and soon even they were obliterated, and the rains continued and the winds howled. And God said, "Vengeance is mine," and all that jazz.'

'That was in the days when God had a bit of go in him. He's finished now. You missed a bit. The top of my left thigh,' said Alison.

'And one day, Tim O'Brien, my great-great-great-great-great-great-grandfather, was standing there and Noah and his ark came up the bay and stopped in front of him. And Noah called out, "Are you Tim O'Brien?"

' "I am," said my great-great-great-great-great-great-grand-father.

' "You're on my list, Mr O'Brien, I'm to save you from the deluge. I have instructions from God. Fetch your wife and the two of you are welcome aboard to join us and have a great dinner of hot stew and apple pie."

'And Tim O'Brien pulled himself up to his full height, and he was a giant of a man, eight foot tall, and guess what he said?'

'I don't know,' said Alison. 'What did he say?'

'He said, "That's all right. The O'Briens have their own boats." '

'I knew it'd be something contrary,' said Alison.

'Their own boats,' chuckled Charlie.

And little Michael, tired of his own efforts, stumbled to his feet and jumped on the centre of the carefully made fort, its meticulous assembly collapsing under his tiny weight.

'No, don't,' said Charlie, jumping to his feet in pointless remonstration. 'It took me ages to make it, and it's much nicer to look at. Look, when the sea comes in it'll fill the moat and there'll be canals and islands and it'll look great.'

And little Michael jumped on the head of the Sphinx, reducing it to peppery sand.

'Nooo,' said Charlie.

'Let him be. He loves trashing things,' said Alison lazily, sleepily.

'It took me ages to make.'

'Well, you made it for him, and if he gets enjoyment out of wrecking it, so be it.'

Charlie watched as Michael scampered about, clearly having a marvellous time.

'I didn't entirely make it for him,' said Charlie. 'I made it partly for myself.'

And little Michael started work dismantling the satellite forts, jumping on them one by one, with great concentration and thoroughness. The third satellite half survived the initial jump, so he jumped a second time to finish it off. Then he jumped on the main fort again, kicking the walls into the moat, laughing with glee and looking to his parents for approval. 'Ukka a me, ukka a me,' he cried, and Alison laughed and Charlie stared. The child jumped up and down on the site until the forts were all levelled, smiling, an infant King Kong towering among ruins. The devastation was complete.

All Orion/Phoenix titles are available at your local bookshop or from the following address:

Mail Order Department
Littlehampton Book Services
FREEPOST BR535
Worthing, West Sussex, BN13 3BR
telephone 01903 828503, *facsimile* 01903 828802
e-mail MailOrders@lbsltd.co.uk
(Please ensure that you include full postal address details)

Payment can be made either by credit/debit card (Visa, Mastercard, Access and Switch accepted) or by sending a £ Sterling cheque or postal order made payable to *Littlehampton Book Services*.
DO NOT SEND CASH OR CURRENCY.

Please add the following to cover postage and packing

UK and BFPO:
£1.50 for the first book, and 50p for each additional book to a maximum of £3.50

Overseas and Eire:
£2.50 for the first book plus £1.00 for the second book and 50p for each additional book ordered

---

BLOCK CAPITALS PLEASE

name of cardholder ....   *delivery address*
....   *(if different from cardholder)*

address of cardholder ....

....

....

....

postcode ....   *postcode* ....

☐ I enclose my remittance for   £ ....

☐ please debit my Mastercard/Visa/Access/Switch (delete as appropriate)

card number ☐☐☐☐☐☐☐☐☐☐☐☐☐☐☐☐

expiry date ☐☐☐☐   Switch issue no. ☐☐

signature ....

prices and availability are subject to change without notice